if jack's in love

STEPHEN WETTA

BERKLEY BOOKS

New York

THE BERKLEY PUBLISHING GROUP
Published by the Penguin Group
Penguin Group (USA) Inc.
375 Hudson Street, New York, New York 10014, USA
Penguin Group (Canada), 90 Eglinton Avenue East, Suite 700, Toronto, Ontario M4P 2Y3, Canada
(a division of Pearson Penguin Canada Inc.) • Penguin Books Ltd., 80 Strand, London WC2R 0RL,
England • Penguin Group Ireland, 25 St. Stephen's Green, Dublin 2, Ireland (a division of Penguin
Books Ltd.) • Penguin Group (Australia), 250 Camberwell Road, Camberwell, Victoria 3124, Australia
(a division of Pearson Australia Group Pty. Ltd.) • Penguin Books India Pvt. Ltd., 11 Community
Centre, Panchsheel Park, New Delhi—110 017, India • Penguin Group (NZ), 67 Apollo Drive,
Rosedale, Auckland 0632, New Zealand (a division of Pearson New Zealand Ltd.) • Penguin Books
(South Africa) (Pty.) Ltd., 24 Sturdee Avenue, Rosebank, Johannesburg 2196, South Africa

Penguin Books Ltd., Registered Offices: 80 Strand, London WC2R 0RL, England

PUBLISHING HISTORY
Amy Einhorn Books/G. P. Putnam's Sons hardcover edition / September 2011
Berkley trade paperback edition / August 2012

Berkley trade paperback ISBN: 978-0-425-24778-5

The Library of Congress has cataloged the Amy Einhorn Books/
G. P. Putnam's Sons hardcover edition as follows:

Wetta, Stephen.
If Jack's in love / Stephen Wetta.
p.   cm.
ISBN 978-0-399-15752-3
1. Coming of age—Fiction.   2. Brothers—Fiction.   3. Fathers and sons—Fiction.
4. Social classes—Fiction.   I. Title.   II. Title: If Jack's in love.
PZ7.W5321f   2011   2011013746
[Fic]—dc23

PRINTED IN THE UNITED STATES OF AMERICA

10 9 8 7 6 5 4 3 2 1

for Julie

If Jack's in love, he's no judge of Jill's beauty.

—BENJAMIN FRANKLIN

I'LL NEVER KNOW FOR SURE whether I'd have fought my brother or not. Maybe I might have killed him. The day came and I made the decision. But I will never know.

It was a fated day. Earlier Myra and I met where we always met, in the woods. The woods! There was something daring, even salacious, about the words. Back then, before childhood had grown menaced by television reports, the woods were where kids went to drink and smoke and cop feels. One said "the woods" with a knowing smile. The words could make a thirteen-year-old's heart pump. Yet Myra and I met that day in tragedy. Can you believe it? I was thirteen and already tragic. What my brother did, what he might have done, was enough to start a blood feud between families; and when I left it was with the resolve to bring him down.

I stomped along the neighborhood streets with a pocket-knife in my hand. I was going to do it for myself, for Myra, for my mother. The world would be a better place without him.

My family, my house, were falling apart, and it was because of him. Probably it was also because of Pop, but I was too young to grasp family dynamics. Then again, maybe my mother might have been less mealymouthed when dealing with us. But I didn't want to factor in her responsibility, not just yet.

Rusty, the neighborhood dog, trotted along at my side, worriedly glancing up at my face. He had an instinct something big was about to go down.

I came around the curve and turned on Stanley Street and walked past the Coghill yard. The usual crowd was there, Witcher tormenters, haters, snobs, bigots, jerks, idiots. They lifted their eyes to watch as I passed. I held my head level, walked with dignity. A new day was arriving and I wanted them to know. No longer would they have Jack Witcher to kick around.

When I came to my street I saw the driveway was empty. (Earlier Pop had mentioned an afternoon job interview, which I took to mean he was visiting his bookie.) The Witcher house stood in shambles, overgrown, peeling, weedy, vandalized. A commode leaned against the side wall. A screen on one of the dormer windows had come unhinged and was hanging at the corner. Shingles were missing. The yard was parched. Dog shit formed punctuation marks on bare patches of earth. This was it, my very own Tobacco Road.

I gripped the pocketknife and went in the house.

"Stan!" I called.

No answer.

I stomped to the bedroom (it fortified my resolve to stomp) and flung open the door.

The floor was littered with socks, with underwear, with paper and tissues, with balled-up wrappers. The drawers on the dresser gaped open.

And then I noticed: The stereo player was missing!

We had been robbed! What a development!

I threw open the door to Mom and Pop's room, tiptoed up the hall, checked the bathroom. I held my breath and thrust open closet doors. At the doorway that led to the attic I paused, mounted the steps and climbed higher into the attic heat. When my eyes came level with the floor I gazed around.

No one was there.

The house was empty.

I came down and rested for a moment on the tattered carmine sofa; and then I went to the kitchen phone so I could call the police. But I put the phone in its cradle before I finished dialing.

What was I talking about? We hadn't been robbed. Nothing even seemed to be missing outside of the stereo player.

My brother had flown the coop. That was it. He was gone: running from the law.

Realizing it did me in, and I sank down on the carmine sofa and cried.

Things had been building up so long. It started when Gaylord Joyner disappeared and everyone began to suspect my brother of having something to do with it; but maybe it started before that, like when I was born, or when Stan was born, or when my parents were born. On the other hand, I'm not sure I cried solely because Gaylord Joyner had disappeared, or even because his sister was blaming the Witchers. I'm not sure I actually cried. I had only recently shed tears with Myra and maybe that had drained me. Besides, what if my maligned brother had fled because he was innocent? Then to hell with them. No matter what, my brother's bullying and vandalizing had made me who I was. Better loyalty to my brother than forget I'm a Witcher.

It wasn't a hell of a lot for sentiment to thrive on, but that is what I had: this crummy house, a redneck father, a psycho brother. And now I tried to conjure up a picture of Stan, worried I had seen him for the last time. I squeezed my eyes shut and waited until an image floated before me. And slowly it came.

Gaylord.

LET ME TELL YOU about Gaylord.

Years ago, Pop would take me and Stan to a wooded area fifty miles north of the city where Civil War battles once raged. History enthusiasts would come out on weekends looking for canteens and minié balls dropped by Johnny Reb some hundred years before, and every now and then you'd come upon them prowling through the woods and the fields with metal detectors. There was a river nearby and the air was swarming with mosquitoes and horseflies and when you were standing by your car that's all you would hear, the insects. Pop liked to go there because he had read, or someone had told him, that UFOs had been sighted in those parts. That had always been one of Pop's dearest dreams, to spot a UFO. Truth is, the Pentagon and the CIA were active in that part of the state, and I think the military might have been testing new spy planes.

Imagine two boys about the same age as me and my brother in that infested air and their pop is waiting by the car and they're walking along the edge of the trees and they come to a swarming field and fight their way into the undergrowth because one of them (the older one) thinks they might find some valuable relics down there. The horseflies are batting their faces, the mosquitoes are sucking their blood, the ticks are biting their legs. And when the smell hits their noses it comes with a stab of fear. But they soldier on because of the occult property of smell that turns vicious odors into seductive perfumes that draw us closer to what by rights should repel us. Wild animals were constantly digging up CSA belt buckles and other metal objects around there, and sometimes we'd hear stories about artifacts unearthed and later sold at auction. No doubt a hundred years ago during the skirmishing some Reb or Yank had lain and died and perfumed the air with his decay, like now. And as the boys drew closer they noticed a discarded shovel (it was stolen from a nearby farmer's porch) and then a shoe and then a hand coming out of the earth and resting there like the root of a tree. Before the younger kid knew what was happening the older brother was hauling ass out of there. And then the younger boy took off after the brother and the two of them ran in a line to the car fifty feet apart, hollering for their pop to come see. As soon as they got there they grabbed their pop and led him along the line of trees to the field and yanked him into the undergrowth with the horseflies and the mosquitoes and the ticks. And as they drew nearer to the smell they pushed their pop forward and he put a handkerchief to his nose and scanned underfoot 'til he saw what they had seen. And out he tumbled, away from the smell, and retched in the brush while his kids looked on and marveled that he wasn't being a man about this. Then he hustled them to the car and drove a hundred miles an hour to the nearest state police office.

We heard about it on the TV that night, me and Pop. We knew Gaylord Joyner was missing and we knew my brother was a suspect, and now we cast a furtive glance at each other. Mom wasn't in the room and Pop was glad of it, because she'd have put it together right away. She was perfectly aware of where he took us to scout for UFOs and she knew exactly how familiar with the area my brother would be. Anyway, we figured she'd find out soon enough.

The headlines were gravely sensationalistic. Don't forget, the victim was a boy who had won a scholarship to Duke University. What an unlucky waste of scholarship. That's all you saw on the front page: "Gaylord Joyner, who was awarded a scholarship to Duke University in the fall . . ." How many times do you have to mention such a mighty accomplishment before the full force of the tragedy sinks in? A young Duke scholar bludgeoned and strangled and buried in a shallow grave! They even made it the caption to his photograph:

"Gaylord Joyner, Awarded Scholarship to Duke U."

Shortly after that, the police issued a warrant for the arrest of my brother, Stanley Kirby Witcher.

1

I THINK I BELONGED TO the last generation of kids that could play outside. There were woods near our house with a livid creek, and at the end of Livingstone was a dry drainage pipe where kids would light cigarettes and use them to lure in girls. My father was unemployed and my mother was known for being ugly. Kids in the neighborhood spat my name rather than said it. They didn't even grant me the compliment of a rude nickname.

One of the first things newcomers learned when they moved in was, "It's a nice neighborhood, too bad the Witchers live here." We didn't live in the neighborhood proper. Our house stood on a piece of macadam that connected one homey drive to another. Ours was the only house on the road.

My father was irregular in his unemployment, although there were times when he made genuine efforts to thwart the luckless demons that attended him. I remember one period when he was employed for a long while, maybe two years: my happiest stretch of childhood. My parents didn't argue as much. My father was at peace with himself. Then one night, just as school was ending, he came home in a rage. He had argued with a man who lived on the tidy street to our right, after nearly driving his battered Ford over the man's dog. The man's name was Kellner.

"I'm gonna fight the son of a bitch," my father said, coming in the kitchen. He had groceries in a bag: six cans of Schlitz and some lettuce and mayonnaise for the burgers hardening in the pan.

"Who?" my mother asked.

"Kellner. Son of a bitch thinks I tried to kill his dog on purpose. I challenged him to a fight and he backed down."

"You're too old to be fighting."

That made me uneasy, hearing my pop talk about fighting. My mother had ushered Pop beyond the rowdiness of his early years, and here he was forty-five and still prepared to defend what I'd already spent my born years defending (I was twelve). I had to slug it out with kids all the time, because of my name, because of my house, because my mother looked like a trout. How I longed for adulthood, when I would be surrounded by civilized people who would inquire, "How are you today, Mr. Witcher?" And now my father had picked a fight with pipe-smoking Mr. Kellner.

He grabbed the phone on the wall and dialed Kellner's number.

"Kellner, you son of a bitch, fight like a man!"

During the pause that followed we could imagine Kellner's reasoned response. "I am not going to fight you, Witcher, and if you keep threatening me I'll report you to the police."

"No one accuses me of trying to kill a dog," Pop said. His tone was indignant, affronted, worn-out.

For me the enmity between Kellner and Pop was of a part with nature and history. Pop had a habit of bringing home stuff he found in garbage cans and abandoned lots—car parts, broken bicycles, tossed-out toilets—and dumping it all at the side of the house. He said he had the intention of "getting to it" someday, but he never did. The junk in our yard drove Kellner crazy. He would cruise past the house in his car just to enjoy the loathing it filled him with. He'd circle the block over and over, nursing his disbelief and outrage. One day he composed a petition demanding that we clean our yard and took it to the neighbors to sign. Pop never forgave him for that (nor did he clean the yard). Kellner wore an ascot and listened to Dave Brubeck records, and in our neighborhood this was enough to give him the reputation for being an intellectual.

"I'm gonna be at the drainage pipe at the end of Livingstone tonight at seven. Be there."

My father slammed down the phone.

"Are you really going to fight Mr. Kellner?" I asked.

"If he shows up."

"You are not going to fight Paul Kellner," my mother said. "Good Lord, how old are you?"

"Old enough to kick Kellner's ass."

"Great. In front of Jack. Some example you're setting."

Pop slumped on the sofa with his arms embracing his shoulders. He was watching footage on the TV of a lugubrious Lyndon Johnson explaining why American boys were being jetted off to the jungles of Asia. My mother pulled my head against her dress, sparing me that male darkness. But I didn't want to be spared. I knew damn well Kellner wasn't going to show up at the drainage pipe, which in itself was a source of shame. Mr. Kellner was a fully developed grown-up and Pop was a schoolyard bully.

In Pop's defense, he'd have veered his car into a tree rather than run over a dog. He loved dogs, always fed them scraps when they came a-begging. Dogs sunned in our yard, fought in our yard, frolicked in our yard, rutted in our yard. Dogs were always hanging around our house. Rusty, Kellner's dog, enjoyed the distinction of being the neighborhood mascot. He and Pop were very good friends.

I went to Pop and said, "How come Kellner thinks you tried to kill his dog?"

"Damn thing ran in front of my car. He says I steered the car towards it."

"Rusty," I said. "Good dog."

"Hell, I ain't got a problem with his dog."

I stared at the worn carmine fabric on the sofa. The antennas on our TV set had been mended with masking tape. One of our front windows was missing a screen.

Mom came to the room and sent me to the backyard. I went outside and perched on the swing and listened to their voices rising and falling. My brother came home about that time, and when he heard them shouting he elected not to go inside.

"What is it this time?"

"Pop wants to fight Mr. Kellner. He just called him up and challenged him to a fight."

"What for?"

"He almost hit Rusty. Mr. Kellner thinks he did it on purpose."

"Rusty the dog? What's Mom shouting about?"

"She doesn't want 'em to fight. Pop told Mr. Kellner to meet him at the drainage pipe."

"No kidding? Is he gonna show?"

My brother grinned. He liked it.

We ate our burgers as a family, in silence. I was sad for the Witchers. Only recently I had visited the Pendleton house and one of the Pendleton boys, Johnny, had afterwards made a point of cleaning the front porch with a hose because I'd been sitting there. Tanya Browning, Susie Kellner, the three Coghill daughters—the very belles of our neighborhood—had all been present (so my informant, Dickie Pudding, later related), and they were giggling and laughing and shrieking encouragingly, "God, Johnny, you're so cruel!"

What was so bad about the Witchers? We didn't listen to country music. We didn't eat chitterlings; we didn't wear overalls. My mother read books by Charles Dickens, Jane Austen. She could play show tunes on piano.

It was Pop, he was the one who made the trouble.

After supper he headed to the bedroom and put on his T-shirt and jeans. When he finally left to go beat up Mr. Kellner, my mother called out that my brother and I should stay behind. But we ignored her, and Pop didn't send us back. He wanted us to see that Kellner would be a no-show.

We went to the end of the street, turned left and circled around to Stanley Street, which ran between the end of Livingstone and the field with the drainage pipe. (There was a worn path that debouched on Livingstone about a hundred yards from our destination, but we didn't take it. Shortcuts, for some reason, were taboo to grown-ups.) As we approached the field we saw Kellner standing next to well-dressed Mr. Joyner, his next-door neighbor and father to Myra, who had learned by now, or would learn shortly, that Mr. Witcher had picked a fight with one of the community's more esteemed dwellers, a man who smoked a pipe and listened to Dave Brubeck. I was confused by shame and pride, feelings intensified by my secret passion for Myra, who was kind when no one else was around.

My brother and I, flanking Pop, stood on the side of the street where it verged on the field. Mr. Joyner strode briskly forward. I was worried Pop wouldn't recognize his role as emissary and would punch him instead of Kellner.

"Look here, Witcher," Joyner said.

Look here! What a civilized sound it had to my ears. It's what decent men in movies said when forced to reason with desperadoes and thugs.

"There are other ways to iron out your differences."

This was no longer a world of Kellners and Witchers. Mr. Joyner might have been Gregory Peck or Gary Cooper. (I guess Pop was Richard Widmark.)

"Stand aside, Joyner," Pop said.

I almost burst out laughing. Mr. Joyner noticed.

"What did you bring your kids for?"

"To show 'em Witchers look out for themselves. *Kellner, you ready?*" he called.

"I'm ready," Kellner feebly responded. You had to feel a little sorry for the man. He was making a stand, he was going to take my pop's pounding. Pop was from the mountains, a hillbilly.

I tugged on Pop's sleeve and jerked my eyes in the direction of home. But Kellner was distracting him. He had removed his navy blazer and folded it neatly across his arm. Now he was placing it on the ground and carefully setting his pipe beside it. He rolled up his sleeves.

My father brushed past Mr. Joyner.

"Witcher!" Joyner called.

"*Mister* Witcher," my brother said. "Kick his ass, Pop."

Kellner positioned one leg slightly in front of the other, raised his arms and began to revolve his fists in the air like a turn-of-the-century pugilist demonstrating fisticuffs.

Pop's eyes bugged out. He gave me a wink and said, "Sheeit," playing the rube, a mortifying tendency whenever he got around civilized types like Kellner and Joyner.

Joyner came between the two men. "I'm warning you, Witcher," he said, like a sheriff.

"Am I gonna have to fight both of you?"

"I'll back you up," my brother said.

"You go home, boy," Joyner said. My brother was eighteen

and soon to begin classes at the cracker college downtown so he wouldn't have to go to Vietnam. He'd long harbored murderous feelings for Mr. Joyner's son, Gaylord, because Gaylord had stolen his girl, Courtney Blankenship. Possibly this made the tone of Mr. Joyner's voice sound more imperious and disdainful than it was. To me his tone was moralistic; he was saying, "Go home, this is no place for a young man." To my brother it was more like "Go, villain. Leave."

Suddenly Joyner said in amazement, "This young man is threatening me."

Sure enough, my brother was pounding his fist against his palm and staring aggressively into Joyner's eyes. Which didn't surprise me. My brother had inherited Pop's feeling for the clan.

"Keep him covered," Pop said, moving towards Mr. Kellner.

"You're encouraging him!"

Joyner blustered in the direction of the crowd gathering on the side of the field, mainly kids who lived on local streets. He was playing to them, gleaning support in a propaganda campaign he'd already won.

"Beat him up, Mr. Kellner!" a pipsqueak hollered from the sidelines.

Kellner desperately charged. He flung himself in the air, putting all his weight into a fist that he sent sailing into Pop's jaw. It staggered Pop for a second. He wasn't expecting it. No one expected it, a sucker punch from Kellner. A shout of "Oh!" came from the sidelines.

Pop rubbed his jaw and grinned. Then he came in swinging. Pow pow pow!

Mr. Kellner flopped to the ground like a tumble of clothes.

The kids on the side couldn't believe their eyes. A grown-up from the neighborhood had just pummeled another grown-up. The entire world had just observed the barbaric effects of a mountain upbringing.

Mr. Joyner seemed appalled, but not exactly eager to press the matter.

"You okay, Paul?" he asked Kellner.

A mumble came from within the sack of clothing.

Pop was staring at a cut on his knuckle.

"Do you need an ambulance?" Joyner asked.

A monosyllable came from Kellner, without the close front rounded sound that might have signified a yes.

Joyner turned sternly to my pop.

"Are you happy now?"

Pop stomped his foot, Joyner leapt back.

We followed him off the field. My brother swiveled his head, grinning in the faces of the stunned onlookers. We marched back to our house, victorious but unpopular, like Wehrmacht infantrymen goose-stepping into Prague.

2

POP BEATING UP KELLNER WAS, I think, the beginning of it all. We bear primal anxieties about our fathers, and it's tough to witness your pop beat up a pipe-smoking gentleman from the next street over. I had visions of the police raiding our house, of my mother, hair wrapped in a scarf, taking us to visit Pop in jail where we'd have to pass snacks and tobacco through cold iron bars. Truthfully, at the time I was more worried about how the news would affect Myra. Myra was everything to me, probably because there wasn't much else.

My brother, meanwhile, was having an entirely different reaction. He'd had a five-year jump on me in suffering rejection from El Dorado Hills, and life had embittered him early. On the way home he kept slapping my father's back. "Way to go, Pop! Did you see Kellner fall?"

My father was a quiet man until he knew you, and a veteran

of Normandy. Probably he had killed people. He'd been raised in Hendersonville, North Carolina.

When we got to the house my brother dashed in before Pop could grab him and told Mom about the heap Kellner made when he fell to the ground.

She was holding on to his shoulder when we came inside.

"Is it true?" she asked.

Pop went down to the bedroom without saying a word.

The next day he was home before noon. He had been fired from his job as a mechanic at the refrigeration company.

My first thought was regret for those Sundays when he used to bundle me in a furry arctic parka and take me into the deep freeze and let me walk amongst the sides of beef. That was part of his job, to make sure the freezers were working properly.

"What do you mean you've been fired?" Mom said.

"Old man Ball told me to go home. Said he didn't need me no more."

"Why not?"

Pop shrugged. Bad luck never needed a reason. But later we found out there was indeed a reason. Mr. Ball was cousin to Mr. Joyner.

My mother's knees gave way and she sank to the worn carmine sofa. Poor Mom. Thin lips, haggard nose, weary eyes, a face that belonged in a Dust Bowl documentary. No one had ever been attracted to her, except for Pop and the manager of the Ben Franklin store. But Pop had a painful way of showing his love. Which is to say he never showed it.

"What are we gonna do?" she said.

"Look for more work. You should too."

"Who's gonna hire you now? You've been fired from every job you've had."

"I'll go to Southside," he said.

He meant across the river. He figured no one knew him there and his reputation wouldn't precede him.

All that week Pop would be at the kitchen table with the newspaper spread before him while Mom paced from the stove to the sink and back. "What are we going to do? Where will the money come from?"

Finally, in desperation, she painted on lipstick and wiggled into a skirt so short and tight it made her knees touch and her calves bow out like a wishbone. Then she made me go with her to the Ben Franklin store.

Short skirts weren't too common back then. Only recently had the first miniskirts made it to the market, and they were designed for girls far younger than my mother. Skirts like hers you saw on tarts in *Andy Capp* cartoons.

We passed the drainage ditch where the kids were hanging out and came upon Myra sitting on the front steps of the Coghill house, among the Coghill lovelies. Alas, the second she spotted my tart-skirted mom she turned away.

In humiliation I fixed my eyes before me, seeing nothing.

We arrived at the Ben Franklin and Mom took care of her business, whatever that was. Why did I have to come? The manager of the store was Mr. Harris. He'd long held a flame for my mother, and he liked it that she looked like a tart.

(When she was growing up in Lakeside, Mr. Harris resided in the house across the street, a henpecked man at the time, now a widower.)

The walk home was brisk, furious. Mom's heels were stabbing the macadam. At intersections, looking both ways for cars, and unavailing of the sting, she dug her nails into my shoulder. When we passed the Coghill porch Myra was gone, and I found the pain of not being able to alleviate the shame of our last encounter worse than the shame itself.

After we got home Mom announced she was going to start work at the Ben Franklin the next week, as a cashier.

Pop didn't say anything. It was summer. School was out, baseball was in. He was on the bed listening to a day game on the radio.

Stan stared for a long time. Mom had whored herself, that's what he was thinking.

"What does that mean, Pop, you're going to be the housewife?"

He got up and left the house.

Later, when the game was over, Pop cut off the radio and rose from the bed.

I ran to the kitchen. I assumed he was going to raise hell with Mom for getting a job without consulting him. But maybe she did consult him, who knows.

He sat at the table. Something long and brown, like a strip of bark, was sizzling in the pan. Through the torn screen of the door we could see the tops of the trees blowing as a storm moved in.

THE WAR AGAINST the Witchers began to escalate about this time. I remember when the war was still cold, when all we had to deal with was the snootiness of our neighbors. Oddly enough, Pop was more trouble then. He gambled, he drank, and perhaps he ran with women. I wasn't positive on the last score, I only knew what Mom and Stan had hinted at. The legendary days of Pop's life of sin belonged to my insensate years, when I was small and assumed all was well in the world. I did have shadowy memories of Pop being drunk, but I loved those memories. Pop was fun when he was drunk.

He straightened himself out only when Mom threatened to leave him for good. He got the job at the refrigeration company and our family was granted two years of domestic calm. Yet that is precisely when the neighborhood hostilities became overt. Maybe no one feared Pop sober. Or maybe it was the increasing militancy of my brother, who rode the streets on his Sting-Ray bicycle, one arm at his side and one arm holding a portable radio to his ear.

Trouble had arisen over Stan's wooing of Courtney Blankenship, a clear signal that the Witchers no longer knew their place. The Blankenships were gentry. Mr. Blankenship was the weatherman on Channel Six, and for a half hour every weekday morning he spruced himself up in a crisp white sailor's uniform and genially hosted a local children's program called *Ahoy, Mateys*, which came on just before *Captain Kangaroo*. The neighborhood, you understand, instantly realized something needed to be done. A Blankenship gal dating a Witcher? It rallied by enlisting the square-jawed charms of Gaylord Joyner. It was as though a committee had been formed to appoint some local squire the task of coaxing Courtney back to the realm of suburban chivalry. Later, when the seduction was accomplished and she had dumped my brother, Gaylord just as casually dumped her, and promptly was awarded the scholarship to Duke University (although I'm not sure there was a cause-and-effect relationship).

A day or so after Pop's pummeling of Kellner, a patrol car pulled up in front of our house. My brother and I were watching through the front window with the missing screen. "It's a cop," Stan called.

Pop jumped from the sofa and took a peek.

The cop stayed in his car, the way cops do, writing his report and mumbling in his walkie-talkie; and then out stepped a skinny guy wearing glasses who seemed no older than Stan. He peered at our house, verified the number, and made an inscription on his legal pad.

Stan and I answered his ring. The cop bent and squinted through the dark screen.

"I'm looking for Mr. Charles Witcher."

"He's not here," my brother said.

"Stan!" Pop called, admonishing him. He swung from the sofa, where he'd rearranged himself after spotting the cop through the window, and invited the officer in.

He turned down the volume on the TV (he was watching *As the World Turns*) and turned to the cop with a cocky grin. He didn't offer a seat or anything, he just grinned. Meanwhile I studied his sandy curls and his red mechanic paws rakishly placed upon his hips and wondered what he was going to do. (Stan and I had inherited Pop's hair and not, for which we were thankful, Mom's orange tangles.) Pop was magnificent, but what made him magnificent was too obscure to understand, exactly. His smile made you an accomplice in mischief that never happened; or you might find yourself laughing at things he said without knowing why. It was always hard to tell whether he was being charismatic, or simply hollow.

The cop introduced himself as Reedy. "I hear you and Mr. Kellner got in a scrap," he said. You could see in his eyes that he was already taken by Pop. My father had that redneck charm so vital to the design of the South. But it only worked on ladies and cops.

"Has Kellner swore out a complaint?"

"No sir, I'm just following up on what I heard."

"Am I in trouble?"

"No sir, I just want to make sure everything remains peaceful."

"Giving me a warning, huh?"

"I'm not taking sides. I just want to know if there's anything I can do to help you and Mr. Kellner be civilized with each other."

"Keeping the peace?"

"Yes sir."

Pop nodded distrustfully. He had the mountain man's suspicion of the badge. He kept out of trouble with the law, and he had taught us not to believe in cops. "Don't mess with 'em, don't call 'em. You get in trouble you can get out of it without 'em."

Now he said, "Boys, disappear."

My brother and I hesitantly headed to our room, with no option but to chart the progress of the conversation through the walls and windows.

The men meandered out to the yard. They kept looking at the roof of the house as though they were discussing home improvements, but it was just one pair of eyes wandering off and the other pair following. Pop's shirt was undone two or three buttons, disclosing his softening chest. His bulging forearms and pinched elbows made me think of Popeye.

We heard the big bedroom door creak open and ran to the hallway. Mom was stepping out, one-eyed from her nap.

"Who's your father talking to?"

"The police," we said.

"Good Lord, what now?" She came and peeked out the window.

Pop was dominating Reedy. He had his arm around the cop's shoulder, and he kept poking his chest, making points.

"What does he want?" Mom said.

"Says he came as a peace officer," Stan said. "Old man Kellner snitched. I'm gonna kick his ass for that."

"You watch it," Mom said. "Look who's in our yard, that's what kicking someone's ass does. And stop saying 'ass.'"

We watched Pop usher Reedy to the patrol car. After the cop got in he sat and wrote in his pad for a while.

When Pop entered the house we filed into the living room.

"Shhh," he said.

We waited until Reedy started the engine and moved the cruiser away.

"Says he wants to keep the trouble between me and Kellner from escalating." Pop winked. "Letting me know he's got my number."

"What's that mean?" my mother said.

"He's Johnny-on-the-spot, that's all. Through with your nap? I'm hungry."

"What's he going to do?" she asked.

"Watch me like a hawk."

"Can we move out of this dump?" Stan said.

Unlike me, my brother remembered a time when Mom and Pop lived in Lakeside with Mom's parents. Those were idyllic days. Grandma used to sing "In the Pines" to put him to sleep. People didn't look down on the Witchers there. We moved to this place about the time I was born. It was the only place I knew.

Leaving the neighborhood became my brother's theme that afternoon. "What's the point of living here? Nothing but trouble comes our way. Hell, let's just move. An apartment would be better than this joint."

"Stop saying 'hell,'" Mom said.

Pop drove to the job he'd been fired from and picked up his

last paycheck. When he came home he said, "Let's go get a hamburger."

"On what, your good looks?"

"Come on, let's go down the drain in style."

We hopped in the battered Ford station wagon, which Pop allegedly had deployed as a missile to take Rusty's life.

"Look at us," Stan said, "unemployed and going out to eat."

We rattled past the neat houses with their tidy yards.

"Everyone around here is related to someone that can destroy us," he went on, thinking of Mr. Ball. (By now we had an inkling it was Pop's thrashing of Kellner that had led to his sacking.) "I hate this dump. Stupid lawns, stupid crew cuts, fucking squares."

"I'm warning you," Mom said.

Pop turned onto Clark, a verdant lane that rolled bucolically towards the newly asphalted four-lane. This was before developers had robbed the neighborhood of its woods. Set deep in the trees was a spanking-new brick-and-wood two-story palace with a concrete drive, carport and swimming pool. It had been completed only the month before. We neighborhood kids had been riding our bikes over to stare at its opulence, wondering at the aristocrats who could afford such a place. It was the talk of the neighborhood, and every time we passed it Mom would say, "Golly, what a gorgeous house."

Now its owners were moving in.

A moving van, yellow and monstrous, squatted under the foliage of Clark Lane.

"Look!" Mom hollered.

Pop slowed so we could see.

In front of the house were a well-tanned gentleman in tennis shorts and a platinum-haired lady in a white summer dress, who appeared to be supervising workers staggering like Atlases beneath furniture.

They might have been hosting a cocktail party. To me they seemed like high-society people, like Thurston Howell III and Lovey from *Gilligan's Island*, only not as old. We slowly cruised past and Mom, unseen, lifted her hand to wave, but decided to brush her hair instead. The daughter, if that's who she was, placidly wound her way through the brawny movers to join her parents: a hippie girl in a paisley minidress and orange fishnets. Her blond hair had so many twists and turns I was reminded of the off-ramps and overpasses on an interstate highway.

Stan's eyes nearly popped out of his head.

He swung his eyes to peer at the retreating tableau. "Who are those people?"

"Looks like they're our new neighbors," Mom said.

"Are they rich?"

"Must be."

He grew quiet.

We went down the highway to a beer joint decent enough to dine in as long as you got out of there before eight. Pop ordered a plate of corned beef and I watched him while he chewed. After a while he said, "Stan has a point. We could get an apartment right cheap. I hear they're not so expensive at Colonial Courts."

"I've changed my mind," Stan said. "Moving would be stupid. The only thing we'd accomplish is allowing them the satisfaction of thinking they drove us away."

We turned to stare at him.

He was already lord of the manor, in his dreams.

3

TROUBLE ARRIVED on the very morning Mom started at the Ben Franklin. She had just stepped out the front door—we were at the table sopping our pancakes in syrup—when we heard a brokenhearted cry come from the yard. We ran and looked. Mom was standing atop a loose slate and staring at the house with her face all askew. For a moment we didn't get it. We knew the house was ratty and it needed paint and it was missing screens; we knew about the junk rusting at the side of the house; we knew about the bare patches in the yard and the overgrown flourishes of ragweed here and there. But why the pain of it should attack her at this particular moment we didn't understand.

And then we stepped into the yard and saw.

During the night, while we slept, someone had spray-painted TRASH across the front of the house. It was near the bottom, under the paneled living room window, clearly visible from the street.

"Son of a bitch," my brother said.

Pop was grinding his teeth. I saw a muscle twitch in his jaw.

"I'll have it off before you get home," he told Mom.

"Who would do such a thing? Who would be so cruel?"

"Kellner was behind it," my brother said.

"Don't you do anything, Stan, we don't know who did this."

"I'll find out," he said.

"There's some paint in the crawl space," Pop said, "go get it."

Pop's temper was inscrutable. You never knew when he would lose it. It blew fierce when he did, but he could take a lot of grief. At the moment he didn't seem terribly upset about the vandalism. He just wanted to get it off the wall for Mom's sake.

Me, I was burning with shame. This was Myra's judgment on me, in bold black letters.

Mom's face was in tears. Pop put his arm around her shoulder to comfort her while three or four dogs loped across the yard, hoping Pop would toss them some scraps.

"You go on to work," he said, "don't you worry about this."

"Why do people have to be so mean?"

Pop couldn't answer that. He just knew if you got lucky enough to catch 'em you could enjoy the pleasure of stomping the shit out of 'em. Whoever did this, young or old, better hope Pop never learned who did it.

Stan had run around to the back of the house to fetch the paint. Now he came marching towards us with two buckets in his hands (*like an old-stone savage armed*, I thought, remembering my Robert Frost from school—I was a straight-A student).

"Set 'em there," Pop said, nudging his chin. "We'll scrape and paint later. Let's cover it up for now."

"I'm gonna kill the son of a bitch that did this," Stan said.

"Stan," Mom said.

The unmistakable rumble of Reedy's patrol Plymouth sounded in our ears and we gazed at one another with questioning eyes. Who did this guy think he was, Deputy Dawg? The cruiser rumbled to a stop and the driver's door cried plaintively open.

Reedy got out, staring at our defaced house.

"Got trouble?"

Pop wasn't very friendly. He eyed the cop and said, "We didn't send for you, this ain't your business."

"Looks like you had visitors in the night."

Pop didn't say anything. We stood in a group. My mother sniffled. The dogs had joined us, excited about the action.

"I guess I'll go to work," Mom said.

"You want to make a complaint?" the cop asked.

"Talk to him," she replied, and walked off with a lowered head, mortified in advance by the scorn she would encounter.

Pop seemed anxious about Reedy's presence. He didn't want people to think we had called the cops.

"We can handle this without you," he said.

Reedy had a squinting, benevolent cowboy face that belied his limited stature. "You sure? Whoever did this is not likely to go away."

"I can handle it. When a law's been broke I'll call you."

"I'd say one has been broken."

Just then a car pulled onto our street, a long, polished Cadillac Fleetwood with the electronic windows sealed to keep in the air-conditioning. As it passed it slowed down a little. On the passenger side, riding shotgun, was the grande dame of the big house, critically examining the writing on our wall. She glanced at the police cruiser and swung her offended eyes to Reedy and to Pop. The stately coupe eased past like a luxury liner, and as it moved along we discerned a network of golden locks turned halfway and trembling in the rear window. They belonged to the hippie girl whose image had by now been burned into my brother's dreams.

"Christ," he said, "she saw."

He had placed himself behind Pop, hoping he wouldn't be spied.

"It's like a billboard telling 'em who we are," he said.

"I can make sure whoever did this gets prosecuted," Reedy offered.

For all I knew, some friend of Myra's had attacked our house. Perhaps at this very second the vandal was laughingly retelling his deed.

Pop jerked his eyes nervously while Reedy lectured him on the efficacy of statements to the police. He didn't like the questions the lawman was asking.

After a while the cop reluctantly drove away.

My brother and I, meanwhile, were spreading paint over the letters that all too soon would immortalize our social status if we didn't get rid of them fast. Even after we finished, the word TRASH still whispered through the thin coat of white.

I moved dejectedly indoors and threw myself on my bed. My brother followed and climbed to the bunk above; he was so quiet I figured he'd fallen asleep. Then, from the declivity in the bunk, his voice rang out, deep and serious.

"I'm gonna fuck Gaylord Joyner up. I'm gonna hurt that motherfucker bad."

4

I HAD GONE to the Ben Franklin to see my mother for a reason I can't remember, probably some message Pop wanted delivered. (Our phone had been cut off.) I found her behind the register, primly awaiting the first customers of the day, while Mr. Harris leaned against the counter contemplating his treasure. When I left the store I glanced casually towards the steps on my right, and lo and behold, there was the angel of my social studies class ascending them—little Myra Joyner, sister to Gaylord.

I waited until she reached the top step and then I took off to follow her.

Before the school year ended, while we were undergoing a discussion in class on the problem of racial prejudice in America, Mrs. Carter had asked us to reflect upon the reasons white people looked down upon blacks. Now, Martin Luther King, Jr., was Mrs. Carter's hero, and she had spent most of that lesson refuting a charge, made by Benny Fisher and backed up by a pamphlet he'd discovered the previous day in his mailbox, that King was funded by Russians headquartered deep in the heart of the Kremlin. (The pamphlet bore a photograph of King in a classroom with others, attentively listening to some lecture: proof, the caption asserted, that King visited communist training camps.) It was progressive Mrs. Carter's commitment to social justice that had led her to embrace me as her cause that year; yet I wondered if her mission to convince my classmates that even Witchers deserved equal rights might best be left alone.

"So why," she was asking, "why is it that white people, even in a society founded on these principles we've been talking about, these principles of justice and equal rights, why is it that so many white people still put black people down? How do racial stereotypes persist even in this day and age?"

The question fell on dead air. No one raised a hand or volunteered a response. And then, to my alarm, Mrs. Carter began to scan the aisles. I dropped my head and shaded my brow, thinking, *Please, don't, don't, don't call on me.* She always called on me—praised my exam scores, my book reports, my mastery of punctuation, my handwriting. She would read aloud my written assignments as models of elegant and concise composition. What she never understood was the outrage her good intentions provoked. Rather than derive edification from my essays, the other students would seethe with the social injury of having a Witcher placed above them.

Oh, what the hell, I already knew what she was planning to

do. Scanning the classroom, pretending to search for someone besides me to call on, that was just a charade masking the lady's insane humanitarianism. Why didn't she drop it? I didn't want to be saved, I wanted to be ignored.

Finally her eyes lighted on me.

"Jack," she called.

I raised my head. "Ma'am?"

"Why do you think white people still have prejudice? How do white people see black people in our society?"

"Well," I said.

I should have told her to go to hell, which might at least have cured her of the urge to raise me up. But I was incapable of institutional disobedience—that was my downfall. Who'd ever heard of a Witcher who obeyed?

"White people see black people as being low-class, as having an inferior social status," I said.

"And why is that?" Mrs. Carter urged, delighted I had taken the bait.

"Well, because black people are denied education and they're not allowed to have good jobs, and that forces them to live in poverty and not get ahead. And then other people see them as stupid and trashy when really they just haven't had the same opportunities that white people have."

Had I let the word "trashy" slip? Like a straight man in a comedy routine I allowed a beat to pass. I'd set up the punch line inadvertently, and now I wanted to get it over with.

It arrived in a whisper from behind.

"Like Witchers."

The class let loose with hysterical laughter while Mrs. Carter glared in hopeless reproof.

"Go on, Jack," she said, kindly.

I shook my head. I didn't have the energy. Mrs. Carter smiled grimly for my humiliation and, having already plucked me from time-serving obscurity, removed the spotlight and placed it on Benny Fisher (the source of the whisper) by forcing him to repeat his rude words aloud. Which, of course, only threw the spotlight back on me.

So there you have it. It might have been an average day in my wretched life (a good one was when I escaped notice), but for the fact that *she* approached after class, ever so carefully and delicately, and spoke aloud the words that would give me direction, meaning and purpose. . . . But more on that later.

The shopping center was built into the side of a long hill with terraced rows of shops that you reached by a series of steps, which culminated where Mr. Gladstein had his jewelry store. This was the direction Myra was heading. I nearly called out to her, but I suddenly remembered how she'd turned away that morning when I was walking with my mother. I wasn't sure I could tolerate that anymore, not from her of all people, and so I followed quietly, keeping a distance of fifty feet between us.

She labored up the succeeding stairways, admiring her reflection in the windows and bouncing lightly like a pogo stick, a peculiar way of walking she had. After she passed Gladstein's she hooked a right, went around the corner.

This left me in a dilemma. I couldn't follow her without

being discovered, because the shops along that pathway led to the end of the line and she'd eventually have to turn back. But there was another problem. People in our neighborhood tended to exit the shopping center through the alleyway in the rear. If Myra was patronizing a store down there, chances were good she'd pass through the alleyway when her business was over. Which meant I could either tail her and be discovered, or lose her.

I felt reasonably certain she was visiting the sewing store. Her mother was an amateur seamstress, and Myra might very well have been sent to pick up thread and pins and other tools of the couturier's art.

Needing an observation post, I impulsively dashed into Gladstein's Jewelry, Inc.

Now this Gladstein was a corpulent, goateed Jewish man, a native of New Jersey with manners distinctly Yankee. He didn't like kids and (there being enough anti-Semitism abroad to keep him on the defensive) he seemed to distrust Southerners. I'd have gladly sought sanctuary from any other storeowner. But there I was. And there he was, sitting behind his glittery glass counter and peering my way with a jeweler's knob in his eye.

"May I help you?"

He had a great bass voice, powerful, nearly godlike. Hearing it reminded me of a recent evening at the supper table, when my mother, out of the blue and in front of Pop, had blurted, "You know, Mr. Gladstein isn't good-looking, but I'll bet a girl could fall in love with him just by the sound of his voice." My brother and I were stunned, and Pop raised his head from his plate in slow amazement. He didn't say anything, he just kept chewing. Perhaps he'd realized that Mom's erotic imagination ran much further than he'd ever credited it.

Now the jeweler was giving me a real good going-over. He removed the knob from his eye. Maybe he was worried I might set a precedent and other young hoodlums would come loiter in his shop.

"I want to buy a ring for the girl that just passed," I improvised, hoping to reassure him and gain some time.

The fat of his pallid neck oozed like peanut butter over the border of his collar. His tie was too thin, too short, ending halfway up his shirt.

"Myra Joyner?"

He knew!

That would be something to reflect upon, later. We in the neighborhood had long pegged Gladstein as a Yankee Jew insolently unconscious of our goy world. He was so preoccupied with his baubles and diamonds that whenever we peered in his window he would hardly deign to acknowledge us. It had gotten to be a joke among the kids in the neighborhood, and one day on a dare Dickie Pudding performed a tap dance before the jewelry store window to see if he would react. (He didn't.)

His sharp jeweler eyes focused closely on me.

"Yes sir," I said. "Don't tell her."

I peeked at the mirrored column that ran the height of the shop's side window. In its reflection I would be able to monitor the front of the sewing store. On the panel in front of me Gladstein's face was hovering quizzically.

"Myra doesn't know that she has an admirer?" He caught the internal homonym. "Ad-Myra," he said, in case I didn't get it.

I found it odd. I wasn't all that comfortable with the man.

I pointed at the mirror. "I can watch from here," I said, wanting him to know so I wouldn't seem rude.

"You're following her!"

"Yes sir. She doesn't like me," I explained.

"Have you told her so? Why play these games?"

His smile carved thinly between his fat cheeks. It was unsettling that a face should be so sharp and fat and crafty and stupid. And his smile made it kindly and malevolent, too. I wasn't sure I liked him, although I had no reason to not like him. He seemed to appreciate what I was up to. He was getting a kick out of me.

I shrewdly formed a strategy to make him my confidant so he wouldn't run me out of his store.

"She thinks I'm not good enough for her. But one time she told me she was proud of me 'cause I make good grades."

"You make good grades, do you?"

Gladstein's cartoon smile etched across his fat jinni's face. And yet his voice was too deep and booming to be playful. It put me on guard. Something about his shop wasn't quite right. It was quiet as a tomb. It lacked the hum of air-conditioning. It was humid. And it smelled.

"You're a lover, not a fighter, right?"

"I fight when I have to."

"A lover and a scholar," he boomed.

I shrugged. Let him talk, if that's all he wanted.

"Would Myra accept a ring from you?"

"I don't know." I swiveled towards the mirror. The sewing shop door had swung open, but it wasn't Myra, it was only a pleasant-looking lady calling farewells.

"You can't spend your life following her like a mooncalf," he said.

"No sir." That was self-evident, but I couldn't figure out how to approach a girl whose superiority to me was practically a family catechism.

"You can't be timid, you have to show women who's boss. That's what they like. They'll boss you if you don't."

I checked the mirror and glanced back at him.

"You're Margaret Witcher's boy."

That caught me off guard. His knowing my mother wasn't surprising (he'd repaired her watch a few times) but his gift for genealogy was. Apparently he noticed more about our world than we believed.

"How much money do you have to buy a ring?"

"Now? I don't even know how much they cost. How much is a diamond ring?"

"Diamonds run high. That's what the business is about, diamonds."

I wondered if the stories I'd heard about Jews were true, and I formed a resentment against him for putting it in my head that I might have a chance with Myra. He wanted to sell me a ring, that's all.

"How much you have on you?" he said.

"Fifty cents."

"Fifty cents. Well, let's see."

He wiggled his finger for me to come close. I wandered unenthusiastically towards him, which meant leaving off my observation of the mirrored column.

Gladstein was on a three-legged stool, his pallid bulk spread under him. He tugged on a fabulous drawer that opened across his lap.

"How old is this Myra whom you admire?"

"My age, twelve. I'm gonna be thirteen in a month."

"So that makes you what, a Gemini, a Cancer? Plus you make good grades in school!" He seemed to find something comical about such slight accomplishment. He kept smiling, demonic and fat behind the goatee. There was a brand of canned sausages with a demon on the label whom Gladstein could be a stand-in for, except he was fatter. And yet he seemed a nice man, for all that. . . . He confused me. I needed time to think about him.

He held forth a silvery ring with a blue agate stone in its center. It wasn't the prettiest jewel I'd ever seen, but at least it was a ring. And who knows, it might give me a new lease with Myra.

"You think this would win her heart?"

"How much does it cost?"

"I can let it go for fifty cents."

"Is that really what it's worth?"

"Kid, this ring is worth nothing. Except it might fit Myra's finger. That's worth fifty cents, don't you agree?"

I slid it up and down my pinkie.

"I might have to hold her down to get it on her, though."

Gladstein roared. He thought that was funny.

"Keep studying!" he bellowed. "Make those grades!" He broke into a fit of coughing, which put the brakes on his laughter.

I handed him two quarters and held the blue stone to my eyes. Never before had I owned anything as precious and grown-up as a ring. That it was associated with Myra made it mystical to me.

Gladstein seemed to be enjoying the enchantment of his profession. "I can give you a charm to go with that if you'd like."

"Sir?"

I wasn't sure I'd heard him right. But he must have thought better of it. He frowned and examined the jewels in the drawer.

Meanwhile I was balancing the ring on the tip of my thumb, upping it into the air. Gladstein ran his hand over his mouth to hide his amusement. Then he got distracted by something behind me.

"She just went by." He jerked his chin.

"Sir?"

"Your girl just went in that direction."

I bolted to the door, hollering my thanks, while he shouted some obnoxious encouragement I couldn't catch.

Myra was heading back the way she had come, descending the steps with her pogo-stick bounce.

5

I DON'T HAVE the faintest notion what I'd have done had she discovered me behind her. But I had a trinket, a gift to offer, and that was as good as a purpose.

She passed the Ben Franklin, and fifty feet later I passed too (keeping my head rigidly advanced, lest Mom see through the window and distract me). Alas, she turned into the A&P, which forced me to cool my heels in the Hallmark shop next door.

The truth is, very few ties of fate bound me to Myra. One: my father and her father hated each other. Two: my brother and her brother hated each other. Three: she had once been kind to me. Four: we had been on the same honor roll during the previous school year.

And look at what kept us apart. She was a Joyner. Her father was a model of square-jawed integrity, her mother the spit and image of Betty Crocker on the packages. Duke University, that Alexandria and Oxford and Weimar of the Carolinas, had spread wide-open arms of welcome to her brother, and probably would do the same for Myra in years to come. *And* she lived next door to the Kellners. Whereas I was a Witcher. My father was a hillbilly, my mother looked like an Okie, and my brother would soon be commuting to a state school on a municipal bus solely to avoid the draft (he was precisely the kind of redneck the politicians liked to pack off to sweltering jungles). We lived in a shack that lacked not only screens and shingles but grass in the yard. And now the word TRASH was painted across it.

Yet within me dwelled an indefatigable optimism. My angel of self-love kept whispering encouraging words in my ears. Had I not caught Myra staring at me in class? Had she not told me with her own lips that she was proud of me for making the honor roll?

That had happened the very day of my humiliation in Mrs. Carter's class, when she touched my arm as I was escaping into the hallway. Think of it, Myra Joyner touching me! That alone might have sufficed to make the day miraculous. And then she actually deigned to speak.

"Benny Fisher is a moron," she said when we made it out to the hall. "I hate it when they make fun of people."

What could I say? I'd assumed Benny was the spokesman for everyone, including her.

"I just want you to know you're the smartest person in class, next to me. Mrs. Carter told me herself. I heard you made the honor roll."

"I always make the honor roll," I said.

"I'm really proud of you. Benny and his friends are idiots. We're not all like that. A lot of us think you're really neat."

"You do?" Where would I find this committee of well-wishers? She never told me and I never found out.

"Yes. And you know the paper Mrs. Carter read in class, the one on *Profiles in Courage*? That almost made me cry when she read it. And when I got home that day I told my parents about it and they think you're really smart."

It was a scene I'd later exert my imagination uselessly to construct: Mr. and Mrs. Joyner listening enthralled while their daughter enumerated the scholastic accomplishments of a Witcher. In that case, why did her parents still not wave to me when they passed in their car? Oh well, at the time it didn't seem important: what was important was Myra's lopsided nose, the down on her cheeks, her sloe eyes warm as charcoal embers.

What was I supposed to do now? Should I invite her to my house so we could study together? Shame alone would never permit it, not as long as Pop's junk was in the yard. Should I walk with her, carry her books, offer her a stick of gum? All I could do was gawk, and not twitch.

"Don't let Benny and his friends bother you," she said. "It really doesn't matter you're a Witcher, not to anyone that counts."

"It doesn't?"

She swallowed her lack of conviction and nodded. Perhaps that was going too far. But she had followed me into the hall to reassure me, and Myra Joyner did nothing by halves.

"Would you like to get together sometime?" I said.

"Maybe we'll talk later," she said. "I have to go now, Kathy is waiting."

"Have you read *Fahrenheit 451*?" I said.

"That's on the summer reading list, have you read it already?"

"I read most of those books a long time ago."

"Wow, Jack. Listen, we should talk more someday. I'd like to talk about books."

"Why not now?"

"I can't, Kathy is waiting."

"Myra," I said, to make her stay.

She placed her palm against my chest and stared deeply into my eyes; and then she left.

What the hell did that mean?

All night I tossed and turned with those sloe eyes still staring at me. When morning came I headed to the schoolyard early, hoping to speak with her. But she had reasserted her usual reserve. She was standing next to the Coghill girls, and she waved only when they became distracted by something. It was a wave that said she saw me, felt me and acknowledged me; and managed to add, *Not now*.

Now, in the Hallmark store, my angel of self-love was whispering once more, encouraging me gently to hubris. If only I could make Myra see me for what I was, she would appreciate me, she would accept me, she would want me. . . .

Her head went bobbing over the top rack of the greeting cards and I sped out of the store to tail her.

At the other end of the shopping center, when you hung a

left, was a brief mall of office fronts (insurance, dentistry) that formed a blind. Behind them ran the alleyway.

Myra crossed and mounted the steps that led to the street, still without the slightest idea that a boy just behind was monitoring her pogo-stick progress with love-swollen eyes. Coincidentally, the sloped street that the steps led to was called Myra Street. I have never figured out why the developers christened it that. All of the other streets in the subdivision were named after famous explorers. Maybe in the old days, when bulldozers were uprooting the farmland so the developers could append our cracker suburb to the expanding town, someone had had a premonition of the brainy bobbing goddess whose feet now were tripping happily along its paved cultivation.

She swung left and right, taking me past the woods behind Dickie Pudding's house and onto a street that eventually curved northwards and plunged downhill to Stanley. In other words, we were drawing close to our separate blocks, and our paths must soon diverge.

Realizing I was about to lose her, if only from a distance of fifty feet, I recklessly called out her name.

She turned, smiling benignly, but quickly knit her brow as I drew closer and she realized who it was. (I hadn't yet garnered the automatically hostile expressions reserved for my father and my brother. Instead I received looks of dismay, of social concern.)

"Yes, Jack," she said, patiently.

I caught up.

"Hi," I said.

"Hi."

"How's your summer so far?"

"Fine," she said.

I stood blankly. What was there to say?

"I have to go," she said.

"Wait. How come you don't talk to me anymore?"

"I should think you know why."

"I don't."

She regarded me with a raised eyebrow, tapping her foot.

"Perhaps you don't remember what happened at the drainage ditch the other day?"

"You mean Pop and Kellner? What's that got to do with us?"

"I can't be seen with you now."

"Why not? It wasn't me who punched Kellner. I can't help it what Pop does."

"You were *with* him."

"Of course I was, he's my father." I didn't want to defend him at this crucial juncture, but I couldn't exactly deny the obvious.

"Fine. I have to go."

"Wait, I have something to show you."

"What?"

I nudged my head towards the woods.

"Let's go over there."

"Where?"

"In the woods, I don't want people to see."

"I am not going in the woods with you, Jack Witcher."

I reached into my pocket and pulled out the ring.

"I want you to have this," I told her.

Myra stared. And then her face changed. She looked up with a softened expression.

"Whose is that?"

"It's for you. I got it at Gladstein's, I was just there."

"You bought this for me?"

"Try it on," I said.

She blinked in astonishment. The flattery implied by my gesture had made her forget her station. The air between us became charged with meaning. I noticed the down on her tanned cheeks softly quivering.

"No one has ever given me a ring, this is my first." She seemed already to understand how fraught with sentiment this moment would be in the future.

"Daddy would never let me wear a boy's ring," she said, "especially not yours."

"Just keep it in your pocket."

Myra kept staring into the blue agate, wrestling with the temptation.

"I can't," she said.

"Sure you can."

"What would it mean if I did?"

"That we're friends."

While she struggled with the burden of that, I decided to go for broke. "Plus we'd be going steady. . . . If you want," I threw in.

"Jack, are you crazy? I can't be your friend, and I will certainly never go steady with you."

"Come on, you're always staring at me in class, I've caught you before."

Tears filled her eyes. "I do not stare at you! Go away, leave me alone."

"You know you like me."

"I can't believe how conceited you are."

"Just take the ring."

She turned and ran.

"Chicken!" I called.

I don't think she heard me, and later I was glad. That would have marred our first romantic moment, for which I'd spent my last fifty cents; and even though the ring still lay in my palm, I can't say I'd been crushed by her. I had seen the tears in her eyes, and my angel was quick to reassure me.

I was ready to cut through the woods to call on Dickie Pudding, the only boy willing to claim me as a friend. But the emotion of the day was too much, so I went home and watched soap operas with Pop. Yet even with Pop I was restless. I'd had my first romantic encounter with a girl! I couldn't stop reliving it.

Somehow I wound up in the front yard kicking tufts of dirt and thinking about Myra. It must have been close to suppertime. Mom was due home any minute and I kept debating whether I should tell her what had happened.

Then I heard a car turn on our road. A horn tapped and a black Continental cruised past, driven by Gladstein. His fat, hot-sausage-demon grin was going a mile a minute. He swung his head to look as he passed and I took a step forward, thinking he was about to stop. But he didn't. He just grinned and waved and stared in the mirror.

Three fluffy dogs were yapping faintly through the rear window.

6

MY BROTHER WAS TALKING to himself, laughing out loud, swaggering about with the plug from the portable radio in his ear. He'd bought a pair of sunglasses that he rarely took off, and sometimes he wore them in the bathroom. We'd hear the toilet flush and out he would spring, grinning behind the shades. Then he might snatch the book I was reading and fling it across the room: *Rush to Judgment, Tai-Pan, The Source, The Fixer, A Texan Looks at Lyndon*—paperbacks my mother would buy at the drugstore rack and leave unfinished for me to pick up. He would accuse me of being a square. He laughed at my music. He assured me cool things were happening in the world, psychedelic things, and told me what a drag it would be if I missed out on them.

One day I went to the living room and found him silhou-etted in the doorway. "Jack," he said. He jerked his head to-wards the yard and we went outside. Silently he motioned me to hop on the back part of the banana seat of his Sting-Ray, and I was happy that my brother was being a brother. How rare that was these days. But it was a fact. Stan Witcher had once been a sweet boy. We had laughed and conspired; he had defended me, amused me.

We sailed along to the woods beside Clark Lane and then shouldered through some brush for about fifty yards, to a small trickling creek. The little patch of woods was well shaded and hard to reach, and if you were willing to brave the ticks and mosquitoes you might find some sylvan privacy there.

We sat at the edge of the creek. My brother took off his sunglasses, set them on the ground and pulled a box of Marlboros from his pocket. Then we lit up.

I was fairly new to cigarettes, maybe a year in. Smoking was an event during which I liked to meditate authoritatively on the relative merits of different tobacco brands while practicing my talent for smoke rings. Stan was diligent about introducing me to new vices, and he always seemed genuinely interested in how I was getting along in them. But now he had no regard for my ruminations. He kept cracking his knuckles and staring back in the direction of the street. Did he have some ulterior reason for bringing me to the creek?

He flicked a half-finished cigarette into the water and pulled the box from his pocket. Only this time, using his thumb and forefinger as tweezers, he brought forth a white-wrapped stogie and dangled it in the air with the satisfied expression of a surgeon displaying a diseased kidney.

"Grass," he said.

I didn't understand what he meant.

And then it dawned on me.

"Is that a joint?"

He nodded, very seriously.

I gaped over my shoulder, half expecting the cops to come crashing through the brush behind us. Drugs were an entirely new social malady at the time, more a rumor than a reality. Stan was probably the first person ever to bring pot into El Dorado Hills.

"Where did you get it? Let me see."

I flipped it back and forth in my hand.

"Where did you get it?"

"I have my sources."

Now I knew why he'd been hitchhiking downtown so much of late. I understood the muttered phone conversations, the hanging up whenever someone came into the room.

"Have you tried it?"

"Of course. In fact, I'm going to smoke this one. Now."

"No!" I hollered.

"Relax, it's not what they make it out to be."

He took a few tokes while I glanced about in alarm. I remembered what had happened the last time he'd brought me to the woods, when he had picked up a rock and brained a squirrel with the same dead-on accuracy he used to deliver sucker punches. I'd gotten all flustered and pained by that and yelled at him to quit. I hated squirrels as much as the next guy, but I couldn't see any point in killing them. And then he whipped out his knife, sawed into the creature's legs and tail, and, using a few rusty nails that he yanked from some moldy boards lying in the brush, he hung the amputated appendages like strips of hairy meat to a tree. What kind of psycho did things like that? And why on earth did I get stuck with him as a brother?

Smoking the joint took forever. He closed his eyes, held his breath and spat air. Seeds were popping. The very burning of the weed was sinister.

When he finally smoked it to a nub, he dropped the roach into the Marlboro box.

"You save them?" I said.

He just grinned.

"Are you hooked yet?" I asked.

He burst out laughing and stared at me with his silly eyes. Which pretty much answered my question.

What would be the next calamity to befall the House of Witcher?

"Let's go home," I told him.

"Are you crazy? I can't face Pop in this condition."

"You better watch it, you'll be addicted in no time."

This well-meant warning brought forth another peal of drug-addled mirth. He wavered his hands like a spook and taunted me: "Look out, I'm stoooooned."

How quickly was I learning the futility of reasoning with a hophead. I turned away, depressed.

"Hey, come on, I wanna show you something," he said.

He put his sunglasses on and leapt across the creek, and I followed. We climbed a slope, shooing away briars until we came to a narrow ridge. After that the ground sloped downwards. We shoved through some branches and leaves and wound up at the other end of the woods; and then we got in a hunkering position and surveyed the newly cleared plot of land upon which Thurston and Lovey had built their palatial homestead. We were staring directly into their backyard.

"Her name is Anya," my brother said.

"How do you know?"

"I was here yesterday. I heard the old lady calling her from inside the house."

"The girl was in the yard?"

"Yeah, she was sunbathing, wearing a bikini."

"Were you high?"

Stan laughed and pushed me over.

We sat cross-legged. It was a hot day, but there was a lovely breeze and everything was peaceful. We watched the large, inclined yard. Close to the house the ground leveled out, and that is where Thurston and Lovey had placed their swimming pool, surrounding it with a green slatted fence. Stan told me the pool hadn't been filled with water yet. At the far end of the yard, near the garbage cans, stood piles of empty boxes and discarded padding material from the move.

"What kind of name is Anya?" I asked.

"Pretty, huh?"

We heard a door whoosh open. She stepped out to the yard, laden with empty boxes she intended to haul up to the garbage area. The moment she stepped outside, Stan's nose jutted like a pointer's. He watched as she marched through the yard in her sandals and white shorts. His nose was quivering.

He whistled between his teeth.

"Quit it, we'll get in trouble."

"This ain't their property, we can sit here all we want."

The hippie girl dropped off the boxes and headed back to the house. Stan whistled again and she stopped. We were behind sparse brush, partially obscured.

She smiled and came over.

"Who's there?"

"Peace," Stan said. He gave her the peace sign.

She kept craning her neck. This time her hair hung in ringlets. She came to within three feet of us.

"Who are you?" she said.

"Peace," my brother said.

Anya laughed and gave the peace sign back. "What are you supposed to be, a hippie?"

"We're the Welcome Wagon."

"You are not," she protested blithely, in an accent more Southern than ours.

"Where you from?"

"Dallas. We just moved in."

"Dallas, Texas." Stan nodded familiarly, as though Dallas were a place he'd been to a hundred times. "You must need someone to show you the town," he said.

"Doesn't strike me there's a lot to see." She nudged her chin at me. "Who's this with you?"

"He's my bodyguard."

Anya found that funny. She gave me a flirtatious wink.

"Hi, Cutiepie, how old are you?"

I scowled.

"Do you smoke grass?" my brother asked.

She tossed him a look. "Now I think you're being impertinent."

Her use of the word "impertinent" made me nervous. It demonstrated clearly that she outclassed us. I could handle "impertinent," but Stan didn't possess my scholastic talents and he resented it when people put on airs. I looked to see what he was thinking, but he only stared at her from behind his sunglasses.

"It's just a question," he told her. "If you smoke with me I was thinking we might have some fun."

"You haven't told me your name," she said.

"It's Gaylord."

Why did he say that?

Anya laughed, unwilling to believe anyone would be named Gaylord.

Suddenly a voice called from the rear door.

"Anya, what are you doing?"

It was Lovey!

"Nothing, I'm talking!" she shouted over her shoulder.

"I have to go," she told us.

"Meet me tomorrow at the creek," my brother said.

"What creek?"

"Just cut through. It's on the other side of the hill."

"Anya, who are you talking to?"

"I have to go."

"I'll be at the creek at three," Stan said.

She walked off in her sandals and tight shorts and my brother watched her from behind with his low-class insolence.

I wanted to get out of there. Lovey was on the back porch standing on her tiptoes so she could see us, and here was my brother in possession of marijuana. And no doubt Reedy was at large, poking his nose into everyone's business. What if Lovey went inside and called him?

We returned to the creek and hung out until my brother came down some.

I was monitoring his high with great anxiety. He made me promise not to tell Mom and Pop he was on drugs. And I didn't tell them. But I wanted to. And the next day he went without me to the creek. He was there at three in the afternoon. He waited for a while, and just when he was about to give up Anya came brushing through the woods from the street side. She told him that if she'd entered the woods from the yard her mother would have seen and called her back.

Stan passed her a joint and she toked on it like she'd been using drugs all her life.

He told me about it that evening. After they got high they made out for a while and he felt her breasts.

I was stunned. I figured my brother had been setting himself up for a fall. I thought he was making coarse, untrue assumptions about Anya, and about girls in general.

I was wrong.

7

MY BROTHER HAD PICKED UP some of the new hippie expressions, like "far out," "outasight," and "dig it." A few of these had already gained wary currency in our neighborhood; others were provided by the groovier television shows. Only recently Stan had hollered, "Sock it to me, baby!" and dashed across the room to sweep my mother in his arms. "Give me a hug, foxy lady! Come on, you sexy chick, hug me tighter!"

I marveled at his brazenness. Who else ever told their mother she was sexy? I mean, wow. The boy had charm— sometimes. (Poor Mom would accept flirting wherever she found it, except from Mr. Harris at the Ben Franklin.)

Stan had the longest hair in the neighborhood, maybe in town. Hair length was a contest among the boys in the neighborhood; most lost out when their parents lugged them to the barbershop. But Pop, he was indifferent to the controversies other dads raged about. He just didn't care that much, and

Stan's hair kept on growing. When you saw hair as long as his it was on garage band record covers or maybe on the hippies out in San Francisco. It wasn't typical in our town, and it drew stares of disapproval whenever we passed by in our smashed-up Ford. "Doesn't that just show you," the old folks would say. "You can't expect people with a car that looks like that to control their teenagers."

During the course of the year Stan grew his hair so long he almost wasn't allowed to graduate, even though the principals were eager to get rid of him; but after he threatened to turn it into a constitutional issue, they decided not to press the matter. It was dawning on people that the war against long hair was over. Soon they would give up on rock and roll and drugs. After that it would be Vietnam, civil rights, homosexuals, pornography. The news kept arriving through our television screens. The world was happening out there, if not in El Dorado Hills: drugs like the planet had never seen, orgiastic music, interracial shenanigans, crazy long-haired gatherings—flowers and dancing and girls blowing bubbles!

Not so long ago, maybe eight or nine months back, my brother had been bawling his eyes out over Courtney Blankenship. That mad affair had lasted one brief season, long enough to scandalize the neighborhood and cause Mr. Blankenship (he of *Ahoy, Mateys*) to seek professional counseling for his daughter. For three breathtaking months the romance between Stan and Courtney was the talk of El Dorado Hills. Courtney lost many of her best friends, and didn't seem to care. What in the world was she thinking? Perhaps El Dorado Hills had been too negligent of my brother's sinewy physicality and Jim Morrison curls. Maybe. But after I saw him bawling over a girl he didn't seem so tough. Actually, it gave me a little heart, seeing my brother vulnerable and crying. But that period passed, and now he scorned Courtney Blankenship for being plastic, square and uptight. Derisively he sneered when he heard her name. He called her "Suzy Creamcheese"—a cocktease, a whore, "the slut goddess of El Dorado Hills." When he learned Gaylord Joyner had already broken up with her he laughed out loud. Not that it softened him towards Gaylord. On the contrary. It was as though Gaylord's sole purpose in pursuing Courtney had been to break his heart, and that was a crime he would never forget.

What this meant was, I couldn't talk to my brother about Myra. Joyners were Joyners, and he hated them all. Besides, he'd grown too cavalier about love to sympathize with romantic feelings. "Let me tell you about chicks, they want it as much as guys but they can't admit it. When they find out they like it, it freaks 'em out, see? Especially when they like getting it from a hippie dog like me. Chicks around here can't deal with their instincts. That's why I dig Anya, she knows exactly where it's at."

Profane talk like that made me hesitate to utter Myra's name in his presence. When had he become a hippie dog, anyway?

There didn't seem to be a soul I could confide to. Mom had been burned too many times to think any good would come of love. Her hope was that I'd find some nice ugly girl, after I turned thirty. As for my going with Myra, that would be reaching for the stars, and she'd never encourage such overweening

62

vanity. Which left two potential confidants: my only friend, Dickie Pudding, and Pop. Dickie Pudding was out, because it would be all over town faster than a telegram if I breathed a single word to him about Myra Joyner. And Pop was too manly to have much regard for feelings. So I locked up my dreams and walked alone.

One afternoon I strolled to the Ben Franklin to see if Mom would loan me a dollar (she wouldn't). As I was leaving the store I decided, on impulse, to visit Gladstein.

Gladstein was the only person who knew about Myra and me—Gladstein, of all people. How had it come about? And yet I was still a little timid around him.

I stopped before his shop window, pretending to browse his display. When I casually raised my eyes, I saw him behind the counter, grinning like a demon and waving me in.

The prissy bell above his door tinkled when I opened it.

"How's it going, little Witcher?"

It was humid and tomblike in the shop, and it smelled subtly of linked meat.

"Did you give her the ring?" He waited happily, his grin parting the bristles of his goatee.

"No sir, I tried to but she wouldn't take it."

The grin vanished and he fingered his whiskers. "I don't get it, it's a nice ring."

He pulled the drawer over his lap. "Let's see what else we have."

"I can't buy another ring, I don't have any money."

"So trade that one in."

He had piles of jewels in there, rattling and jingling, and he

kept waving his hands over them. I wouldn't have been surprised if a turbaned muscleman had appeared and granted me
three wishes.

"She said she won't take a ring from me. My pop beat up
Mr. Kellner and now our name is mud."

"Like the doctor who treated John Wilkes Booth, his name
has been Mudd ever since."

Gladstein let out a hoot of laughter, but I got the joke only
later, when I thought about it.

His face grew serious.

"Why did your father beat up Paul Kellner?"

"Kellner said Pop tried to hit his dog with his car. But it's
not true, Rusty ran in front of it. He's kind of a dumb dog."

Gladstein nodded. "That's a serious charge, trying to kill a
dog." He owned three white mutts, Peek Shoos, Yatzis, some
name like that. I'd observed them yapping through the rear
window of his Continental many times. Otherwise I didn't
know a thing about his domestic arrangements. I didn't even
know if he had a wife.

"Boy, you know, I don't know what I'd do if someone tried
to hurt my dogs. I just don't know."

"Pop didn't try to hurt anyone's dog."

"Of course not, I'm just pondering human motive. Well,
Witcher. We have to do something about you and Myra Joyner.
Have you kissed her yet?"

"Oh no. She would never let me kiss her." I asserted this
solemnly. "All I want is to talk to her. Maybe I can kiss her later."

"No-no-no-no-no-no," Gladstein said. "First you kiss her. You have the rest of your life to talk to her."

"I don't know about that, she hasn't been that friendly to me since Pop beat up Mr. Kellner."

I trailed my finger across the counter. He was a weird guy, but at least he let me talk about her.

"Witcher," he said, "look at me."

Unwillingly I met his eyes. He held them on me for a long time, making sure I understood their gravity. They tended lugubriously downwards, hanging above pendulous bags of flesh.

"Do you want to kiss her?"

"Yes," I said. The sibilance I placed on the trail of the word took me by surprise. Do we know ourselves? Are we privy to our own impulses? All I had wanted up to that moment was to spend time with Myra, to speak with her. That's all.

"Listen to me. If you want to kiss her you can't think of anything else. Imagine kissing her. Form a picture in your mind. Meditate on it and it will come true."

He turned to the trinkets in his drawer and ran his hands through them. He was muttering, speaking. . . . I think he was talking to his jewels.

I popped my knuckles, looked around.

By and by he returned to me.

"You have to learn how to use your mind. Anything you want you can have. It's all in your power, you just have to want it."

"Yes sir."

"Don't 'Yes sir' me. Listen to what I'm saying."

"I am listening."

"But you aren't believing. Do you have the ring?"

"Yes sir," I said. It was in my pocket. (It never left my pocket.)

"Give it to me."

I did, and Gladstein replaced it with a golden band that had a ruby-red stone glinting in its middle.

"What's this for?"

"It's a trade. Take it instead. Give it to Myra."

"You sure it's okay?"

"Witcher. Listen. Picture the girl in your mind. Don't let that image go away. Stay focused. And keep this ring in your pocket. It is magic. When you give it to her she will let you kiss her."

Filmy sweat had covered me. The smell of linked meat grew stronger. I remembered the red demon on the sausage can. I couldn't meet Gladstein's eyes.

Tiny whimpers came from the rear of the store, breaking the tomb-quiet spell.

"My babies are waking up."

"Your dogs? You bring them to work?"

"You've seen my dogs?"

"I see them in your car sometimes."

"Okay. Tell me what you're gonna do."

"When?"

"When you see Myra."

"Kiss her," I intoned.

Gladstein smiled. A gleam was in his eye. "And you're going to give her this ring."

"Yes sir."

"Next time I see you you'll tell me that. We'll laugh about it, we'll have a good time. But I don't want to see you 'til you've kissed her, understand?"

"Yes sir."

"Witcher. Look at me. Stop looking away."

He stared at me with his baggy eyes. I tried to keep mine level.

"The will is in the eyes. Do you understand?"

I nodded. I didn't understand. I didn't know what the hell he was doing.

"Good. Now go."

I turned.

My feet were reluctant. I had all sorts of questions. But I didn't know what to ask. I moved towards the door in a fugue state.

The rest of the day passed in a dream. Could it be Gladstein was a demon? And yet he seemed to be on my side. He was rooting for me. He wanted me to kiss Myra.

I mentioned him to my mother that evening, in a tone of idle curiosity. I was passing his shop, I said. I went in to look at something and had a chat with the man.

Pop was napping on the carmine sofa.

She gazed at the window and said, softly, "He's Jewish, you know, but he sure has a beautiful voice."

I went to the bathroom and examined the ring and its red

stone. I clenched my eyes to form a mental image of Myra. And something miraculous happened. Myra appeared. She was in the bathroom with me. I could smell her talcum. I could see the down on her cheek. I wanted to kiss her. She said, "Yes! Yes!"

And I kissed her.

I stepped into the hallway. My fingers were trembling. What just happened had scared me. I paced until my mother asked what I was doing.

I didn't want to go to my bedroom because my brother was in there listening to his wild funky music.

I slipped outside.

Immediately a cold dog nose nudged my bare shin: Rusty.

I walked in the dusky light to Lewis Street with Rusty trotting beside me. The older kids were out, sitting on their porches and riding their bikes. Through the dusky air cicadas and frogs and crickets were croaking with all their might, as if engaged in a talent competition. Bats swooped angular against the pale glow of the sky. I reached the Kellner house and Rusty slowed down, disappointed that I'd brought him home. Then I moved along, glancing furtively at the house next door, where Myra lived.

I walked up to where the street met the two-lane.

I came back. When I passed her house I prayed, "Myra, Myra."

I wanted to see if she would hear my voice. I fingered the ring. I watched the windows of her house.

I headed home and got in bed. But I couldn't sleep. The excitement was too portentous. I picked up my discarded shorts from the floor and slipped into them. The ring was in the pocket, and I wanted to sleep with it next to my thigh.

8

POP GREW UP LISTENING to mountain music. He used to sing me a song by Merle Travis called "Kinfolks in Carolina" and I would think, "That's me, I got kinfolks in Carolina." But we rarely visited them, and they seemed about as fantastic as the Beverly Hillbillies. Pop had outgrown his mountain culture and he didn't enjoy going back. His people were hard-shell Baptists who never approved of his youthful carryings-on. They hadn't accepted Mom either, because when Pop took her to meet them she told them she didn't believe in God.

I wanted to know more about Pop's wild years. It made him heroic, that he had once been bad. My brother told me that during the war, when Pop was overseas, he had carried on with a French gal. My daddy with a French gal, that seemed so exotic. But it was a secret I wasn't allowed to let Mom in on. Before he was packed off to Europe, when he was stationed in Alabama, Pop had begun listening to blues, and after the war he taught himself to play some harmonica. He had a small record collection, Slim Harpo, Howlin' Wolf, Little Walter, but somehow in the midst of those drinking and gambling and cheating (maybe) years he'd lost his precious 78s. Those were the days of the great blues labels, King and Chess and Excello. Pop still got mad when he thought about what he'd let slip away.

Some evenings he'd come in our room and groove along with what we were playing on the stereo. The records in the house belonged to my brother, who could afford to buy them because of the dough he made as a bag boy at the Safeway store; but mainly he bought inexpensive 45s rather than albums: garage band hits, British invasion singles. Later his taste in music changed and he began coming home with soul, funk and psychedelic music, which Pop didn't like that much.

One evening Pop went to a seafood shack at the edge of our neighborhood (a year later it was torn down and replaced by a 7-Eleven) and saw Snead sitting at an adjacent table. Snead was a fixture in the neighborhood, a big black man whom people would hire to paint their houses and rake their yards and haul off their garbage. He had five children—the one in the middle was my age—and he lived in a two-story wooden house behind the seafood shack where Sneads had been since the Civil War. If aristocracy is determined by the number of years a family has survived in one place, then the Sneads had everyone beat. There had been two Snead houses originally, until one branch sold out to the developers. Our Sneads, the descendants of those who remained, were the sole black family in El Dorado Hills; but they lived far enough on the fringes for everyone to regard the neighborhood as appropriately segregated.

The two men fell to talking, one topic led to another, and soon the subject of music came up. Quickly they grew emotional. Snead shouted, "Yeah, man, dig it!" Pop hollered out Big Bill Broonzy's name and Snead brought up Son House; and finally one of them intoned the hallowed, the sacrosanct, the august and most high name of Sonny Boy Williamson. Tears poured forth, and next thing you know, Pop had run home to fetch his harmonica.

He headed to Snead's and Snead broke out his electric guitar and they jammed until three in the morning, with Mrs. Snead watching from behind her horn-rimmed glasses. After Pop left she warned Snead nothing good ever come of associating with white folks and later Snead told Pop what she said. But it was cool. The neighbors had no way of knowing what was happening in a Negro's house on the fringes. It was the next week, when Pop brought Snead to the Witcher house (an infant was sleeping in Snead's house and they didn't want to wake him), that the controversy began.

At first it wasn't all that obvious what was going on. The weather was cool and Pop and Snead were still jamming indoors. True, Snead's pickup was parked outside the house, but it might have been he was inside painting or doing some plumbing, unless anyone paused to wonder how it was that low-class people like the Witchers could afford to hire a black man to do their chores. But maybe no one did. People in comfortable circumstances imagine their own comfort is universal.

Then the weather grew warm and Pop and Snead hauled lawn chairs out to the front yard. There they would perch with a cooler between them while they played the blues on balmy nights and the neighbors cruised past, appalled. Frankly, up to the time Snead came around I hadn't exactly thought of Pop as an advocate for civil rights. Not that he was a bigot: he wasn't, and considering where he came from, that was quite an achievement. It's just I never got the impression he cared one way or the other. He was too busy not paying the bills and scrounging for work. Then one day Mom raised concerns about what the neighbors might think if Snead kept coming to the house, and that's when Pop took a stand.

"Let 'em think what they want, they don't like us anyway."

He was having fun, maybe more fun than he'd had in years. Snead and Pop sounded right good together, if you like homemade blues. And soon it got to be something more than music. Something else was happening. Maybe it was because Pop was as much an outsider as Snead, even though he never had to ride at the back of a bus. I once heard Snead tell Pop, "It's what they do to your head, that's how it works. It's when they don't have to tell you you don't have rights 'cause you don't think you do nohow." Whenever they got tired of jamming, they'd set their instruments aside and begin to speak about life, money, philosophy. In the early hours of the morning they'd be out in the yard speaking in deep voices, with their cigarettes glowing among the lightning bugs. I could hear them through my window when I woke up in the dark.

A white T-shirt and blue jeans was Snead's uniform. I never saw him in anything else, and he always kept a cigarette between his lips, to the point I wondered if it was the same one all the time. It never seemed to burn down, and I never saw him take it away. It hung on his lips even when he played the guitar. He used to bring his records over and Pop would fetch Stan's stereo player and we'd sit in the living room listening to Bo Diddley, Muddy Waters and Chuck Berry. Snead's blackness would fill the room. Ashes from his cigarette would fall on the rug, giving Mom a fit. The way he squinted over his smoke caused monstrous wrinkles to appear on his face. I had seen him crunch beer cans in his fist. He looked mean, but he was nice enough.

One evening when he was over and I was still awake, I asked him about Gladstein.

It happened that Snead, with the well-known Snead practicality, had bought himself an industrial buffer, and some of the stores in the shopping center had contracted with him to wax their floors. He had a regular gig cleaning Gladstein's shop on Saturday afternoons: waxing, buffing, squeaking a wiper along the window. I used to pass the shop when Snead was inside swinging his buffer: Gladstein would be behind the counter, straddling the three-legged stool and giving him an earful.

"You know Mr. Gladstein, don't you?" I said.

Snead squinted over his smoke. "Mojo Man."

"Mojo Man," I repeated.

"You know the song."

I guess he meant "Got My Mojo Working." We had just listened to it. But what was it supposed to mean? Had Gladstein gone to Louisiana and got himself a mojo hand?

Pop was grinning, trying to figure Snead out.

"Cat's got magic," Snead said.

"Gladstein does?"

"Keeps dogs in his back room. I have to clean their shit up, smells like a goddamn kennel."

"What kind of magic does he do?"

"Listen to me, little Witcher, I don't go poking my nose into what shouldn't be poked into. See no evil, dig? I stay clear of jive like that."

That's all he said. It was frustrating as hell.

"You mean he has magic rings?" I said.

"What?" Snead gave me a look. "It's past your bedtime, little Witcher."

He turned to Pop. "Cat's got diamonds in the store, rings and shit. Some of 'em worth more than five thousand dollars."

"Think so?" Pop said.

"Diamonds as big as the Ritz," Snead said.

"He can really get five thousand for a ring?"

"You know, most of it's cheap-ass costume jewelry. He keeps the expensive stuff in the back. He's got a safe back there you'd have to dynamite to break into."

Pop didn't say anything. He looked at Snead, thinking things over.

When Pop started thinking, he could burn a hole right through you. He didn't even realize he was doing it. Now he picked up his harmonica and brought it to his mouth with his eyes still on Snead. He began to blow a tune and Snead strummed along.

9

To try out Gladstein's magic ring I needed Myra. But it was summer vacation, which meant she could be anywhere. For a few days I hung out at the Ben Franklin hoping she might pass the plate-glass window on an errand for her mom. I was tempted to consult Gladstein, but he had ordered me not to return until I had kissed her. Going to her door and ringing the bell was out of the question. Nor would it be a good idea to pass the Coghill porch, where Myra reigned jointly with the beauties who lived there. She would find it mortifying to be greeted by a Witcher in the presence of Coghills.

Another possibility was to frequent the small wooded area behind Dickie Pudding's house, where I might waylay her if she passed. I took to the woods, and immediately Dickie spotted me through the glass in his storm door. He called my name and came up to join me.

"What are you doing?"

I was squatting beside a bush with a copy of *Death Be Not Proud* in my hand.

"Sitting here," I told him.

"No lie," he said. Of the neighborhood kids Dickie was the shortest in my age bracket. His parents made him take tap dance lessons and enter competitions, which had earned him the reputation for being a mama's boy. Bullies were forever collaring him and forcing him to dance.

"I'm thinking things over," I explained.

"What things?"

"Just things."

Dickie sat beside me. It was a Saturday; his father was home from work and we saw him through the trees gathering together a hose as a preface to washing his car. Mr. Pudding shaded his eyes—pointlessly, since the sun was behind a cloud—and peered in our direction. Then he broke into a grin and came towards us. I found this extremely irritating. I wanted Myra, not the Puddings. Of course, I was on their property, so I guess they had a right to be there.

"Little Witcher!" Mr. Pudding shouted.

"Hi, Mr. Pudding," I said.

"How are things at Witcher House?"

"Fine."

Mischief hunkered deep in his eyes. Mr. Pudding had tight, wavy hair, a dark complexion and a Roman nose, ethnic traits in our part of the world. In spite of such swarthiness he vaunted a proud Anglo-Saxon heritage. One day not long before, he had left the house and ventured into Southside, where he'd signed up with the KKK. This was a secret Dickie confided in me after I swore on a stack of Bibles not to tell (a speech act without any real authority, since multiple copies of the Good Book were not readily available). Mr. Pudding had a pleasant face and beady eyes; he coached a failing Little League team; he listened to music that had banjos in it. And yet the Puddings were deemed respectable because they'd added an extension to the rear of their house.

"I see Snead's been visiting your folks lately," Mr. Pudding observed.

There, I thought, it's out. People are already talking.

I didn't say anything.

"What are they doing, singing the blues?"

"Yes sir," I said.

"Ain't nothing wrong with singing the blues. Kind of like Charley Pride," he added, although I couldn't follow the reasoning. "Don't you think they should be doing that someplace else, though? There's a time and place for everything, your father should know that."

Dickie was averting his eyes.

"Pop does what he wants to do," I said.

"Well, you should bring it up with him, tell him what I said."

My pop could kick your ass into the next county, I was thinking. But I didn't say it. Mr. Pudding was one of the few men in the neighborhood willing to acknowledge Pop. Sad as it sounds, he was one of the good guys.

"I don't think he'd listen to me," I said.

"Why not, aren't you the brains of Lee Elementary?"

My grades were the subject of frequent comment in the neighborhood. That a Witcher should make the honor roll was an anomaly in social logic. My brother certainly never made the grades. In fact, because of his legacy my teachers (Mrs. Carter aside) hated me even before they knew me.

I reminded Mr. Pudding that we were starting junior high in the fall and that Lee Elementary was irrelevant. He nodded absentmindedly, already thinking about something else.

"Snead's not such a bad colored fellow," he allowed. "The Sneads aren't bad people."

"No sir."

"But don't you think Snead of all people would know better?"

"Better than what?"

"Than to come in here if it's not for work."

I shrugged. It was none of my business. I decided that would be my policy when dealing with the Snead scandal. And there was sure to be trouble. The amiability of Mr. Pudding's face had been replaced by tight lines formed by so many disciplined years in the wilderness of the dialectic of white supremacy.

"Y'all come on down, we'll throw the baseball in a while," he said.

Abruptly he spun and went towards his house.

I was surprised to have gotten off that easily. Dickie seemed so relieved that I half expected him to leap up and do a soft-shoe. But what had made Mr. Pudding get so preoccupied? We watched him pass indoors. I worried he might be phoning his fellow Ku Kluxers that very moment to convene an emergency konklave. The last thing the Witchers needed was the KKK on our ass.

Dickie and I sat in silence. There wasn't much to say, even though our eyes kept searching for what the other was thinking.

He claimed he had something to do and left me sitting by the bush.

By now I didn't care whether I saw Myra or not. Of course, that is precisely when she appeared, in the moment of my perturbation. Too demoralized to call out, I watched while she made her progress through the trees.

Mr. Pudding had thrown me for a loop. If the Puddings had such a hard time with Witcher ways, what prayer would I have with Brahmins like the Joyners? My father entertained Negroes. We were broke. Only last night Pop had admitted to Mom that he'd lost fifty bucks to a bookie, and Mom had hit the ceiling. He was supposed to have been in Southside applying for a mechanic position; instead he was betting on baseball.

By the time I found the resolve to catch Myra, she was gone. I dashed out of the woods and hurried to the end of the street. She wasn't anywhere in sight. She'd already turned the corner onto Myra Street.

For a moment I was too deflated to keep going. But then I reached in my pocket and felt the ring. . . .

I caught her as she was passing through the gateway that led to the alley behind the shopping center.

Within moments I had her against the brick wall, next to

the insurance agency. Her eyes were focused on the red stone in my palm. I was passing it this way and that before her eyes, hoping it might perform some mystical agency on my behalf.

"I can't," she kept saying, "I can't."

I held the stone under her eyes.

"That isn't the ring you showed me the other day."

"It's yours," I said, "take it."

She sucked her teeth in frustration. She was all too aware of the ostracism suffered by Courtney Blankenship before Gaylord came to rescue the silly fool.

"Did you get it at Mr. Gladstein's?"

"Keep it in your pocket, no one will know."

"Leave me alone, Jack. What you're doing isn't right."

"What am I doing wrong?"

"You're a Witcher, I'm a Joyner."

I couldn't believe she would put it so baldly. Of course, it was exactly what I believed. In the depths of my being I subscribed to the same class distinctions she did. It's just I got no advantage by believing in them.

With nothing else to lose, I shoved in to get a kiss. And she slapped me.

She put her hand to her mouth.

She started crying and ran off.

I went on home.

An hour later the electric company shut off our power.

That night I slept in torrid darkness. The big window fan in our dining room was unable to blow. There were no lights in the house, and the candles only made it hotter. Outside my window I heard the voices of Pop and Snead, unnaturally loud. They were drinking beer, smoking cigarettes.

I kept waking up hot and thirsty, half expecting a glow at the window, and the sound of flames flapping in the night as they consumed a cross raised by Mr. Pudding.

10

ON MONDAY, Pop went downtown to pay the bill so our lights would be turned back on. (He was supposed to have paid it the day he visited his bookie.) Even then he had to get the money from Mom, having gambled his own away.

It's a curious thing about Pop, when he had a job he was a dependable worker, regular as a clock, never took a sick day. It's only when he lost work that he suffered his moral collapses. Once that happened he couldn't motivate himself to do anything. It was as though he regarded his time off as a deserved vacation.

My mother had spent most of her adult years raising kids. Until the previous year she had babysat a few brats from her old Lakeside neighborhood, but now that I was old enough to look after myself there was no reason my parents shouldn't both work full-time. The real challenge facing our family was Pop's rehabilitation.

All day Sunday she paced about the hot house moaning and wringing her hands. "What are we going to do? All the food in the icebox has spoiled."

I was behind her, wringing my hands in accompaniment. Pop said I was a worrywart just like her.

I decided to go to the wooded area off Clark Lane, where my brother had taken me the day we met Anya. The brackishness of the creek and the brambles along the way tended to discourage recreational visitation, which made it unlikely my solitude would be violated by beer or tobacco delinquents. I wanted to be by myself so I could think about why Myra had slapped me.

When I left the yard Pop was lying in a chaise lounge beside the house, deprived of the electricity that might have allowed a little Chuck Berry to go with his beer. Mom was still inside, pacing through the rooms.

As I was cutting off the road to go into the trees, Dickie Pudding rode up on his bicycle. My heart sank.

"Where are you going?"

"Down there."

I pointed into the woods.

He kicked his stand down and followed me through the foliage.

We were thirty feet in when I smelled marijuana and stopped in my tracks. "Let's go back," I said.

"What's that smell?"

"Let's go back."

"Wait, there's someone by the creek."

"Dickie!"

I gestured frantically. I used hand signals to indicate the perils of approaching strangers in the woods. But Dickie was determined. He took a half-squatting position behind some fern leaves. "Come here," he whispered, "it's some guy with a girl! Jesus, they don't have their clothes on!"

I took off for the street. Dickie came behind me, giggling and calling. "Witcher, come on, you have to see!"

I stood by his bicycle. He joined me.

"It's your brother. He's got a girl with him and she has her top off. "

He was breathing heavily and sweat had beaded on his upper lip.

I nodded ruefully. For my brother the gates of Hell had opened wide, and he was determined to take as many girls with him as possible.

"Let's go back and watch," Dickie said.

"You don't know what you're getting into. If he catches you spying he'll kill you. He'll bite your ear. He'll gouge out your eyes. That's the way he fights."

The joy in Dickie's eyes slowly extinguished. We stood on the street in the fly-plagued sunlight. On the shoulder of the macadam, tar was bubbling up. No breeze whatsoever disturbed the trees.

Dickie pedaled off. I went home and sat in our backyard, without shade. Dogs approached with suffering tongues, asking me to do something to help. Our home was dark, dead. The fan blades in the window moved half a rotation whenever a rare wind passed through them. Not even thoughts of Myra could save me from my torpor.

Mom went to the drugstore and brought back Popsicles, which we had to finish right away to keep from melting. She told me she'd come upon Mr. Gladstein in the aisles of the store and he had inquired about me.

"Have you and Mr. Gladstein become friends?"

"Yeah, he's a pretty nice man," I said.

Oddly, this was the succor I needed, to hear that Gladstein had inquired. It was good to know he was on my case. It invigorated me. If it hadn't been Sunday I'd have gone directly to his store. I wanted to let him know Myra had slapped me.

I went to the spigot at the rear of the house and saw my brother cutting through the yard. Lately he had developed a new way of walking, throwing back his shoulders and bouncing on his feet lightly, like a boxer. When you looked at him he jerked his eyes away, hard as ice.

He came up to me. "You've been invited to a party. Next weekend. Pool party at Anya's. They're getting it filled this week. She told me to invite you."

"She wants me to come?"

"You can bring a guest. But only one person. And don't bring Dickie Pudding."

He strutted away, rolling his shoulders.

I sat on the grass in a state of wonder. Anya had invited me? A girl who lived in a mansion?

Myra, I thought. I can invite Myra.

The next morning I was at Gladstein's shop before it was open.

His Continental pulled in at the top of the hill and coasted to his spot and parked. When he got out, the Yatzis dashed to where I was, yapping like sopranos.

"Witcher!" He was happy to see me.

"Go ahead and open up, I'll come back later," I told him.

"No, come in."

He unlocked the store. "I have to go to the safe," he told me.

He pushed open the door that led to the back room and closed it behind him. I heard slamming sounds and an occasional yap. Then he reappeared with a narrow wooden box clasped in front. He pulled out the display jewels and arranged them in the window, carefully examining each bauble before he placed it in position. He greeted the jewels by name. He asked them how they had slept. Air whistled through his florid nostrils whenever he breathed out.

After he finished arranging the window he waddled to the stool behind the counter. Using a tiny key attached to a chain at his neck he leaned forward and unlocked several drawers just underneath. He pulled each drawer open and examined the accessories inside. Then he pushed them shut.

"Now," he said.

He blinked. He didn't seem to remember who I was.

"It's me. Little Witcher."

"Yes."

"Don't you remember Myra?"

A dim torch seemed to light in his eyes. "The Joyner girl, yes. How is she?"

"She's all right."

I had the feeling he still hadn't come around completely. "You gave me a ring," I reminded him, "you told me I should kiss her."

"Yes. The red ring, that's right. And did you kiss her?"

"She slapped me when I tried."

"Ah," Mr. Gladstein said. He placed his hands on his thighs, perplexed. "The bane of man's existence, Witcher."

"Yes sir," I said. I guess he meant women. "Are you married?" I asked him.

"There once was a Mrs. Gladstein, but she passed away. Then I moved to this place. That was a long time ago."

"I'm sorry," I said.

"And now you have your life. It is the time for youth. Old men must step aside, that is the way of the world. The torch has been passed to a new generation, as our late president once said."

I wiped my forehead, already filmy with stagnant air. What he had just said depressed me.

Gladstein held forth his hand. "Let me see the ring. I assume she refused it."

"Yes sir."

I handed it over.

Gladstein examined it. He turned it back and forth.

"Stay here."

He rose from the stool with a soft yodel and headed for the

back room. The dogs back there yapped and whimpered riotously, as though they hadn't seen him in weeks. I heard clicking, whooshing, and what might have been a refrigerator door slamming shut.

Gladstein returned. He pulled the rear door to and climbed on his stool.

"Next time you see Myra try this."

He handed me a ring set with a clear crystalline stone large as a buttercup. I had never seen anything so magnificent.

"This is a diamond!"

Gladstein winked. "Looks genuine, right?"

"Is it fake?"

"It's crystal, but she'll never know. How old is she, twelve? Try that one on her."

"Should I give you money? I don't have any."

"It's a trade, Witcher. Remember? You paid fifty cents."

I stared at the stone.

"All right, let's go through this routine once more. What are you going to do when you see her?"

"Give her the ring."

"And when she has accepted it?"

"Kiss her."

"Are you imagining that in your mind?"

"Yes sir. I'm trying."

"Good. Now go. And this time don't come back until you've kissed her."

"But—"

"Go!" Gladstein boomed.

His voice could have filled a cathedral.

I opened the door. The prissy bell tinkled.

"Witcher!"

I looked back.

"What's your mother's name?"

"Margaret."

"I saw her at the drugstore yesterday."

"Yes sir, she told me."

"Come here," he said.

I went.

He whispered a syllable into my ear, an incantation he had devised. I was not to divulge the syllable. Ever. To anyone. I was forbidden to utter it aloud. Doing so would bring me harm. Wonderful things will come to those who respect the power of words, he told me.

I left the shop, silently chanting my syllable.

And I never did reveal it. Not once. Not to anyone.

11

THE NEXT TIME I SAW MYRA she was in her usual place on the Coghill steps.

The Coghill beauties had arranged themselves in a circle in the sun. Johnny Pendleton, one of the neighborhood's more virulent Witcher haters, was loitering about their yard, amusing the girls with his native wit and sophistication. He was wearing madras shorts, loafers and an alligator shirt he had purchased at Gary's Fine Clothing for Men, an upscale haberdasher located in the shops at Dogwood Downs, on the way into town. Not quite sixteen, he was between my brother and me in age, although by rights he was Stan's contemporary. His great distinction in the neighborhood was that of being younger brother to Gaylord Joyner's best friend. It made him a peer of the realm.

As I passed I made a purely subliminal attempt to signal Myra to meet me in the woods behind Dickie Pudding's house.

This dire message I endeavored to communicate with facial tics and eye movements, and Myra, sensing what I was up to, turned to speak with exaggerated directness to the Coghill on her left. Perhaps my intensity had made me brazen. I kept repeating Gladstein's syllable in my mind, fixing my sights on her.

There was a flurry on the porch. The Coghill girls had been disturbed, and now they disdainfully took notice. Johnny Pendleton glanced over his shoulder. His chest expanded righteously and he strolled to the edge of the Coghill yard, snarling and ogling me.

"What are you looking at, Witcher?"

The alligator grinned sardonically from his pumped-up pectoral, well informed of my social inferiority.

Pendleton was on the high school wrestling team and could easily have manhandled me. Nevertheless, legends about my brother's eye-gouging and nut-squeezing tended to keep the older kids at bay. It was well known that Stan would spend his might and his vengeance upon anyone over fourteen who dared to molest me (and indeed, I had once or twice protected the identities of malevolents who'd crossed me, without their even knowing I'd spared their lives). There was, at any rate, little reason to worry about the Pendleton menace with Stan behind me.

I kept leaning to the side, trying to locate Myra.

She had her head averted, rigid with embarrassment. Pendleton saw what I was doing and turned, bewildered, to look at her. Then he looked back at me.

"Get out of here before I kick your ass, Witcher."

"Try it," I said. I kept walking while Pendleton stalked at the edge of the yard, riled by his bloodlust.

"We know who Witcher likes!" one of the girls taunted, and everyone laughed, except Myra.

I stooped behind the bush in the Pudding woods and presently she came along, bobbing thoughtfully. She was gloomy and upset and acting as if she were unaware of my presence. Of course, she knew damn well who was lurking in the verdure.

I popped up and called her name. She peered nearsightedly, pretending not to place who I was. And then she said, "Oh, it's you," determined to finish the charade.

"What do you want?" she said.

"I have to ask you something."

To my surprise she stepped into the woods, albeit gingerly, looking for crawling insects and slithering snakes. She came a few yards in and I took an encouraging step in her direction. Immediately she held up a forbidding hand. For a girl of twelve her haughtiness was pretty damn authentic.

"Why did you look at me when you passed the Coghills'?"

"I want to talk to you."

"Don't ever look at me like that in front of everyone."

"It's a free country, I can look at you if I want. But if it bothers you I won't, maybe."

"I don't want you looking at me like that in front of Kitten and Karla," she said, referring to two of the three Coghills. Why Kathy didn't count was a puzzle to me, but these complexities of caste seemed to exceed my comprehension.

Myra kept watching me with her hands on her hips. And

yet, as my angel of self-love whispered, she was here, right? She had followed me, hadn't she?

"Okay, so what did you want?"

"I have a new ring for you. This one's a lot nicer."

"Oh, Jack." She clucked her teeth. "Don't you ever get the message? There's no way you and I can . . ." She decided to leave unuttered what might follow the predicating term.

"Just take a look at it," I said.

She snuck a quick peek.

"Come closer," I said.

She did. And then she thumped her hand against her chest.

"That's a diamond!"

I smiled.

"Where did you get it, from Mr. Gladstein?"

I didn't say anything, choosing to be enigmatic. She gazed at the stone, all hypnotized by its luster and its luxury, and I said, "Listen, the new people that moved in have invited me to a pool party at their house on Saturday. Do you wanna come as my guest?"

"What new people?"

"That moved into Clark Lane."

"You mean you actually know them?"

"The girl's name is Anya, they just moved here from Dallas."

Myra bit her lip. An intricate display of emotion passed over her face. Her eyes peered into mine . . . she began to say something . . . stopped . . . opened her mouth. . . . Her lip trembled—and she burst into tears.

"Why are you crying?" I said, thunderstruck.

"Because I want to go to the party," she sobbed, "and I can't."

"Why not?"

"Because of your brother. He threatened to beat up my father."

"When?"

Then I remembered—the evening at the drainage ditch . . . Stan punching his palm, grinning at Mr. Joyner. At the time I had indeed assured myself it would come back to haunt me, but so much had happened since then that I'd nearly forgotten about it.

"Well look," I said, "we can't let what other people think hold us back."

"Hold us back from what?"

She drew up her shoulders. How dare I refer to us as *us*.

She proudly stared away and I allowed myself the opportunity to examine her profile. That she was still lingering made me think I might have an advantage, and silently I began to chant my magic syllable. I believe my lips moved . . . she bit her lower lip, watching me . . . I locked my eyes on hers . . . didn't let her look away. I must have chanted ten times before I eased up.

She blinked.

"Here." I stretched out my hand. "Take the ring."

She reached—snatched back her hand—reached once more.

"It won't bite."

She took it. "It's too big, this is a grown lady's ring."

Nevertheless, the ring was now on her finger. Had any Witcher in the history of our race realized the glory that was mine?

"Keep it in your pocket."

I took her bare brown shoulders in my hands.

"Don't you dare kiss me. Don't you even try it."

"If you're going to take my ring you have to kiss me."

In some corner of my mind I saw Gladstein perched on his three-legged stool, watching and applauding.

"Why were you staring at me just now? That was so weird."

"Because you're beautiful," I said.

I moved in and got my kiss.

Gladstein nearly fell off his stool.

When I drew back, her eyes remained pensively shut, evaluating, as opposed to savoring, my kiss.

She blinked her eyes open. . . . And then she began to dictate the terms.

One, she would accept the ring, but only for a few days. Two, she would come to the party, but I was not allowed to pick her up at her house. Three, I was never to tell anyone, ever, that she had gone to the party with me.

I nodded, overwhelmed by her skill in romantic administration. And those were just the major terms. Now she got down to the nitty-gritty.

We had to figure out some way to sneak her into the pool. One good thing, Clark Lane was fairly secluded, but she nixed the idea of going through the woods: too many ticks. Probably I should just leave getting to the party to her. Another thing, she'd have to wear a bathing suit under her clothes so her parents wouldn't see.

I stood there slackly attentive while she arranged the details. She asked if my brother would be at the party and I explained he was the reason we were invited in the first place.

"That girl *likes* him?"

She wrestled with the enormity of that, and then she told me that Stan must not be allowed to speak to her. "Just tell him. If he speaks I won't acknowledge him. And God help him if he says anything nasty about Gaylord."

Passionately I shook my head. That would never happen, I swore.

She then informed me that she would keep my ring until the party, at which point I'd have to take it back. It did not mean, repeat, did not, that we were going steady.

"What does it mean, then?"

"It means I'm your friend until the party. We'll take it from there."

This girl had my head swimming. I wasn't even able to relish the kiss.

She held up the oversized ring and smiled. "I'll bet in a couple of years I could grow into this."

"It's yours," I avowed, "forever!"

She gave me an exasperated look. "What did we just agree on?"

"Okay, fine. I'm letting you know, that's all."

Through the trees, from down at the Pudding house, sounds of conversation drifted up. Myra grew alarmed.

"What time should I be there Saturday?"

I told her one in the afternoon.

And she vanished.

She pogo-sticked right on out of the woods.

Dickie Pudding and his brother entered as she exited, punch-ing their fists into their baseball gloves.

12

I HURRIED TO GLADSTEIN's to tell him the news. As I dashed past the Ben Franklin, hoping and praying Mom wouldn't spot me, out through the door strolled Pop, bestowing the favor of his crooked grin upon the world. He must have stopped in to hit up Mom for money.

"Whoa, hoss, where you off to in such a hurry?" he said, collaring me.

"Up there." I pointed up the hill.

I didn't want him to know about my friendship with Gladstein. Or about the ring. Or about Myra. In Pop's presence my most ardent schemes seemed preposterous and I no longer wanted to admit to them. Maybe it was because I was small and he was big and I was years away from attaining that easy masculinity he had brought down from the mountains with him. Frankly, I didn't think I'd ever have it. I was full of the nervousness that creates neurotic ambition, whereas Pop was impervious to ambition. Even Stan's masculinity was hard rather than easy. Stan hated being who he was, and his virility was manifest in his inclination to tear off noses and swallow ears and spit out eyeballs. Seducing girls was his social vengeance. Stan never forgot he was a Witcher, and shame had made him proud. But Pop, he took life as it came. He was a democrat, a man among men, and without bigotry. There was a socialist streak in Pop; he didn't think of the things he owned as possessions. If you wanted what he had, you could have it. But he expected the same of you. Probably that was his problem in life: the world is not a socialist place, fundamentally. Fundamentally the world is competitive and ruthless and striving, and he found the ambitions of others heartless and cold. His easy attitude made everything you dreamed about seem vain, grasping.

"What do you mean, 'up there'? You keeping secrets from your old pop?" His eyes were teasing me, having fun.

"I'm heading up the hill, that's all."

"To Gladstein's?"

It surprised me that he knew. I glanced through the plate window of the Ben Franklin and saw Mom at her cash register, waving enthusiastically and blowing kisses. She almost looked pretty.

Pop said, "She tells me you and him are becoming best friends."

"He's all right."

"You going to see him? I'll come along with you."

"No!"

Pop's company was the last thing I wanted. For the first time ever, I was putting another grown man before my father. I guess in some remote way I felt guilty about it. But it was a fact: I would happily divulge to Gladstein what I would never confide to Pop. I didn't even want to be in the same room with them both.

"I'm just stopping in for a minute," I explained. "I have something to tell him."

"Why?"

It was a good question. Why would I be calling on a merchant Jew who dealt in costly diamonds and kept fluffy dogs and retailed unintelligible Yankee jokes?

"I have something to tell him real quick. You wait here," I said.

"I wanna see the man's shop, I've never been inside the place."

He steered me onward, and my heart fell accordingly. The only reason I wanted to see Gladstein was to tell him what had just happened with Myra. And if Pop was around I'd be loath even to bring up her name. Then again, I was worried Gladstein might bring it up. Discretion was hardly a trait the megaphone-throated jeweler could claim.

Pop walked up the steps beside me and we turned in.

"Little Witcher!" Mr. Gladstein called.

The prissy bell tinkled over our heads. Pop turned to look.

"And who do we have here, the famous Mr. Witcher?" Gladstein said.

Pop ducked his head, being humble. He came forth with an outstretched hand.

"Yes sir, very pleased to meet you."

"The annihilator of El Dorado Hills," Gladstein boomed.

"I wouldn't know about that," Pop said. "Sure is a nice place you have here."

He'd barely glanced at it.

"I understand you're the annihilator of Kellners," Gladstein boomed, unwilling to give anything up.

Pop gave me a shove and laughed. "What have you been telling this man?"

I stared hard at Gladstein. I begged him with my eyes to shut up.

Pop gazed all about, rubbing his hands. "My, you got some gorgeous jewelry here, you sure do." He stared through the glass-top counter at the riches and splendor of the House of Gladstein. "Look at that gold necklace there." Pop whistled. Then he wandered over to gaze at the stuff in the window.

As soon as he turned his back, I glared furiously at Gladstein. I put my finger against my lips. I cut my arms through the air like an umpire calling out a base runner. I popped my eyes at him. Gladstein was startled. But then his Buddha smile returned. I think he got the message.

Meanwhile Pop was before the show window, entranced by all the glitter and gold. He kept muttering, "Golly gee, mm-mm-mm, ain't that pretty." He sounded like Andy Griffith. It made me ashamed in front of this Solomon of the towns of Jersey.

I turned my attention to Gladstein. He raised a questioning brow, inquiring mutely about Myra. The ring, the kiss. Had I?

I gave him the thumbs-up sign and he nodded, reassured.

Pop returned to us. "Mr. Gladstein, is it all right if I ask you something? I don't know a lot about jewelry and I'm curious. How much would the most expensive item in this store sell for?"

"That's not easy to say. Some of these items I sell on consignment. Then again, I might give wholesale prices to customers who buy several things at once."

"Yes sir. I see. So you negotiate on your prices."

"You might say that."

Gladstein didn't like these questions. He gave my pop the once-over.

"Are you interested in something in particular?"

"Well, my wife's got a birthday coming up," Pop said.

"How are you gonna—?" I stopped, not wanting to embarrass him.

He pointed through the glass counter. "That gold bracelet, how much would you ask for that?"

Gladstein peered down, reluctantly. "For that I might ask a hundred and fifty, but it's a very nice piece of work. The other bracelet, the silver one, that's a good piece. I wouldn't ask more than forty for that. Maybe thirty-five." I think he was trying to steer Pop to a manageable price range. He was shrewd enough to know what a man could pay. Besides, anyone could see from the way Pop was dressed what he could (and could not) afford. He was wearing a light-blue work shirt unbuttoned halfway, with its tail out on one side. His trousers were rolled at the bottom and they rested on his scuffed-up work shoes.

He kept playing the unassuming workingman. "Well, I still got a couple months before the old lady tacks on another year. You know Miss Witcher, works at the Ben Franklin?"

"I fixed her Timex last month. Demagnetized it."

"I hear you been keeping an eye on my boy." Pop put his arm around me, the proud father. It was phony as hell. Not that he was a bad pop, it just wasn't his way.

Gladstein demonstrated one of his demon grins and Pop blanched. It was the first time he'd seen it. "Boy keeps me entertained. Gives me the lowdown on the neighbors. Kid's better than Rex Reed."

Pop gave me a squeeze. "I better not get wind of you telling him anything else about me. Man won't have anything to do with me when you're through."

They both chuckled manfully.

To me it just seemed weird. I cracked my knuckles and looked away.

Pop became serious again. "You have everything in the store on display? Everything's in the showroom?"

Gladstein's eyebrows came together. "What you see is what you get."

I fidgeted uneasily. Gladstein had just lied. I knew damn well he kept jewelry in the safe. I knew it from him. I knew it from Snead. What's more, Pop knew it, so I didn't understand why he asked in the first place.

Pop put out his hand and said, "Well, listen, I gotta run. Just wanted to meet you, been hearing so much about you."

"It's been a pleasure," Gladstein boomed.

I wanted to stay behind to tell Gladstein about Myra, but Pop lugged me through the door with him. I stared helplessly back, and the jeweler jerked his thumb in the air.

Outside, Pop said, "Come on, I'm running by Snead's before we go home."

He took me across the lot, which inclined so steeply that people would put on their emergency brakes when they parked. We jumped in the dented-up Ford, and Pop gathered the trash from the footwell and tossed it in the back. Then he got her started.

"Why are we going to Snead's?" I asked.

"Got something to give him."

"What?"

Pop shrugged. "Just something."

I turned away, depressed. It was the second time I'd heard a grown-up lie today.

I had mixed feelings about going to see Snead, anyway. I was worried Mr. Pudding would find out and use it when he presented his case against us at the klavern. And yet I was eager to see how Snead lived. I'd never been inside a Negro's house.

We went down Karen Drive and forked off on the two-lane blacktop that led to the seafood shack.

Snead's driveway was dusty and long. It ran past the seafood shack and down into some trees. Through the trees you could see his house and his truck.

Pop honked the horn and Snead came out with his son Robert, the one my age.

Snead said, "Take little Witcher inside, show him your room."

Robert took me upstairs. I noticed two beds and figured he must share the room with a brother not present. There didn't seem to be anyone else in the house, although I could hear voices outside.

Robert stared at me and I stared back. The house wasn't much different from a white person's.

He showed me a model plane he had put together. Next he showed me a basketball. Then he showed me a catcher's mitt. I kept complimenting him.

We stood there and didn't say much.

Through the window I saw Snead and Pop below, talking seriously.

"Wanna go out back and throw the ball?" Robert asked.

"Sure," I said.

But then Pop hollered it was time to go.

Robert turned bashfully away and I told him I'd see him later.

When Pop and I were in the car he said, "Now why would Gladstein tell me he has everything out in the showroom? He's got something in that safe he ain't talking about."

I said, "It ain't your business, Pop."

He shot me a funny look. He wasn't used to hearing me take that tone. Later I felt conflicted about it, and I prepared justifications in case he challenged me. But he must have dropped it. He probably didn't want to talk about it any more than I did.

13

NOW THAT I HAD KISSED MYRA, my sole purpose was to do it again. For the rest of the week I was harassed by longing. I lived solely for the pool party at Anya's. I was intolerant towards time. Clocks made me angry, calendars provoked my wrath. On Friday afternoon when the clock struck one I said, "Twenty-four hours to go." It seemed an eternity. I had no idea how the situation would play itself out; whether, for instance, I might find an opportunity to get my skinny girlfriend alone beside the brackish creek in the woods, or whether I might cop a little hug beyond the trees. But Myra was so squeamish and afraid of critters, and it might strike the others as rude if I stole her away from the party. I just didn't know; I hadn't been to that many parties.

The pool at the house was kidney-shaped. Even though I'd seen it when the house was being built, it was still smaller than I expected. Anya's family name was Taylor. Nevertheless, as her parents insisted, "Please, call us Tillie and Basil." Some Taylor kinfolk local to town were present, the only people the Dallas Taylors knew so far, unless you counted Stan and me. Their number included a humble man, a decent woman, a dour son and a pious daughter. As practicing Methodists they considered these newcomer relatives shamefully immoral because of their conspicuous consumption and manifest taste for go-go accessories. (The pendulous jewels dangling from Mrs. Taylor's ears matched her snow-white bathing suit. To top it off, she had painted white lipstick on her lips, which in the self-effacing world of El Dorado Hills belonged solely to graven fashion models like Twiggy.) I suppose this is why they kept to themselves at a table near the western lobe of the kidney. Mrs. Taylor, or Tillie, kept calling me Jackie, although I was pretty firm about it being Jack. Basil, a martini drinker, picked up on it, and he took to bellowing "Jackie Robinson!" "Jackie Wilson!" "Jackie Mason!" whenever his eyes lighted on me. Apparently he'd challenged himself to come up with a different "Jackie" every time he bellowed.

I was tossing sticks in the pool to amuse the Taylors' golden retriever, a dog that seemed to enjoy no restriction from the family water (at least no one stopped me). Myra still hadn't arrived, and just when I was approaching the verge of despair— it was one-thirty—Tillie called from the entranceway of the fenced-in pool: "Oh, Jackie, your friend is here!"

I leapt up and escorted Myra to the chaise lounge where I'd been reclining. She nodded in all directions, smiling a graciously frozen smile for everyone except Stan, who was smirking beside Anya in the pool. Only that morning had I admitted to him my date would be a Joyner.

Myra perched on the edge of the chaise, tentatively lowering her skinny butt so that it barely touched the metal frame. I interpreted that as a lack of commitment.

"Are you wearing your bathing suit?" I said.

"Yes," she said. She had a pink blouse and blue jeans over the suit.

"You wanna swim?"

"Not yet," she replied, curtly.

Her frozen smile of graciousness reappeared as Tillie brought her a Coke with a slice of lime.

"I suppose you're too young for a highball," Tillie said.

"Yes ma'am."

It occurred to me that Stan and Anya were drinking booze. I'd been wondering why their beverages were clear, whereas mine was Coke-colored.

Tillie sat nearby. Myra swung herself in that direction, deliberately excluding me so that she could chat compulsively with Tillie about Gaylord and his scholarship to Duke. Whenever I tried to get a word in edgewise she ignored me and kept her back rigidly turned away.

I fell quiet and sat abandoned, depressed. In the pool Stan and Anya observed my plight and took to whispering.

My eyes met Basil's. He was on the other side of the white metal table, smiling mellowly into his martini.

"Jackie Gleason!" he bellowed.

Finally Anya clambered out of the pool and padded over on

wet feet. She perched on the chaise lounge, her back nearly resting against Myra's, and purred huskily in my direction, "Hey there, sexy."

Myra swung her head.

"Dear, have you met little Myra?" Tillie asked.

Anya didn't take her eyes away from me.

"Hi," she said distractedly. She kept smiling at me. "I just came over to say hello to this sexy hunk here."

Myra twisted around a little more.

Anya flicked water at me, giggling.

I stared back in amazement.

Myra's gracious smile began to falter.

"If only you were a couple years older, no telling what I'd do," Anya said.

Never in my born years had a woman's eyes shone at me so shamelessly. She licked her lips and walked her fingers brazenly up my thigh. "I'm just thinking. How old are you, twelve? That means when you're eighteen I'll be twenty-four. That's not such a bad age difference. When you turn eighteen give me a call, okay, big boy?" She cut her eyes at Stan. "At least he'll be legal then."

Stan said, "All right, come on back, quit ogling my brother."

She gave me one last glance.

"Why is it the cutest guys are always unavailable? Oh, well." She sighed and padded back to the pool.

A tiny laugh issued from Myra's lips, petering out on a note of despair. Her shoulders heaved weakly . . . her defeated eyes met mine. She had met the competition, and she was sorry.

Now she clean forgot about Tillie. The palace gates of her conversation flung wide, and for the next half hour I was regaled with tales of Coghills, Kellners, Joyners, Pendletons and Blankenships. This was my first honored glimpse into the lives of the Top Five Families of El Dorado Hills, and I listened raptly enough. When she reached a lull in her reporting, I asked if she wanted to take a dip in the pool and she cried, "Yes!" She stripped down to her lovely baby-blue bathing suit in three seconds flat. Her tanned limbs had become so friendly, so welcoming.

As we jumped in the pool I heard Tillie say, "Look, they're so cute."

Anya made horny eyes at me. "Better not let him get too close," she told Myra.

We splashed about, giggling and throwing water. From time to time I spied the Taylor kin watching through hooded eyes. Not once had they condescended to enter the pool. In fact, they were all buttoned up and collared as if for January. They had paid this odious call to their Texas cousins without the slightest intention of swimming.

After a while Myra had to pee.

She asked Tillie if she could use her bathroom, and Tillie said, "Yes, let me show you where it is. You come too, Jackie, I want you to see the house."

"Jackie Kennedy!" Basil bellowed.

We stepped into the pastel splendor of the Taylor house. To me such a lavish spread belonged to some glossy magazine devoted to fabulous mansions and country gardens in a faraway land of opulence, like California. The kitchen had a built-in stainless-steel range, and a floor so gleaming and polished you could actually see your image peering back at you. A luxurious reflected cat rested on the linoleum, languidly licking between its nails. A system of intercoms connected the assorted spacious chambers—three baths, four bedrooms—telephonically. The entire house was uniformly chilled by central air. Grandfather clocks ticked and bonged.

The front room was enormous, with a sloped ceiling that belonged to a hunting lodge or ski lodge. In the corner stood a Steinway grand piano with enough space around it for a concert hall.

I pointed. "Can you play that?"

"Oh, that," Tillie laughed. "What a pointless expense. We got it for Anya, but she won't go near it. All she wants is that wild rock and roll."

"My mom can play songs from *Showboat*," I said.

"How wonderful," Tillie said.

We stood in the center of the room, stretching our necks. Even Myra had been subdued by the grandeur of the Taylor palace. She was shivering in the air-conditioning, a towel wrapped around her.

"Poor dear, you need to tinkle. Just down the hallway, first left."

Myra broke into a trot; she needed to go bad.

I stood next to Tillie.

"This is a nice house you have."

She sighed. "It will do. Oh, Jackie, if only you could have seen how we lived in Dallas!" The pain made her grievous, and I shook my head in sympathy.

Then she said, "I should return to the other guests. You wait here and escort your friend to the pool when she's ready."

I waited in the living room. Now that I was alone it had become quiet, gloomy, cavernous. It even made me slightly afraid.

Myra took an awfully long time, until finally I heard sounds coming from the distant hallway. I crossed the room to meet her.

"Where's Tillie?"

"Outside," I said.

We stood in the refrigerated house, gazing about.

"What a nice place. Basil must make a lot of money."

"He's a lawyer," I said. "All this seems creepy to me, I don't know if I'd like living here."

Myra came close. The goose bumps on her flesh brushed against me and I draped an arm around her. "Thanks," she said, "it's so cold in here."

I spun her around and kissed her madly. I put my tongue in. I was like a man in the desert sucking water out of a cactus. Before I was even close to finished, she pushed me away.

"We should go back. We shouldn't be doing that in here."

She let me hold her hand as far as the dining room, and when we passed into the gleaming steel kitchen she released it with a placating pat.

Outside was a loud commotion.

At the door we were met by Tillie, coming in. "There you are, dear. A young man is looking for you. I believe it's your brother."

Myra gaped at me. We stepped outside. At the entrance to the pool stood Gaylord.

He ran his eyes up and down me contemptuously.

"Get your things," he said to Myra. "You're coming home."

14

WITHOUT A WORD Myra bowed to her brother's command. She went into the pool and gathered her clothes and murmured a thank-you as she passed Tillie. I was outside the pool, observing her through the slats. I was eager to defend her, but as soon as I began to speak Gaylord cut me off.

"Do I know you?"

I'd have liked a word with Myra. I didn't want her to get away before I could show her that I was concerned, that I heeded her, that I would protect her. How had Gaylord learned she was with me anyway?

Myra cast a worried glance at her brother and darted past me with declined eyes. Stan, behind her, appeared at the pool gateway. He watched as Gaylord and Myra walked down the sloping yard to Clark Lane.

It all happened with silent efficiency. Social equilibrium was being quietly restored, thanks to Gaylord's moral authority.

The trouble was Stan. His eyes were burning Gaylord Joyner's back to a cinder, and Gaylord could feel it. I guess it was too much for the Joyner pride. Just as he reached the side of the house, right before he might have passed out of sight, he spun and returned my brother's scowl.

"Got a problem?"

In a flash Stan was in front of him, standing chest to chest with him.

Gaylord stepped around him.

Myra was already at the street, shivering and mortified by the drama she had caused. My brother descended the slope at Gaylord's side, glaring at his profile with insolent joy.

Gaylord was afraid of my brother's retribution. Why wouldn't he be? He had been brave enough when it belonged to the unforeseeable future. Perhaps he was hoping he could put it off until the end of August, when he would be ensconced in a tobacco-gothic dormitory at Duke never trespassed by Witchers. Besides, he had a sister to protect from life's darkness (even though it was her susceptibility to guile that had brought about this unhappy situation in the first place). Stan, of course, had nary a qualm about Myra's gentility. Nor was he in the least shy about revealing the baseness of Witcher blood in front of Basil, Tillie and Anya. The moment offered too many opportunities to provoke the apocalypse about which he long had dreamed.

When they reached the street he grabbed Gaylord's shoulder and yanked him around.

Gaylord violently flung my brother's hand away. "Don't touch me, Witcher."

My brother grinned and I felt my stomach go soft. Oh boy, did I recognize that grin.

"Now who's got the problem?" he said.

"Look, we'll settle this later."

"I want to settle it now," he said, gritting his teeth in Joyner's face.

"Not in front of my sister. We'll settle it later, I said."

"That's how you're gonna pussy out? You're gonna use your sister?"

"Gaylord, let's go," Myra called, quivering.

"You know damn well she shouldn't have been at that pool."

"I don't have anything to do with that. This ain't about her anyway."

"You stay away from her. I don't want her around you. Or your brother." Gaylord was wagging a moralistic finger in the air.

"Quit pointing at me, you fucker."

Stan slapped the finger away. A fist might reasonably have sailed in behind the slap, but for our being distracted by Tillie. She was wandering towards us, upset that her party had been disrupted. She had witnessed the slap, and now she was hollering something none of us could understand.

We exchanged glances.

"Ma'am?" Stan said.

There came the rumble of a powerful motor.

We turned and looked.

Reedy's Plymouth was coming around the corner!

My brother swore. The other people here had no idea how

the cop had been hounding us, so to them his appearance was a miracle, a deus ex machina. Gaylord's relief was plain. He stared at Stan victoriously, gloating over the justness of the heavens.

Myra seized the opportunity to dart a glance in my direction. I made an urgent expression, gesturing with my hands, and she cut me off with a quick jerk of the eyes. *Not now, you fool.*

Reedy climbed out of the cruiser, cowboy face a-smiling. The Taylor cousins had gathered to watch the seedy drama their Texas relatives already had wrought. Meanwhile Anya was coming down the slope, staring hard at Reedy. She didn't like cops.

"What's the problem here?" Reedy said.

"Who said there's a problem?" my brother snapped.

Reedy was imperturbable. He nodded amiably, staring all around.

I couldn't figure out what this lawman was up to. He was always cruising through the neighborhood, preaching peace and asking the kids if they could "dig" what he was saying. His favorite expression was "Do you think you can hack it?"

"Everything is fine," Gaylord said. "We had a disagreement and it's over. I'm heading home now."

"He came to pick up his snotty little sister," Stan sneered.

"Is that any way to talk?" Reedy said. "You're Charles Witcher's son, aren't you?"

Stan's face became grim, taut. No doubt he expected a schoolyard taunt to follow. Now even cops were joining in on the fun?

"Your father's a decent man. How would he like it if he heard you speaking that way?"

"He hates Joyners more than I do, so don't worry about it."

Gaylord placed a shielding arm across Myra's shoulders. He smiled ruefully and shook his head. "You can't reason with this guy," he said.

"Joyner"—my brother pointed—"you're lucky he's here. If it weren't for Deputy Dawg I'd fuck you up good right now."

Up by the house, the Taylor cousins, like a wheezy chorus, performed a dramatic intake of breath. I guess they weren't as used to it as I was. Even Anya was gazing at Stan a little cock-eyed.

"This isn't the only time he's threatened me," Gaylord said. "That whole family is crazy. His father physically attacked Mr. Kellner not long ago."

Reedy nodded gravely. "Well, things aren't always that black-and-white. There are gray areas," he said.

We creased our brows, expecting further wisdom. But Reedy was finished, he had said his piece.

Stan turned to the cop. "See the way they always put down the Witchers? That asshole Kellner accused my father of trying to kill his dog."

"Let's watch the language," Reedy said.

"In front of my sister," Gaylord said, "a twelve-year-old. The guy has no class at all."

That did it. Stan blew. He took a step forward and raised his fist, but Reedy snatched his biceps. It made a sound like a slap.

"Easy."

"Easy nothing. Next time I lay eyes on that son of a bitch I'll kill him. You hear me, Joyner?"

Anya took Stan's arm. "Come on, let's go back to the pool." She tried to steer him towards the yard.

But Stan wasn't through. He twirled and pointed. "Keep that in mind, Joyner. If I catch you on the streets you're dead. I mean anytime of day or night. You see me coming you better run."

Tillie frowned, her bejeweled whiteness exceedingly out of place in El Dorado Hills. She was standing beside the cop's idling cruiser, putting it all together: Reedy, the cop car, the morning when her Fleetwood drifted past the house that had TRASH painted on it. Stan's behavior was allowing her insight into the young man her daughter was involved with.

"I'm leaving now," Gaylord proclaimed.

He began to walk Myra away and I fixed my eyes on her (at some point during the commotion she had wiggled into her clothes) and waited for her to cast a look behind. But she kept walking. When she and Gaylord got to the corner they hung a left.

"Oh, dear," Tillie said.

Anya and Stan returned to the pool. The Taylor cousins had disappeared. Down the sloping lawn staggered Basil, glass in hand. He had missed everything.

Officer Reedy said, "Better tell your brother he shouldn't make statements like that. That's the sort of thing that's liable to come back on him."

"Yes sir," I said.

"Why must people be so ugly with each other?" Tillie asked, pensively.

Officer Reedy reached a finger to the brim of his cap and nudged it back. "I want y'all to stay calm. There's no need for all this fighting. Be rational, you people."

He returned to the cruiser, still muttering, and put it in gear.

Tillie held out her hand, offering it to me. That's how she was going to lead me back to the pool. Me, a Witcher! I was all flustered and moved by the gesture.

Meanwhile Basil was drunkenly leering and rattling his glass. Apparently he found it comical that a cop had been to his house.

He grinned in my direction.

"Jackie DeShannon!" he bellowed.

15

THE LOGIC THAT GOVERNS the urge to throw a party, if urges can be considered logical, was pretty much nullified by the incident. The Taylor cousins bade frigid farewells; Basil staggered into the house and never reappeared; my brother dipped sullenly into the pool to receive comfort from Anya for his rage and frustration; and Tillie brought me, either through absent-mindedness or a bizarre compulsion to destroy my innocence, a mixed drink. I sipped furtively at the thing while the wet golden retriever grinned conspiratorially. I was quite excited to be drinking it.

Tillie was all out of sorts. She asked if my brother very often got into fights.

"Nah, he just doesn't take any crap from anyone," I said. I suppose the drink had relaxed my tongue.

"But why would anyone give him crap?"

"Well," I said. How to explain it? Maybe Dallas was a decent town where people didn't observe the blood distinctions that set classes apart. And if these sweet, boisterous Texans weren't wise to such things, I certainly didn't want to be the one to teach them. Why should I train Tillie in Witcher hatred?

She asked how far away we lived, and that's when it hit me she hadn't put it together yet. She still didn't realize that Stan and I were the kids who lived in the house with TRASH painted all over it. (That was still discernible from the road, and would be as long as we kept using cheap paint.)

"We live over that way," I said, gesturing towards Europe.

Tillie said, "I see," and threw a disturbed glance at the pool, where her daughter was earnestly counseling Stan. He was listening with a tight face and nodding curtly.

Meanwhile I was sipping rapidly from my well-loaded drink.

"That policeman, that Reedy fellow, he seems a nice man," Tillie said hopefully.

"Yes ma'am," I agreed.

And then, without any warning, she burst into a torrent of tears.

I stared, thunderstruck, and then I glanced nervously at Stan and Anya. They were too wrapped up in their conversation to notice.

"What's the matter?" I said helplessly.

Tillie buried her face in her hands. "I'm sorry, Jackie, I shouldn't be crying in front of you. I'm homesick, that's all."

"You miss Dallas?"

She nodded and dabbed at her eyes, while I consolingly patted her arm.

I took another hit of my drink.

"I don't think we're going to fit in here," she said. "This place is so provincial."

"Provincial," I repeated. I knew the word, but Tillie's use of it was enlightening. A new social concept was birthing in my brain, and I had a momentary feeling of superiority to El Dorado Hills. Outside, beyond the city limits, were other places, other towns: New York, San Francisco, Dallas.

Bravely Tillie tightened her lips and stanched her tears. She sniffed one more time and the crying fit was over.

"Well, I like you, Tillie. You and Basil and Anya, y'all seem like real nice people."

"Oh, Jackie, if only everyone were as sweet as you. And your little girlfriend. Why did that young man take her away? Is it a sin to be at a pool?"

"Her parents are real strict," I said.

"Oh," Tillie said, irritated, "people." She flapped a hand through the air.

The drink she'd fixed was potent and I was getting a nice high. It made me downright loquacious.

Tillie and I talked through the afternoon, sealing our friendship, while in the pool Anya and Stan deepened their own intimacy. The sun was burning bright in the sky.

Later, as my bejeweled hostess grew introspective, I took a moment to reflect on the day's events. Myra was still in possession of the ring! She had told me she would give it back today, and didn't. True, the appearance of Gaylord might have preempted its return, but I had a feeling that if things had been allowed to take their course she'd have kept it anyway. That kiss in Tillie's living room had changed everything.

I wanted to discuss it with Gladstein. I saw where the sun was, and figured his store might still be open if I headed there right away.

"Do you mind if I leave?" I asked Tillie.

"Of course not. You run along. It's time for me to do my correspondence, anyway."

I dashed inside, changed into my street clothes, bade a quick good-bye to Stan and Anya (who barely noticed), and took off.

It was nearly seven, closing time on Saturdays. Alas, I'd forgotten that Snead came to clean that day. It occurred to me only when I passed the Ben Franklin (my mother was off work) and spotted his truck in front of Gladstein's.

As I was mounting to the top of the steps the two men came out of the store. Gladstein was locking up and the Yatzis were bouncing about like Ping-Pong balls in a wind tunnel.

"Little Witcher!" he called.

Snead squinted over his cigarette.

Bashfully I approached. The drink had pretty much worn off, and Snead, who very well might act as spy for my father (you never could tell), was spoiling everything by being present. Once again I was to be prohibited from pouring my heart out to my mentor.

"Awright, little Witcher, how you doing."

"How you doing, Snead."

"Where you been, kid?" Gladstein asked.

"Swimming. You know that new house on Clark Lane? The people there let us come to their pool."

"Shit, little Witcher, you swimming with the rich folks?" Snead grinned.

"Yeah." I came close to telling him about the mixed drink, but I decided to stay on the safe side.

"Your brother went too?"

"He almost beat up Gaylord Joyner but the cop came and stopped him."

"Deputy Dawg?"

"Yeah," I said.

Gladstein's mutts were pawing frantically at his fat legs. "Where are those people from?"

"Dallas."

"Dallas," he said scornfully, "don't talk to me about Dallas, that's where they shot our president."

"Shit, Mr. Gladstein, you can't blame the whole town," Snead said. "That was that lone nutcase, that Oswald cat."

The men moved towards their vehicles. Snead was carrying a bucket and some rags. In the back of his truck, on the flatbed, you could see the handle of the buffer poking up.

"Jack Kennedy was the best president we've ever had." Gladstein raised his eyebrows, impressing the point on Snead.

"Fine with me, I ain't arguing. Why did your brother want to beat up Joyner?" Snead asked.

"You of all people should know what I'm talking about,"

Gladstein went on. "Jews and blacks have to stand together, right? I can't stand prejudice in the South. Abhor it. I moved down here to protest the injustice of the place. When my wife died, I said to hell with it. You know where I live? In Jefferson Ward. I figured that would show these bigots a thing or two."

Snead swiveled his cigarette. "You shitting me, you live in Jefferson Ward?"

"I never told you?"

"Nah, I never heard tell where you live."

Gladstein nodded, somber, proud.

"You take your Continental into that neighborhood? You a brave man, Mr. Gladstein."

"Oh, they're good people."

I didn't quite understand. I had heard of Jefferson Ward. It was downtown, a neighborhood forbidden to white people. They called it Niggertown in El Dorado Hills. But this was the first time I'd heard that Gladstein lived there. Perhaps if I had been older, if I had traveled beyond the confines of El Dorado Hills, the incomprehensibility of a white man in Jefferson Ward would have struck me more powerfully.

Gladstein was all exercised by now. "I figured if I moved into one of these lily-white neighborhoods like El Dorado Hills I'd be no better than anyone else. People have to do it themselves, the government can't do everything. That's why I bought in Jefferson Ward. I haven't had a moment's problem there. They're good people, Snead."

Snead squinted over his cigarette. "If you say so."

I don't think Gladstein grasped how uncomfortable Southerners were made by straightforwardness. Snead didn't want to discuss it. Integration was fine on the news, but who ever heard of a white man with money moving to Jefferson Ward? It was a bit like Dickie Pudding's tap dancing.

Gladstein kept watching Snead's face, expecting to be congratulated for his subversion. But Snead never gave a thing away. I liked that about him.

"You don't approve of my living in Jefferson Ward?"

"I ain't got no problem with it. You do what you want, Mr. Gladstein."

"You should visit me. Come see for yourself."

Snead didn't reply.

The jeweler frowned and shook his head. "Black people down here don't want change any more than the white people."

"Nah, people gotta live, that's all," Snead said.

Gladstein looked around for his mutts and started pensively in the direction of the Continental. I kept my eyes on him, wondering whether he'd remember to ask about Myra. There were so many things I wanted to tell him.

He stuck his key in the car door and the dogs leapt happily inside.

Snead said, "I ask you, Witcher, can you imagine a white man parking that car in Jefferson Ward?"

"I don't know, I ain't never been there."

"Shit, man *lives* there. He must have a lucky horseshoe.

Man's got some kind of magic if they let him live in Jefferson Ward." He laughed. He stared at Gladstein's car as it pulled up to the top of the hill to exit onto Karen Drive. He gave the sky a saturnine shake of his big, tough, squinting head. "Damn fool," he said. "Thinks he's doing black folks a favor."

16

I NEVER DID LEARN how the Joyners came to know about the pool party. And yet it was easy to imagine Myra spilling the beans to a Coghill and that Coghill repeating it to a Pendleton who would report it to another Pendleton who would then ferret the news to Gaylord Joyner. And if the neighbors had by now learned that Myra was associating with a Witcher, well then, what were wars in the jungle or assassination conspiracies or long hair on boys to prove the world was going mad?

I kept pining for her. For a week I haunted the woods behind Dickie Pudding's house, gazing at the street and listening for her step. I wandered the terraced slopes of the shopping center, climbing up, climbing down. In Gladstein's Jewelry I stayed near the corner mirror and studied the sewing store, hoping against hope.

Gladstein, happy about the power of his ring, told jokes to

cheer me up. "You kissed her, Witcher, and you told me she'd never let you."

"Plus she came to the party as my date," I said.

"A date with Myra Joyner, you Don Juan!"

Nevertheless, society had dictated its will. My girl had vanished.

I heard rumors she had been grounded and couldn't leave the house. That made me feel a little guilty, but also triumphant. I was tapping into the same evil forces that drove my brother. Maybe I'd become as expert at seducing girls as Stan and Pop. What if someday I got a French gal!

Meanwhile Anya had fallen for Stan, the way girls do for violent, reckless boys. She came to the house to meet the folks. She bore witness to the pallid TRASH legend showing through the watery paint and shook her head, muttering bad things about the philistines of El Dorado Hills. "In California people have tons more money than here. Everyone is free in California, they don't have all these small-town hang-ups."

Mom didn't approve of such worldliness, no matter if the girl was defending us. Why would she be bringing up California? It must have something to do with those hippies. Pop inscrutably eyed her, appreciating what a chip off the old block Stan was; he was remembering that French gal, I'll bet.

Anya, she gazed at where the screen should be, at the tattered carmine sofa, at the car parts beside the house, at the weeds in the yard, and yet all she saw was Stan: his sinewy muscles, his brooding lips, his long hair, his contempt for the plastic suburbanites of El Dorado Hills.

Wow, man. Women.

One afternoon while I was watching soap operas with Pop, I spied a familiar head through the window and I bounded up for a closer look. Kathy Coghill loitered stealthily on the street, gazing towards our house. I raised my hand in greeting and she glanced tentatively away at that very moment, unaware she was being watched. Then she took a quick step to the side, yanked open our mailbox, tossed something inside, and hurried off in the direction of Clark Lane.

She was around the corner by the time I got to the yard. I opened the mailbox and took out an envelope with my name on it, *Jack*, composed in flowing cursive, by a hand possessing the deepest artistic feeling.

I took it to my room.

The note read:

> *Dearest,*
> *They've got me locked in the house and I can't get out! I'm about to go crazy! I can't think of anything but you. Rescue me!*
>
> M

What was I supposed to do? I paced about my room, stunned at the way she'd converted so efficiently from reluctant fawn to eager beaver.

I left the house by the back door. I didn't want to have to answer questions from Pop.

I hurried to Lewis Street and scrutinized the windows of

her house, darkened under the afternoon sun. I walked up to the two-lane and retraced my steps. There was no movement at the curtains, no perceptible life. Both Joyner automobiles were missing from the driveway. I went to Stanley Street and passed the Coghill residence, espying nary a Coghill. The entire neighborhood was as dark and sweltering as a ghost town in summer.

I headed for the woods next to the Taylor house where in solitude I might consider my scheme to kidnap Myra and hide her in the abandoned shack on Baskin Road. The main problem would be the distance. I was still only twelve, after all. Even my brother had only occasional access to wheels, although he did possess a driver's license. (Recently Anya had been letting him drive her GTO.) And then I realized Stan's confederacy would be crucial to any plot to free Myra from Joyner propriety. If, say, he could borrow Anya's GTO and be waiting at some corner while I rounded her up, then I might ferry her to Baskin Road. But it would be necessary for me to visit her day after day. I couldn't just leave her in the shack. I would have to feed her, care for her.

I rested my head on my knee by the hot banks of the creek. A chorus of cicadas, growing loud and fading off in turn, stepped up the volume. Things were biting me and landing on my skin. Angry wings buzzed at my ear.

Suddenly I heard voices through the woods, thrashing sounds, stoned laughter. Stan and Anya were hurrying towards me from the direction of the street side. I stood on my feet, guilty of violating a space that belonged to them.

"Jack!" Anya called.

"What are you doing here?" Stan said.

It was late afternoon; Stan had just got off work from the Safeway store. He was wearing an unnaturally wide grin on his face.

"Just sitting here thinking."

"About your little Joyner chick?"

"Oh, come on, it's groovy," Anya said, "he's sensitive, he's got feelings." She gave me a hug. I smelled her sweat and her powder.

"Kathy Coghill put a letter from Myra in the mailbox while I was watching TV. I saw her through the window. Myra's parents have got her grounded and now she wants me to rescue her."

"Rescue her! From her house?"

"I guess," I said. "All of a sudden it's like she's in love with me." I showed them the note.

Anya laughed. "It's so cute! Look, she says she can't think of anything but Jack."

"How does she expect you to rescue her?"

"I was thinking I could take her to the shack on Baskin Road and hide her."

"How would you get her there?"

"I'd need a car, I guess."

I looked at Anya, and she immediately figured out what I was angling for.

"Oh no, I'm not playing any part in that."

"Why don't you help the kid out?" Stan said.

"That would be kidnapping! Look, my dad's a lawyer, you can get in big trouble for that."

"No one would call it kidnapping, they're just kids."

Stan read the letter and handed it over. "Have you talked to the girl?"

"No, I just got it. Kathy Coghill left it in the mailbox and took off."

"What are you gonna do? You need to come up with a plan and write her back."

"What kind of plan?"

"I don't know. Get her to sneak out of the house after dark, meet you outside. Set up a time, make sure the old man and old lady are in bed."

"And then what? Could I bring her to our room?"

His sunglasses peered in my direction. Truth is, I didn't really expect him to agree to my bringing a twelve-year-old to the room. Stan had little tolerance for the wholesomeness of twelve-year-olds. Occasionally he would slap Dickie Pudding around simply because he didn't like the way he whinnied when he laughed. But now we were speaking of a girl whose presence in our house at night would bring shame and devastation to the entire Joyner family. And he liked that idea.

"You could hide her in the room 'til we come up with something better. Taking her to the shack on Baskin Road is a possibility. We could put her up for a few days, bring her food and water."

"Yeah, but . . ."

I looked at Anya.

"N-O spells no," she said.

"Shit, man," my brother said. "Like, wow. We'll get you and the little Joyner girl fixed up. It'll be a gas when Gaylord finds out his sister split for a Witcher."

Later that afternoon, as I was approaching the house, I noticed the red flag on the mailbox jutting in the air.

I found another envelope inside, with my name in Myra's hand.

I took it to my room and opened it.

> *Darling,*
>
> *Write me back and let me know what you're going to do. Kathy will pick up your letter. Leave it in your mailbox. Please do something. Write me! I must see you! I'm going mad!*
>
> *Love, You Know Who,*
> *M*

I gnawed my nails, terrified of failing her. How had she reached this state of abandon so quickly? Was it my kiss? Was my kiss that good?

What if Myra's parents made her go to a psychiatrist too? This was the madness of Courtney Blankenship all over again!

I found some paper in the wooden desk by the window and wrote a reply. *Dear Myra*, I began, forgoing the "dearest." I had decided on a no-nonsense approach.

Stay calm. I am working on a plan. Will you be able
to climb out your window at night? Maybe tonight or
tomorrow? I will rescue you and hide you somewhere
so we can be together. We will get jobs and make
money and buy a farm. Don't worry.

Your boyfriend,
Jack

I dropped the letter in the box and put up the red flag.

At midnight it was there. And again at eight the next morning. But sometime later, I don't know when, the flag went down and the letter was gone.

A Coghill abetting a Witcher to elope with a Joyner: what a revolution was taking place in El Dorado Hills!

17

THE ANSWER DIDN'T COME until the afternoon, when I heard the mailbox lid creak on its hinges and spotted Kathy Coghill rushing past the window. I left Pop in front of the TV (he was too involved in *As the World Turns* to notice the daytime drama under his nose) to retrieve the missive lurking in the cryptic depths of the box. I read it in my bedroom with my shoulder against the door to bar intruders. Myra said she was ready to do whatever I wished. However, she did make one small adjustment to my plan. Her bedroom being on the second floor, she couldn't very well slip out of that window; on the other hand, the den window behind the house would suit nicely. Her parents went to bed early, but to stay on the safe side I should wait until after midnight. But we couldn't do it tonight, she added, because her parents were going to a play at a local supper club and would be out later than usual. Otherwise, and this is exactly how she put it, *I am yours.*

My heart pounded when I read that line. Had she truly written those words? In a daze of ecstasy, of apprehension, I roamed up to Gladstein's shop. I was so preoccupied that I forgot to look in on my mother when I passed the Ben Franklin.

The prissy bell tinkled, the Yatzis yapped, Gladstein shouted a greeting.

But I didn't say a word.

I placed the letters on the counter for him to see.

He beetled his brow and read what I'd given him.

"My my," he said, "the magic works."

"Is it really magic?"

Gladstein remained silent awhile, thinking, and then he said, "If it works, it is magic."

He let me ruminate on that, watching me with a smile. One of his eyebrows was quivering like a Cupid's arrow about to be shot into the air.

"You have quite a situation here," he told me, "a damsel in distress, and she's locked in an attic. What are you gonna do about it?"

"I guess I have to help her. This whole mess is because I kissed her."

"You'll get no argument from me, Witcher. I may not look like Paul Newman, but I once had my day." He was from Atlantic City, he said, where horses dive off boards and Miss Americas ride the boardwalk in shiny new convertibles. They smile in their bathing suits with their arms in the air, like movable Statues of Liberty, and all the while the great ocean is lapping behind them. Atlantic City is a world of fun rides,

Ferris wheels and roller coasters; people from Atlantic City possess an innate sense of beauty, Gladstein told me. As a young man he'd gone on a romantic quest for a Miss North Carolina whom he met while employed as a bellboy in a hoity-toity hotel. One afternoon while the beauty queen was in the hotel's lounging area—she was with a few other contestants—she suddenly expressed, loudly and within earshot, a desire for cotton candy. She'd glanced directly at him, batting her lashes in case he didn't understand. Gladstein, being young and vigorous and strong, had instantly leapt to the occasion. He abandoned his post, dashed to the boardwalk, procured a sticky bale for his Tarheel queen, and rushed back holding the fluffy confection aloft. Meanwhile his boss had been pacing the lobby, incensed. He fired Gladstein on the spot for leaving without permission. "But what did I care? I was in seventh heaven. I asked Miss North Carolina for her phone number and she told me she wasn't allowed to date. Instead she gave me the address of her parents' house in North Carolina and said I could write her there. And you know something? Every week for three years I sent that gal a letter to Rocky Mount, North Carolina. And to every letter I sent she penned a gracious reply, thanking me for the cotton candy I had lost my job for. I would think, Ah, these Southern gals, so sweet, so soft-spoken. Then in one of her letters she expressed a racist sentiment and I never wrote her again."

"What happened to her?" I asked.

"She married a local baseball player. They have a minor league team in Rocky Mount."

"So you married someone else."

"Local Jewish gal. We were hitched for twenty-five years, before the cancer got her. Good woman. Class. Social consciousness, compassion for the poor, the oppressed."

I tried to imagine her. All I could picture was a woman with a rag tied around her head.

"You're really against prejudice, huh?" I said.

"Of course. Aren't you?"

"I guess. I got a friend whose dad is in the KKK. He doesn't like it 'cause my pop is friends with Snead."

Gladstein arched that quivering eyebrow. "Your dad's a friend of Snead's? Well well, what a world. I wouldn't have pegged your father as a liberal."

"I don't think he calls himself that. He voted for Johnson, and I think for Kennedy. He's a Democrat," I said. I wanted Gladstein to like Pop. I figured a report on his voting record might do it.

Gladstein nodded and looked away, full of heavy musings I couldn't possibly understand.

Finally he tapped the Myra letters on the counter.

"All right, to the matter at hand. You've kissed Myra, so what next?"

"Well, now I have to rescue her."

"From what?"

"From being grounded. Her parents don't want her going with me."

Gladstein folded his arms. His chest rose and fell with his breathing.

"Have you felt her breasts?"

"No sir," I said awkwardly. That a grown man should speak of breasts to a child in El Dorado Hills was unheard of. Only foulmouthed brats spoke of breasts. I hadn't given Myra's breasts a moment's thought. I wasn't even sure she had any.

"Well," Gladstein said.

There was a shrug in his voice: a sigh for the fatuousness of romantic boyhood. "To each his own, I suppose. But I should think you'd want to touch her breasts. Certainly I would have at your age."

"Did you touch Miss North Carolina's breasts?" I asked.

Gladstein roared with laughter. "The mountains of North Carolina, hey, Witcher? Asheville on the left, Boone on the right!" He hacked out a laugh and slapped his thigh.

My face was hot as a furnace.

"Listen, Witcher. She has the ring, and that means she is in your power. Whatever you want her to do, she will do. Look at me, Witcher, you're looking away."

I obeyed.

He handed over Myra's letters. "Don't forget these," he said. "And here, take this." He pulled a golden bracelet from the drawer and dangled it before my eyes.

"What is it?"

"It's for her. Take it, it's junk. Otherwise I'll throw it away."

"No, don't throw it away."

I pocketed the bracelet, dazzled by his bottomless stock of trifles.

"Listen, do you want to see her breasts or not?"

"I do," I said.

"Then you must think of them constantly. Make it a prayer. Do not let her nipples out of your mind. Smell them, taste them. Picture her blossoming young tits. Myra's breasts are yours, Witcher."

"Yes sir," I said.

Gladstein's baggy eyes released me. I left the shop.

18

THE NEXT NIGHT, the night I had arranged for Myra's rescuing, Snead paid a call at our house.

My heart sank as his truck pulled up. When I sent my final instructions to Myra I hadn't reckoned on his being at the house. I had told her I would come to her yard at midnight, or shortly thereafter. I was to hoot three times like an owl, and she would climb out the den window.

Around ten I went to my room and pretended to go to bed.

It was a cool night and the fans were off and I turned out the light and listened to Snead and Pop and Mom under my window. They had a cooler out there and I would occasionally hear the soft pressurized sigh of a beer can jabbed by an opener. The guitar-playing didn't last very long that night, there was conversation instead. More and more the music was simply an excuse for Snead and Pop to get together.

Their voices kept lulling me, and several times I was close

to falling asleep. Around eleven I heard my mother say good night. She folded up her lounge chair and came inside.

Usually at midnight Snead would head home, but sometimes he stayed as late as two or three in the morning. The thought made me tense with anxiety. I heard the sound of cigarette lighters thumbed open, the scraping of flints, the clicking of lids, hands rummaging through the slushy ice in the bottom of the cooler for the coldest beers, the springy metal of a lounge chair whenever one of the men shifted in his seat. Each time I heard a noise I hoped it meant Snead was rising to leave.

"Go, Snead, go," I prayed.

Stan was out somewhere with Anya, and I was alone in the room.

The men's voices were murmuring, late-night voices, indistinct; and then I realized they were talking about Gladstein. Several times I heard his name. Snead said something about Jefferson Ward and they started laughing.

"Good God," my father said, and they laughed some more.

Their voices grew lower and I strained to hear. I felt defensive for Gladstein, sorry he was so out of place in the world.

Pop made a remark and Snead laughed, and then he began to croon a blues song.

He broke off. "What did you say?" he responded to one of Snead's murmurs.

"Man wants me to come out and see him. In Jefferson Ward."

"You gonna go?"

"I ain't gonna go calling on no white man in Jefferson Ward."

That set off another round of guffaws.

"That would leave his place ripe for the picking, Snead. The store all by itself."

Snead snorted. After a while he said, "I gotta go."

"Naw, don't go."

"I gotta get up in the morning."

"Come on, stay awhile."

"Naw, I can't."

"Go, go, go," I prayed.

Ten minutes passed. Why can't people leave when they say they're going to?

Finally the metal of the lounge chair creaked as Snead urged his bulk upwards. The voices retreated to the edge of the yard. I heard a door slam and an engine rev. Snead's truck pulled away.

Even though it was after midnight I still couldn't leave. I had to wait for Pop to gather the things from the yard and come down the hall and go to the bathroom. I needed to see the dark at the crack of my door before I could take off.

Finally I tiptoed down the hall and slipped out the front door.

By the time I got to the Joyners' yard it was almost one in the morning. A sleepy bark came from around the side of the Kellner house and quickly I whispered Rusty's name.

I crouched by the cars in the driveway (the Joyners' blue Chevrolet Impala, Gaylord's cherry-red Mustang convertible gleaming in the porch light) and Rusty approached, growling low in his throat. But it was okay: as soon as I held out my hand the menace melted away and he slavishly began to lick my fingers. His tail was swinging like a metronome. I let him lap me for a while and then we trotted together around the side of the house.

I stood behind a magnolia tree and eyeballed the darkened den window.

"Myra!" I shouted in a whisper.

Nothing happened.

I hooted three times into cupped hands, sounding unnaturally like a hooting Witcher. I could imagine Mr. Joyner waking up and reaching for his gun.

Nothing happened. I hooted again, but I needed to clear my throat; it came out too raspy.

Then I saw a motion at the window. The screen was raised, a bundle flew out.

Rusty's ears perked up.

A skinny limb thrust over the sill, and another, and Myra leapt to the ground. She snatched the bundle and ran athletically through the dark to greet me behind the fragrant magnolia. We were all excited by our daring, bonded by our transgression, and passionately we kissed.

We headed to the front yard. A car came down Lewis Street and we ducked behind Gaylord's Mustang until it was past. Myra was gripping me breathlessly, holding on for dear life. I was already thinking about her breasts.

After the car went by, we jogged to my house, staying close to the side of the road so we could hide in case other cars came. Rusty ran ahead, looking back deliriously, ecstatic over the unexpected late-night adventure. When we got to the yard I sent

Myra to my bedroom window and went back to shoo him off. I stomped my foot and tossed a stick past his head. His tail drooped, he stared in bewilderment. I hated being mean to the dog, but I was afraid his presence would provide a clue to Myra's whereabouts once the family realized she was missing. Rusty tended to follow Myra wherever she went.

It didn't matter, my exertions proved futile. He whined indignantly and went to Myra. She was against the house, twisting her head to watch me.

"Why are you doing that to Rusty?" Myra said.

"I don't want him to stay, he'll give you away."

"But he's here all the time. Nobody will think anything."

"Maybe," I said.

I knelt beside her, feeling all emotional. I moved my lips towards her and we started making out. While we were kissing, my hand went creeping towards her breasts and I pulled it away.

"I didn't think you were coming. I was in the den with my bundle, I must have waited an hour."

"Snead was here. Him and Pop were in the front yard and I had to wait 'til he left."

"Why does your dad like him so much?"

"Why shouldn't he?"

She didn't answer and I said, "Pop isn't prejudiced, he isn't like people around here. He isn't like Mr. Pudding."

Myra nodded, as if in favor of the idea.

"What did you bring in the bundle?" I asked.

"PJs, my toothbrush, Band-Aids, aspirin."

We kissed again, only this time I couldn't control myself.

I placed my hand on her blouse, above her tiny right breast, feeling the slightest rise.

Myra pushed me away.

"What are you doing?"

"Touching you."

"Well, don't."

"What's wrong?"

"Do you want me to go home?" she said archly.

I leaned my head against the house, hurt. Then I remembered something. I hitched up and felt inside my pocket and came out with the bracelet Gladstein had donated to my cause.

"Here," I said.

"What is it?"

"It's yours."

Myra caught her breath. The golden bracelet gleamed in the faint moonlight.

"Oh, Jack," she said.

She slid it over her skinny arm and held it aloft. We sat for a while, listening to the glowing sounds of the warm night: crickets and frogs, faraway automobiles, dogs barking at shadows on the streets.

"I've been wearing your ring," she confessed, "I put it on at night and sleep with it, and in the morning I take it off."

"So you're my steady girl?"

"Yes!" she cried.

We kissed again, and I dangled my errant hand in the air to keep it away from her breast. It was making its own decisions.

By and by we heard the sound of an engine from the direction of Clark Lane and broke out of our kiss. Parallel beams shot past the house. There was a deceleration and the car came to a halt out front. It was Anya's GTO.

Myra began to panic and I shushed her.

"It's my brother," I said.

"Oh God, your brother."

"It's okay, he's on our side," I said.

"If Gaylord finds out—"

We kept watching. Stan was driving, and now he flung open the driver's door while Anya climbed from the passenger side and went around to take the wheel. Beside the car they sullenly kissed.

Myra shielded her eyes. "We shouldn't be watching this."

After Anya coasted away I dashed to the yard and nabbed Stan.

"I have Myra with me! Open up the window so we can get in."

He didn't say a word. He went in the house, and a few seconds later the window was raised.

"Hey, little Joyner." He gave her a wink.

Myra didn't respond. I cupped my hand and she put her foot in it and Stan pulled her up. I tossed her bundle through the window and climbed in behind her.

The three of us stood in the dark room, baffled, amazed. Stan switched on the desk lamp.

Myra squinted at me. She squinted at Stan. She squinted at the bunk beds. Then she burst into tears.

I shushed her and lowered her to the bed. I put my arm around her.

My brother, for once, behaved chivalrously. He gave her one of his monogrammed handkerchiefs from the dresser drawer. Then he went to the kitchen and brought back a glass of water and some cookies. I thought that was right nice. I was surprised he did it.

Myra thanked him politely. She took a gulp of water and said, "I'm so scared."

"Want me to take you home? Maybe we can sneak you back in the window."

"What if they already know I'm gone?"

"Aren't they asleep?"

"Daddy looks in on me when he goes to the bathroom. He might know by now."

That made me kind of nervous.

"What are we going to do?" she said.

"I don't know. There's a deserted cabin on Baskin Road, I was thinking we could take you there."

"To a deserted cabin? What if it's got mice!"

She cried again, only this time a lot harder.

It was too much for my exhausted nerves. I looked at my brother. He was sitting backwards in the chair, with his chin against the back. He made a scornful sound through his nose. "What the hell did you sneak out of the house for? You expect a luxury hotel?"

"Shut up," I told him.

Myra became dignified. She looked at me coolly, not bothering to answer. "I need to sleep," she said.

She curled up in my bed. I sat beside her and patted her shoulder. Stan turned out the top light and climbed to the top bunk and went to sleep in his clothes.

I stayed next to her for a long time, unsure what I should do. Should I remain as a sentry? Curl up beside her? Finally I curled up beside her.

A snore came from the top bunk.

Myra rolled around to face me.

"I think I should go home in the morning," she whispered.

"Okay," I said.

"I won't tell them where I was."

"Won't you get in trouble?"

"Yes."

"I'm sorry," I said.

After a while I said, "Will you still be my steady girl?"

She was quiet.

"I must be going crazy," she said. "I like you. I really like you."

"Even though I'm a Witcher," I said.

"Oh no, you're too good to be a Witcher."

She fell asleep after that. Her leg twitched once or twice.

I stared at the declivity above, where my brother was sleeping. What did she mean I was too good to be a Witcher? Why did my victory have to be so unpleasantly qualified?

I had a suspicion there would be hell to pay.

19

IT WAS WAITING in the morning.

We heard a pounding at the door and my mother shouted, "What did you lock the door for? What are you doing in there?"

Myra's face, all scrunched up, turned to look at me.

"Is Myra Joyner with you?"

I peeked out the bedroom window, the one that faced the front. The Joyners' blue Impala was parked outside. Rusty was sitting on his haunches, grinning at the house.

"It's your parents."

Myra didn't let a second pass. Just as she had efficiently obeyed Gaylord at the pool, now she leapt up, snatched her bundle from the desk, transferred the bracelet from wrist to pocket, and, with a neat, lovely swipe at her hair, swung open the bedroom door.

My mother and Mr. Joyner were in the doorway, with Pop hovering a few feet behind.

"Okay, young missy, we're going home right this minute," Mr. Joyner said.

I stepped forward.

"I want you to know one thing, Mr. Joyner. It's my fault. I talked Myra into it."

"I don't doubt that in the least. Come on, Myra."

He pulled her into the hall. One of his eyebrows was arched upwards like a rocket ship about to fly towards the sky. For a few seconds he looked crazy—genteel Mr. Joyner looked crazy! His eyes were churning at me. He had a weird grin on his face. He kept darting glances, at me, at Pop, at Mom, at Stan, with a wild, trapped expression. It was as though he had just got his first glimpse of the minor demons of Hell. Never had I felt such contempt coming from an adult. I realized I was taking my prideful place in the Gallery of Witchers. No longer would the neighbors pity my low birth. I had grown into my fate. I was behaving as my blood had bound me.

Pop didn't like the way Joyner was looking at me. He put his hand out and Joyner yanked away, as if a Witcher touch might prevent his escape from the abyss.

And then it was over, just like that. Myra didn't even say good-bye. We heard the screen door slam (letting it slam was a deliberate insult) and we heard the Joyner car move off.

Rusty barked twice and stayed in the yard.

"Damn dog gave us away," I said.

"He didn't need the dog to find out where she was. He knew where she was the second he saw she was gone. And quit saying 'damn.'" Mom was furious. "What's been going on between you and Myra Joyner that I didn't know about?"

"She's my girlfriend," I said.

Pop laughed triumphantly, unable to check himself. Mom gave him a livid frown and he wiped his mouth.

She spun back to me. "You do not bring young girls into this house to spend the night. Are you out of your mind? And you," she said to Stan, "what are you thinking of, letting him bring a girl into the room at night?"

"Don't lose your wig, they kept their clothes on."

"That's not the point! I should hope they kept their clothes on!"

She stared my brother down and returned to me. "You do not go with that girl, do you understand? Joyners and Witchers do not mix."

"What book of the Bible is that in?" Stan sneered.

"Listen to you. You should know better than anyone about what happens when Joyners mix with Witchers."

He opened his mouth to make a retort and faltered and looked away. That might have been a low blow on Mom's part.

At any rate, the upshot was I got grounded for an indefinite period of time. The yard would form my front and my rear boundaries. Mom pointed them out like an avenging angel.

I shrugged. If ignoring Myra's cries of distress meant not getting grounded, then getting grounded was worth it. Besides, my birthday was only days away and I felt pretty sure I'd receive a pardon when it came.

My brother, meanwhile, had got all agitated, and he pulled me into the room.

"Did you see the way that son of a bitch looked at you?"

"He was mad 'cause I kidnapped his daughter," I said.

I could put myself in Mr. Joyner's shoes well enough. Myra was a hothouse flower, a precious fruit. I'd be mad too if some kid came and plucked her away. But my brother was remorseless. He said I hadn't forced Myra to do a damn thing. She was the one who started it with her goddamn letters.

"What was she doing leaving notes in our mailbox? She was asking for it, that's what she was doing. And then you told the old shithook it was your fault."

"Well, I'm the boy and she's the girl."

"What difference does that make?" Stan burned quietly. Then he said, "You know what I'm gonna do? I'm gonna go strolling past the Joyners' house. I'm gonna walk up and down the street until Gaylord comes out."

"What for?"

"So I can kick his ass."

"Man, don't do that, that'll just make it harder for Myra and me."

"Oh, get over the skinny twit, will you."

He left the room.

After a while I realized I was just sitting there, staring ahead. That's when it dawned on me I wasn't allowed to go anywhere.

I sauntered meekly into the kitchen, where Mom was slamming plates to the table, preparing breakfast in a rage. Through the window I saw Pop's head passing back and forth as he re-arranged the junk at the side of the house.

She was making a point of not speaking. I cleared my throat and kept staring until her movements grew less furious. I made my eyes big and childlike.

She darted me a look, and a tight-lipped smile softened her frown. I was her baby boy, and I knew how to play that card.

She let some time pass, maintaining her indignation, and then she said, "You're setting yourself up for a fall, you know that, don't you."

"With Myra?"

"Who do you think I mean?"

I thought about it.

"But she took my ring."

"What ring? Where did you get a ring?"

"From Mr. Gladstein."

"How can you afford a ring from Mr. Gladstein?"

"It only cost fifty cents. It's junk, you know, costume jewelry."

I wanted to abbreviate the details of my transactions with Gladstein, lest she become militant. I remembered how she had once hauled Stan and me to the drugstore, forcing us to return certain items we'd lifted.

"Mr. Gladstein doesn't keep junk in his store."

"Yes he does. He was getting ready to throw out a bracelet the other day and I took it and gave it to Myra."

"Why on earth are you giving jewelry to that girl? Can't you see she's using you? She's just getting what she can out of you.

Don't mess with the Joyners, the Joyners are snobs. She's just slumming with you, boy." I was ready to jump in and defend Myra, but she cut me off. "Don't you let those people take advantage of you. You're a good boy, you hear? You don't come from trash." Suddenly she was walking towards me and shaking her finger in my face, all riled up. "They can paint whatever they want on this house, but my mother and father were the nicest people that ever lived. They may not have had much education but they had good morals and they never hurt a soul. They gave a lot more than they ever received and I never heard them complain about it once. These narrow-minded people that live around here don't know what they're talking about. You're a good boy, you hear?" And then she hugged my head, giving me a monkey-shine.

Mom was a right sweet old gal, although she had Myra all wrong. And even if she didn't have Myra wrong (and a part of me was beginning to wonder), that wouldn't change anything. I wasn't going to quit the girl 'til I felt her breasts.

"Did I ever tell you how I met your daddy?" she said.

"In a bar."

She laughed. "It's the only time in my life I ever went in one."

I knew the story by heart, I'd heard it a hundred times. It was the only time she ever smoked a cigarette, that night in the bar.

"Pop probably thought you were gonna be a lot of fun 'cause you smoked and drank," I said. "Or so he believed."

Mom was laughing at the memory. "We were in a booth in the rear of the bar, the Lakeside Lounge, you know, out on

Lakeside Avenue. He talked to me all night and bought me dinner, tried to make me drunk. And you know what I was telling myself that whole time he was running his mouth?"

"You're gonna marry that man. You've told me this story a thousand times, Mom."

"But do you know why I wanted to marry him?"

Actually, I didn't. It was a new wrinkle. She had never explained that.

"I knew he'd never get it in his head he was too good for me. He has an inferiority complex a mile wide. Most people can't see that, but I saw it right away."

"You mean you fell in love with Pop because he has an inferiority complex?"

"Plus he was good-looking."

I stared at her speechlessly and she said, "What are you looking that way for? People fall in love for far dumber reasons than that."

It made me feel funny, to think Mom didn't fall in love with Pop for his charm. What are women made of? Is that why Myra liked me, because I was lowborn, humble?

I went to my room and meditated on the mysteries of women, deeper than all the philosophies of humankind put together.

20

THE COOL WEATHER KEPT ON, and the indistinct tones
made by Pop and Snead played like music beneath my window. I'd be in and out of sleep, listening to their voices without
making the slightest sense of what they were saying. Baseball,
cowboy boots, blues records. I sort of half got it, floating in and
out; and then I heard Gladstein's name and I sat up to listen.
Snead was telling Pop about the safe in the rear of the store.
He knew the combination, the spinning numbers that would
let you into that box like a magic charm.

"How'd you find out?"

"I was cleaning up where he keeps the dogs. Cat has the
combination on a sheet of paper, it was tucked under the blot-
ter on his desk."

"No shit. So you rich now, Snead? You done pocketed a
diamond?"

They laughed, and then they lowered their voices to a whisper, so I couldn't catch what they were saying. That was frustrating. I wanted to know what they thought about Gladstein, whom I regarded with a kind of proprietary interest. He was mine. He belonged to my world. I knew things about him no one else did, and whatever Snead and Pop were saying I should be able to hear, by entitlement. I strained my ears and they kept murmuring, and occasionally my friend's name would slip in.

I crept out of bed and crouched under the window so I could eavesdrop.

I heard my father's voice: "Hell, Snead, all you gotta do is find a good fence."

He said it in a joshing tone, but it made Snead uneasy, I sensed it.

At the time I didn't know what "fence" meant, and I assumed the subject had been changed. I thought they were talking about doing yard work.

Snead said something about a man who lived in Hopewell who had a fence (or that's what I understood) and Pop asked what the man's name was. Snead told him, but I couldn't make it out. They sat for a while without saying much else. Pop tooted on his harmonica once or twice and Snead neglected to pick it up on the guitar. Pop blew a little longer and then he quit.

They were off the subject of Gladstein and their silence had started to bore me. I was about to go stubbing back to bed on my knees when Pop said, "You know, if you were visiting him at his house then I'd know he wouldn't be snooping around the store. If I'm gonna do the thing I wanna know exactly where he is."

"How you expect to get in?"

"Through the alley door, no one will see. I can get that door open in thirty seconds flat."

"What about the houses on Myra Street?"

"Man, they got those tall shrubs along the chain-link back there. No one can see through the shrubs, especially after dark. All I need you to do is find out if he has an alarm rigged to the door. If he does we have to figure out how to shut it off. Or maybe you could slip back there and unlock the door when he ain't looking, right before you leave. Then after the two of you leave I'll come and tamper with the lock to make it look like it's been jimmied."

Up to that moment I'd been struggling to apply sense to what they were saying. Now I felt the blood in my face. My stomach grew queasy. I returned to bed, not wanting to hear. But their mumbling kept drifting in and soon I was back under the window, unable to stop myself.

"All you gotta do is call and let me know. Call from Gladstein's when you get there. Tell him you need to use the phone, pretend you're calling your wife. We can set up a code. 'Hi, honey, you want anything from the store on the way home?' So I'll know the coast is clear."

Snead didn't say anything for a while.

Then he said, "I don't know, Witcher, this could be more trouble than it's worth. I got a mortgage, I got a baby sleeping in the crib."

"What's the trouble? You won't even be there. There won't be no risk at all, for you. If anything goes wrong I'll take the fall."

"You're talking about a felony."

"What the hell, I do the work, you get half. Just relax and let me take care of things."

"This is hard time we're talking about. I don't wanna do no time."

"Man, there ain't no time to do. Anyone gets caught it'll be me. You know damn well I wouldn't sing, I'd just cool my heels in jail. That old treasure would be *buried*, man."

"I never said you would sing."

"In the mountains they used to say Witchers ain't snitchers. That was a saying where I come from."

Pop laughed, Snead didn't.

"Listen, you think about it. Take your time. I ain't gonna put your baby in danger. I got two sons myself. If I didn't feel so sure about this thing I wouldn't even mention it."

They were quiet a spell.

I got afraid of what I was doing. I was afraid they could hear my heart, maybe feel my body warming the wall. I crawled back to bed and slithered in. I pulled the sheet over my head. For a half hour their voices kept on mumbling, and then I heard the springy metal as Snead got up from the chair to leave.

Pop came in the house. A line of illumination appeared at the bottom of my door when he turned on the hallway light. Then he swung open the door to check on me, which he would do sometimes before he hit the sack.

I saw his form peering into the dark.

"You awake?"

I let out a groggy murmur, pretending to be asleep. I didn't want him to suspect I'd heard anything.

"Your brother with Anya?"

"Yes sir," I said.

His head wavered in the light, searching to see, and then he pulled the door to.

The hallway light went out.

I lay there with this big need inside of me. What was I supposed to do? Witchers ain't snitchers. But the need was in me. I could hear it hollering. This was big, and it made me sorry Mom had got herself mixed up with a man who had an inferiority complex. And wasn't that exactly what came of inferiority complexes? The inclination to knock off jewelry stores instead of finding a job? Wasn't this precisely what Witchers were supposed to be about?

I wondered what Stan would do if I told. He'd kick my ass for telling, that's what; and then he'd let Pop know I squealed. And Mom would leave Pop if she found out, and I didn't want him getting left. And Gladstein would call the police. And Pop would go to the pen. And I didn't want Pop to go to the pen.

I remembered how when old man Joyner was giving me that scornful look Pop had made him quit. Just because I kidnapped Myra didn't mean Joyner could treat me like dirt. Pop had made the old man understand that. He looked out for his own. That's where Stan got it, from Pop. No one would put me down as long as Pop was in the world. But there was also Gladstein, living in Jefferson Ward with the black people and letting me have his throwaway jewelry. And the way he took care of his yappy dogs. Not to mention he acknowledged my mother in the grocery store. *And* he was tolerant of Pop, when all Pop was doing was casing his store.

I had to speak with Pop and let him know what I knew. Which might keep him at bay. But boy. How did a kid have a conversation like that with his pop?

Maybe I would do it on my birthday. Pop was extra nice on birthdays. He would take me to ice cream parlors and minor league games and let me have sips of his beer when Mom wasn't looking. The year before, when I turned twelve, he had let me puff three times on his cigarette. That's how I started smoking. I had always wanted to smoke like Pop, drink like Pop, roll up my sleeves like Pop. But I didn't know anymore. I just didn't know.

21

IN THE MORNING, at the table, I sat there wondering how to broach what I knew. Pop was all pop-eyed and abstract, chewing on his toast. When Mom left for the Ben Franklin he hardly said a word; but then, there hadn't been much between them for some time.

Stan picked up his cereal bowl and drank the flaky milk in the bottom and gasped and set it down. He smirked mysteriously and left by the back door.

Meanwhile I was staring at Pop's profile. Because I had just observed something peculiar. The handle to my coffee cup was shaped exactly like his nose. In profile Pop resembled a coffee cup. I had never noticed that before. Somehow it rattled me and rendered me incapable of further communication. I set down my cup and left the house, remembering only when I reached the edge of the yard that I was forbidden to go beyond it.

I sat on the porch, near enough to the TRASH legend to serve as an illustration of its essential truth.

Rusty got up under my arm and licked my face, and I said, "Hey, Rusty, how's Myra?" He was my sole connection with her. It gratified me to imagine he'd just returned from licking her.

No longer were my letters being footed by Kathy Coghill to Myra. Being grounded, I could no longer scout the Joyner house and gather gossip on the streets. All I could do was imagine the ways in which she might hate me. I had got her in big trouble by smuggling her to my bedroom and I figured she must at least be tempted by resentment of me. Her parents no doubt were feeding her a steady course of anti-Witcher propaganda and I wasn't sure she'd be able to withstand that. And don't forget Gaylord, whom she regarded as next in line to the Prince of Wales. Myra would audit respectfully any forensics her brother made against Witcherdom.

It seemed hopeless, in a way. And yet my instincts kept telling me nothing was lost. Myra was a good girl, docile, obedient, sweet-tempered—until her family turned its back. And then she became willful as all get-out.

I decided to write her one more note. I went to my room and penned the following:

> *Darling,*
> *Don't believe anything bad anyone says about me.*
> *I want what is best for you. You and I should be*
> *together as boyfriend and girlfriend. Let us not let*
> *them keep us apart.*
>
> > *Yours truly,*
> > *JW*

The challenge would be getting it to her. I toyed with the idea of taping the note to Rusty's collar and sending him off like a carrier pigeon, but how could I be sure it wouldn't fall into the wrong hands? My next idea was to slip the note in the mailbox, raise the flag and hope that Kathy Coghill would come along. That seemed to have a chance: remote, but a chance. So I ran the note to the box and sat on the porch and waited.

I sat for two hours. The day grew hot. Our house stood alone and the sun beat down hard on us because trees, for some reason, refused to flourish in our yard, no matter how many times Pop tried to plant them. By noon there was no shade whatsoever. I was sitting in a T-shirt and dungarees. Even Rusty had abandoned me for cooler pastures.

It wasn't just that Kathy Coghill was nowhere in sight—where was Dickie Pudding? Where was Tim Hodges? (He lived on Raleigh Lane, a big, red-pawed country boy who belonged to a clan of deer hunters. One afternoon, when there was no one else around, he had hung out with me briefly, until dinnertime.) Didn't anybody care that I was stranded? I grew more and more dejected, sitting there.

I am a Witcher, I reminded myself, and Witchers walk alone.

Just as I came to that conclusion, an old Rambler pulled onto the road, slowing down as it passed. Johnny Pendleton was at the wheel, driving on his learner's permit. (The car was a secondhand gift from his parents.) He swiveled his head and grinned as the Rambler puttered by. Three boys from the wrestling squad were with him, and in unison they hollered, "Wi-i-i-i-tch-e-e-e-er," following it with a wicked laugh.

That did it. I got up and went in the house, passing Pop on the sofa watching his soaps. I threw myself on the bed and fought away the tears.

Soon there came a rap at the door and Pop stepped in.

"What's the matter, sport?"

"Nothing." I stifled the grief.

"Those boys giving you a hard time?"

He sat on the edge of the bed.

"You heard them."

"It was the Pendleton kid, right? Hey, you know what you do next time you see him? Don't say a word, just walk up and kick him in the balls."

I rolled my head over the pillow and looked at him. "That's dirty fighting."

"Fighting's supposed to be dirty. Fighting's about winning, fair or foul. I ain't kidding, don't say nothing, just knee him in the balls. That's what Stan would do. You notice anyone picking on Stan?"

"No one likes Stan."

"You can't control whether people like you or not, but you can sure as hell make 'em respect you."

"By kneeing them in the balls?"

"That'll make 'em afraid of you. That's where respect comes from, from people fearing you."

I wasn't sure I bought this. It was the exact opposite of what

Mom taught. She taught that respect comes from respecting others. On the other hand, I was plenty respectful to others and in return I received nothing but abuse. So maybe Pop was right.

Having a man-to-man like this seemed a good time to bring up Gladstein, but somehow the words got stuck in passage. Maybe it was because Pop was being sweet when I needed him to be sweet. He was smiling and massaging my shoulders with his big, competent hands.

"We should go out and kick some ass together someday. This is the snottiest gang of people around here I ever met."

"Why are they like that?"

"Deep down inside they wanna be like us. I know it from experience. It's like rich women when they go after the stable boy."

"You think so?"

Pop had a pretty basic way of understanding things. I never wanted to believe life could be as basic as he said it was, and every time it turned out he was right I told myself it was probably for the wrong reason. And now I was telling myself the same thing about Stan, because his thinking was getting to be a lot like Pop's. Except Stan's was even more basic.

"Stop and ask yourself," Pop went on. "Why do you think the girls out there are always falling for you and your brother?"

"Like Myra?"

"Yeah, like Myra. And that Blankenship girl who used to be so crazy about Stan. And look at the way this Anya chick is mooning over him."

There might have been something to what he was saying.

We Witchers did all right with the women, when you considered how off-limits we'd been deemed by society. Yet it never occurred to me we might be the objects of envy.

"I really like Myra," I said. "And I think she likes me too. I mean, I don't think she sees me as the stable boy."

"I wasn't saying you're the stable boy." Pop laughed aloud at the idea. "You're the smartest Witcher I've ever seen," he said. "Must come from your mother's genes, 'cause it sure ain't on my side. But don't forget you're a Witcher. The minute you get too big for your britches they're gonna remind you who you are. We Witchers have to stick together, you got that?"

"Witchers ain't snitchers," I said, and regretted it, because quoting him might give my eavesdropping away. But he just laughed. I guess he figured he had told me himself.

"That's what they used to say when I was growing up."

"Yes sir."

"Don't let the bastards get to you. That's what they want, they want you to think you're dirt. I'm telling you, next time you see that Pendleton punk you knee him in the balls, you hear?"

After that he left the room, worried about what he might be missing on the soaps.

I lay for the longest time, confused and apprehensive. What was I to do about Gladstein? I wanted to be with him, to hang out at his store. I missed Myra. Hell, I missed Tillie, Basil, Anya. And where the hell was Dickie Pudding? Some friend he turned out to be.

Maybe I should just forget what I'd heard the night before. It didn't seem proper to glean such bad intelligence through eavesdropping. The act forfeited the knowledge—perhaps. I lay with that awhile, but it didn't work any miracles in my soul. All I could think about was Gladstein. It would be disloyal to let him down. Yet somehow I couldn't bring myself to speak with Pop.

Try harder, I told myself, be a man. . . .

And then I heard the squeaking of rusty hinges.

I leapt to the front window.

Dashing from the mailbox was Kathy Coghill with my letter in her hand.

22

THE EXPECTED birthday reprieve arrived, and Pop made plans to take me to an ice cream parlor across town. Mom and Stan and Anya would be coming along too.

On the day of the event I headed to Gladstein's. I'd been longing for him almost as much as for Myra. Guilt over Pop's intentions was eating away at me, and I hoped that if I offered Gladstein my earnest friendship I might in some way assuage my feelings.

"Little Witcher!" he shouted when I came in his store, which set his dogs to yapping in the back room.

"Hi, Mr. Gladstein."

"Where the heck have you been?"

"I got grounded for a few days. My parents caught me with Myra in my bedroom."

It sounded so adult to be saying such things.

"And how are things with little Myra? Did you do what I told you?"

Gladstein had a beam in his eye.

"Touch her breasts? She wouldn't let me. I put my hand just above her blouse but she made me take it away."

"How large are they?"

"I don't think she has much."

"Well, she wouldn't. How old is she?"

"Twelve," I said. "Today's my birthday," I added.

He congratulated me heartily and began rooting through his drawers for a present.

"No, don't do that. Do you have a burglar alarm?" I asked.

His head shot up.

"Why do you ask?"

Perhaps I'd asked too suddenly.

"No reason. I'm just wondering what would happen if someone tried to break in here. You have a lot of expensive jewelry and stuff, right?"

Gladstein glanced about furtively. "Don't tell anyone, Witcher. There's an alarm above the door in the back that doesn't work. Fella I took the lease from told me I should fix it, but I keep putting it off."

I popped my knuckles, trying to think of something to say. I'd been hoping a good alarm system would deter Pop so I wouldn't have to get involved.

"Do you have a lot of money?" I asked.

"I'm well-off enough. I could close this place tomorrow, I don't have to work. Why do you want to know?"

"You mean you do it for fun?"

"I need something to do with my time, right? Life is long. You'll see."

He studied me with his lightning-bolt eyebrow, pondering my nervousness. To distract him I took out Myra's latest note and laid it on the counter. This had been delivered by Kathy the day before.

It read:

> DJ [I think this stood for "Dear Jack"]:
>   Every time I see you I get punished. Everyone tells
> me you're wrong for me. I'm grounded until school
> starts. I still wear your ring at night.
>   Love, M

"She wears the ring!" Gladstein gloated. "I told you, Witcher, there's magic in that ring. Do you say your incantation?"

"No sir," I said.

I had forgotten all about my syllable.

"Well, no wonder. If you had been saying your incantation none of these things would've happened." He beetled his brow. "Snead thinks I should be worried because I park my car in Jefferson Ward. Keeps ribbing me about it, white man driving a Lincoln. Do you wanna know why I'm not worried?"

"Why?"

"Because I'm protected." Gladstein tapped his temple.

"You mean you say an incantation?"

He tapped his temple, emphasizing his point. "It's why I'm

not worried about the store. Power, Witcher. It's up here, the power of the will, the power of the mind. Keep saying your syllable."

When I left the shop I was silently chanting my incantation.

On the way home, still under his influence, I found myself moved so powerfully to do something that I could barely control myself. It was to stroll past the Joyners' while chanting my syllable. I knew it would be risky, and yet the urge grew stronger with every step I took. I was hoping Myra might pick up my vibrations and appear at a window. Just to wave, just to exchange a glimpse. I didn't ask for much.

The minute I turned on her street I sensed something wrong.

The Joyners' house was about a hundred yards down, and in front of it a small crowd had gathered. People were milling about a police cruiser. Rusty was among them, barking excitedly.

Something told me to turn back. A voice in my head (my mother's) kept warning me I'd find nothing but trouble in that direction.

I made out a Kellner or two, a number of Joyners, and in the middle of them all, my brother. Everyone was shouting hoarsely, livid and out of control. And I thought, Stan. Who else could unite the neighborhood in such fury? Five or six people beside the cruiser were speaking at once. In the Joyner yard loitered several bystanders, Gaylord, Bruce Pendleton, Mrs. Joyner, who were supplementing accusations made against my brother with commentaries of their own. On the front porch, flanked on either side by maiden Coghills, stood Myra, who flapped her hand like linen on a line as soon as she spotted me; but then she recalled the venerable crowd she was among and turned away, mortified by her lapse in judgment. But so what? I had seen her joy before she could hide it.

"Oh God, here's another one of them," a lady's voice said.

It was Mrs. Kellner.

Stan's eyes blinked in my direction, too preoccupied to notice me. Then he smugly surveyed his accusers, playing the offended victim and thoroughly enjoying the havoc he had wrought. I knew my brother all too well.

Reedy was trying to calm everyone down. He had his hands out and he was saying, "All right, one at a time, please."

"He's been going up and down the street all afternoon," someone hollered, "mocking everyone and acting like a damn fool."

"All he wants is trouble," Gaylord shouted. "He keeps calling me to come out and fight."

"I have a right to walk anywhere I want," my brother said.

"He's harassing us," Mrs. Kellner said. "You should arrest him for harassment."

Myra was focused on the action so she'd no longer have to acknowledge my presence. Then Karla Coghill saw me and her eyes went wide. With malicious joy she whispered in Myra's ear and Myra, with the usual self-possession among her kind, didn't even bat an eye. I couldn't help but admire it; I mean, later, in tranquil recollection, when I wasn't so desperate.

In the meantime Reedy was trying to gain control of the situation. "Why do you have to walk up and down this particular street?" he asked. "Why can't you walk somewhere else?"

"I feel like it, that's why. This is America, if I wanna walk up and down this street there ain't a single law on the books says I can't."

"Still, you can't go around harassing people."

"Who's harassing who? These people are crazy. I ain't bothering them, they're harassing *me*."

The entire crowd erupted into catcalls, finger-pointing, fist-shaking.

"They believe you're menacing them," Reedy hollered over their voices.

"I ain't doing nothing, I'm just walking past their houses."

Reedy turned powerlessly to the crowd. What could he do? A guy has a right to walk in his own neighborhood.

"Sure, he's acting innocent now, but you should see the way he keeps acting. He makes all these smart-alecky faces at us and then he starts pulling down his pants—"

"What are you talking about, lady?" Stan shouted. (It was Mrs. Kellner.)

"It's true, he does grab his pants," Gaylord judiciously broke in, eager to speak the truth. "He doesn't pull them down, he just sort of yanks 'em."

My brother shrugged, as if this part of the argument didn't concern him.

"Why are you yanking at your pants?" Reedy asked.

"I ain't got a belt, I'm hitching 'em up. Is that against the law?"

The crowd pleaded furiously to refute the lame excuse and

Reedy tugged nervously at his fingers. Stan passed a hand over his mouth, concealing a smile.

And then someone, a lady I'd never laid eyes on, turned a vicious frown in my direction. "Look, there's his brother!"

Everyone swung around.

Reedy seemed relieved to see me on the scene. He wiggled his finger for me to come closer.

"Why don't you take your brother on home?"

"I can't make him do anything. I just got here, I don't even know what this is about."

I wanted people to understand I'd played no part in my brother's evil machinations. (He gave me a wink, which I refused to see.)

"Tell your brother to stay away from us," Mrs. Kellner said.

"Miss Kellner, I can't—"

"Oh, you're just a pint-sized version of him. You Witchers are all alike, you're nothing but trash."

In the yard, Gaylord sputtered and turned away. Probably he was laughing because soft-spoken Mrs. Kellner had been brought so low as to shout meaningless insults in public. Even I found it kind of funny. Everyone was amazed at how into it she was. Two or three kids broke out grinning. Yet wasn't it pathetic that such a pleasant lady would let the antics of a Witcher bring her down?

Unfortunately, Stan had observed Gaylord's sputter, and to him there could be only one cause for it: Mrs. Kellner's insult to his brother. Before Reedy knew what was happening Stan was running towards Gaylord and tackling him to the ground. His fist rose once and came down on Gaylord's lip. The second time he raised it Reedy clapped a viselike grip around it. In a flash he had Stan upright, with his arm behind his back.

"All right, let me go!"

Myra gave me a look and I stared helplessly back. That's all that occurred between us. There wasn't any time after that.

The crowd had pulled away, scared of the violence, and now everyone spoke at once. Myra and Mrs. Joyner were tending to Gaylord's bloody lip, and suddenly Myra dashed inside the house.

Reedy, meanwhile, was trying to negotiate a peace between Gaylord and my brother. Gaylord handsomely refused to press charges, which earned him the esteem of the entire crowd and allowed it to draw a contrast between the behavior of Joyners and Witchers.

"You know I could haul you in for this," Reedy told Stan. "I can think of three charges right off the top of my head. Give me thirty seconds and I'll come up with three more. Now get out of here. If you bother these people again I'll get a court order to restrain you."

Stan formed an *f* with his lips and teeth, but he didn't say it. He just stalked off, leaving me to struggle with the dilemma of whether to join him.

It wasn't as though the neighbors would accept my solidarity, if I even offered it. I knew damn well nothing would cause them to differentiate me from Stan. Besides, I didn't want to take their side. But I didn't want to take my brother's side either, not as long as Myra was around.

She came running out of the house with the first-aid kit, and as she handed it to her mother her eyes drifted towards mine. I guess she couldn't help herself. I put earnestness in my expression, devotion, concern, love, heeding, adoration. But not so much as to give her away. And she nodded invisibly. Her eyes flickered before she turned to her injured brother.

And then I followed my bully brother home.

23

NEUMAN'S WAS a blindingly parti-colored ice cream establishment whose regal banquettes made even the tallest and most substantial of our citizens appear puny and trite. There might as well have been a sign at the door, "The management requires you to leave your despair outside." Frosting, frivolity and fluorescence were the essence of the Neuman universe. The nightmare of history had nothing to do with the place.

Deep inside the cushioned pleats of a corner booth sat Pop, Mom, Stan, Anya and me. Our special guest that day was Tillie, who at the last minute had claimed my birthday as an affair she simply could not miss. In hindsight I suspect she only wanted to check out the Witchers, since there seemed no end in sight to her daughter's infatuation with Stan. Nevertheless, I was flattered to have earned the enthusiasm of such a magnificent dame.

She had driven the Fleetwood to Neuman's, with Stan and

Anya making out in the backseat. In the parking lot, where we all met, I discerned a restrained frown on her face while she watched my mother climb out of the Ford. But she brightened up considerably when she saw Pop. There was a spark in her eyes, and I decided I would watch these two closely.

Sure enough, once we got settled on the banquette and my mother's face had disappeared behind the elongated menu, the flirting began in earnest.

"I hear you're looking for work," Tillie said.

"Yes ma'am." Pop's chin was on his fist. He was chewing gum, which made his head bob. He gave her one of his crooked grins. "You got something?"

"You mean work?"

She giggled.

I shot a look at Mom, but she was puzzling over Neuman's encyclopedic list of sundaes.

"Pop's a mechanic. Not a grease monkey, a mechanic," Stan said. This had to do with some private joke between him and Pop, and they guffawed raucously.

Tillie eyed Stan witheringly and turned to me with a smile. "How about Jackie boy. Thirteen years old!"

"Yeah, congratulations," Stan sneered, "your best years are behind you."

Anya elbowed him. "Oh stop. And how about little Mary, are you lovebirds still going at it?"

Mom's eyes peeked up from the menu.

"You mean Myra," I said. "I don't think we should be talking about her."

"You better not be seeing that girl," Mom said.

"But she's such a little darling," Tillie exclaimed.

Mom bit her tongue and hid her face behind the menu.

"The Joyners are crazy," Stan said. "They sicced Reedy on me just 'cause I was walking past their house. What kind of justice is that? Do we still live in America?"

"What are you talking about?" Mom said.

"I popped Gaylord good." Stan brandished his fist.

"You got in a fight with Gaylord Joyner?"

"I was walking past their house and they called the cops. I wasn't doing nothing, I was just walking along minding my own business."

"Did Officer Reedy show up?" Tillie asked.

"How is it everyone seems to know Officer Reedy?" Mom said. "What's going on that I don't know about?"

"I was out for a stroll and I walked past their house and they up and called the cops, like for no reason at all. Then Gaylord got smart with Jack and I had to pop him one."

"You were there too?" Mom said.

"I tell you what, let's change the subject," Tillie said. "Who besides me is having a banana split?"

"Please, I'm trying to have a conversation with my boys."

Mom's eyes darkened. I don't think she liked Tillie.

"I was just walking along," I said, "and I heard all these people hollering at Stan. There was this big commotion, Rusty barking and all. And then I saw Reedy's cop car. And then Stan punched Gaylord and we came home."

Pop grinned. "You punched Joyner in front of Reedy? Boy, you got balls made of—" He caught himself and said, "You got guts, that's for sure."

"What is the problem you have with that young man? You almost punched him when you were at my house too," Tillie remembered.

"When?" Mom said. "When did that happen?"

"It ain't no big deal. Gaylord got on his high horse one day because Jack brought Myra to the swimming pool."

"That happened before I got grounded," I intervened. "Come on, Mom, it's my birthday."

We grew quiet. Mom pursed her lips, studied the menu.

Tillie clasped her hands. "So who's getting a banana split?"

"Say, you know why the banana split?" Pop said.

She laughed and touched his arm, thinking that was the punch line.

"I'm getting a hot fudge sundae," Anya said. "What about you, birthday boy?"

"I'd have never believed you're old enough to have two teenage sons," Tillie said to Pop. He was two or three years younger than Mom.

Mom looked up to see if she was included.

"And how old are you, Stan, I can't remember."

"Old enough to go out with your daughter."

Tillie pretended to laugh.

"I'm thirty-nine and holding," Pop said.

"Oh, you!"

Tillie squeezed his wrist, dead set on touching him. I kept checking with Mom, but she was lost in the menu. Her forehead was all crumpled now with wrinkles and worry.

"Maybe Basil knows of a job," Tillie said. "He hears about all sorts of things in his line. I'll ask him when I get home."

"He's a lawyer?"

"Sometimes his clients tell him things, pass on tidbits, you know."

"I'd appreciate it if you spread the word. I can do just about anything, plumbing, heating, refrigeration."

Mom was working her lower lip, which she tended to do whenever the topic of employment came up. All Pop did was lie around watching soaps all day. And now I knew he had other ideas about ways to make money. Every time I remembered Gladstein I felt a pang for his trusting nature.

I shot Pop a glance, which must have caught him off guard, because he was staring back with a look that made me go cold. It was as though he were remembering thirteen years earlier, before I came into the world. Maybe he'd realized it was kinship and kinship alone that made us friends and not enemies. Whatever it was, he didn't bother to rearrange his face. All he did was send me an unconvincing wink. And then I had a weird idea. I thought, This man would kill me if I gave him the occasion. I don't know why I would think a thing like that. Maybe I was schizophrenic. Maybe I needed a psychiatrist. But it was a scary thing to think and it made the universe grow dark and cold.

Tillie jerked on Pop's sleeve to get him to order from the

gangly kid who was waiting on us. I stared at the table, wanting to be out of there. I wanted to tell Mom that Pop was planning to rob Gladstein. I wanted this thing off my shoulders.

Everyone was just sitting around, not saying a word. We'd already run out of things to say. Tillie seemed embarrassed. She was rubbing her fingertip over the table like she was erasing a dirty word.

All of a sudden I blurted, "I've been smoking cigarettes. One or two a day, sometimes more. I do it in the woods, I just sneak right off and smoke. A lot of times when you think I'm going to the store what I'm really doing is smoking. . . . Sometimes I cut classes so I can go in the woods and smoke by the creek."

I have long since wondered what fatality it was that caused those words to cross my lips. Because fatality it was, and from that moment on my family was never the same. Did my pop provoke it? Was it the look in his eyes? Was I throwing down some gauntlet? But why would I do that? I was only thirteen. I still needed a roof over my head—three hots and a cot.

I shot a look at Mom, who was sipping from her water. Slowly she brought the glass away, while Stan narrowed his eyes, giving me a warning lest I tell tales. "What is this, true-confession time?"

"I'm just saying I smoke. Right?" I looked at Pop.

"Since when did you start smoking?" Mom's hand went to her head, caressing an instant migraine. "Lord, these kids, I give up. Why on earth are you . . . ?"

"Why on earth are you telling everybody you smoke cigarettes, you damn weirdo," Stan said.

"Stop saying 'damn.'"

"Pop let me puff on his cigarette last year at my birthday and I've been smoking ever since."

Mom turned to Pop. "Is that true?"

"Well heck, it might be. I might of give him a puff. But I didn't know he was smoking. It's not like I been letting him."

Anya burst out giggling. "He's so cute!"

Her eyes were weird and I realized she was probably high. She and Stan must have smoked a joint before they rode over.

There followed an uneasy silence that lasted intermittently until the ice cream came. I was trailing my finger in the condensation on the tabletop, wondering why I had told them what I did. To snitch in front of Pop and Stan was the worst thing a Witcher could do.

The waiters brought me a banana split (Tillie, enforcing her gaiety, had insisted I order one) with a festive candle jutting out of the fudge. The entire staff was singing "Happy Birthday" and everyone joined in except Stan, who folded his arms in disgust. The whole Neuman's crowd sang along. It was a tradition there. It was why people came, for stuff like that.

When the song was over Anya let out an inappropriate whoop and Stan swore at her.

I made ready to blow out the candle.

"Did you make a wish?" Tillie said.

I wished for Myra.

Everyone in the parlor applauded.

Later, after everyone in our party had gobbled down their ice cream and headed to the bathroom, Pop, Tillie and I were hanging around just inside the front door, where people could sit until their table came open. A cigarette machine was in the foyer and Pop went over and bought a pack of Salems.

"You can't have one," he told me when he came back.

His tone was joking, but he wasn't happy with me and I knew it.

"You're not corrupting minors anymore?" Tillie asked him.

"This boy doesn't need any corrupting. I oughta whip him good when I get him home," he joshed.

Tillie laughed and rested her hand on his shoulder. "I'll bet you're good at giving whippings."

Pop grinned. He looked at me, proud of himself. He could get a rich gal anytime he wanted, and he was glad I was there to see it.

And I was thinking, Sure, like any other stable boy.

24

THE NEXT NOTE from Myra arrived in the morning.

DJ,

Is it true? Was it your birthday yesterday? Dickie Pudding came to my window and he said it was your birthday. If I missed it I am so sad. [She drew an "unhappy" face.]

Why is your brother so crazy? He is making everything worse. Yesterday Gaylord told me you aren't so bad, but he can't stand your brother. He said as long as your brother acts so crazy no one will approve of you. Can't you talk to him and make him be nice?

To answer your question [she was referring to a note I'd Coghilled to her the previous day]: Yes! I can't say I am in love, but, Yes! I do have feelings for you. I don't want to say I am in love because I am not sure

what that means. Are you? I think I am too young to
have feelings that strong. But I definitely am in like
with you. Well ... I have to go.

Love and kisses,
You Know Who, M

This letter, in which for the first time a girl (and not just any girl) had professed herself mine, I slid under my pillow. For two days I walked about in a stupor, my heart swollen with emotion.

I went to Gladstein's to show it off, but something peculiar was happening when I arrived.

He had customers.

I had never seen customers in his store, at least not since I started to visit. It never occurred to me that his establishment, like any other, might enjoy, occasionally, a visit from clientele. Now some dowdy couple was peering at wedding rings and petulantly bickering over what they liked and disliked while Gladstein diplomatically chimed in when compelled. Nearby hovered a sinister character, a tall man in a dark suit and sunglasses. He was flicking ashes into a saucer Gladstein had provided.

Gladstein gave me a backhanded wave, more dismissal than greeting, and I walked home.

However, I found the compulsion to show the letter off overpowering.

At home I found Stan listening to James Brown, clapping in rhythm and strutting about the room like a turkey. I perched on the bottom bunk and watched. Ostentatiously I unfolded the letter and perused it, figuring he would probably snatch it from me when he passed. And he did.

Then he stopped his strutting. He pulled the needle off the record. His lips were full, slightly malformed. He reminded me of a scornful Renaissance bust I'd seen on a school trip to the National Gallery in Washington.

"So she thinks I'm crazy," he said.

"Well, so what, everybody does."

I figured that much would be obvious.

"Fucking Joyners, man. The little twit sits around talking to Gaylord about me. And look at this, you're all right but I'm not. Those motherfuckers."

"Well, what do you expect? You act so crazy they get the wrong idea about you. Heck, Stan, you *want* people to think you're crazy."

"When did you start taking up for the Joyners?"

"I'm just trying to explain why people see you the way they do."

"Everybody likes you for that, right? That's the deal you got, you're gonna sell out me and Pop so you can run around with your skinny little Joyner snot."

"I ain't selling out anyone."

"Don't deny it, you piece of shit."

Before I knew it he had me collared on the bed and his knee was on my chest.

He thrust his face in mine and pulled my eyes to his, full of hate.

"You fucking traitor. What were you doing squealing on Pop last night?"

"I wasn't squealing on Pop, I was squealing on myself."

"Fuck that shit, you told Mom he started you smoking and now she's not speaking to him. Look, you say anything about me smoking grass I'll fucking kill you, I swear to God I will."

"I ain't gonna say anything, let me go."

He released my collar and took his knee away.

"Punk snitch," he said.

"She's my girlfriend, I can't help it."

"She's Joyner's sister. Which means she's the enemy. If you wanna slobber over the brat go ahead, but don't come crying to me when she tells you to get lost. Fucking punk, you and me are through."

"What do you mean?"

"I don't recognize you as a brother from now on. You're just the kid who lives here."

I sat up straight. I could still feel where he had grabbed my neck.

Stan left the room.

I found Pop in the kitchen, smoking a cigarette.

I guess I'd been too wrapped up in Myra and her letters to notice, but whatever good feelings my pop and brother once had for me had distinctly diminished. Pop hadn't spoken much since Neuman's, and now, in the kitchen, he barely acknowledged me. If Mom was mad because of what I'd told her, and if she was showing him she was mad on top of that—what was there to say? I was a Witcher and I had told tales. She sure wasn't helping any.

"Did Stan come through here?"

"He went out the front."

Exactly what I expected to do when I found him I don't know. I wanted to justify myself, apologize, make up. I didn't want to leave things the way they were.

I checked the south end of Lewis Street. No one was on the road aside from Rusty, who peered from the distance, vaguely wagging his tail. I wandered to the drainage pipe, past the Coghills', into the woods behind Dickie Pudding's house, and then all the way to Myra Street. I doubled back, detoured into the woods, came to the brackish creek where Stan and Anya liked to tryst. I hopped across and hiked up the incline, and when I came to the edge of the woods I peered into the Taylors' backyard. There was someone behind the slats in the fence surrounding the pool. I heard splashing sounds.

I sat on the ground, and soon I saw the whiteness of a bathing suit emerge from the pool and move to a chair.

That would be Tillie.

I sat for quite a while, batting away flies and thinking about what it meant to be a Witcher. The worst thing was, I had broken a code that Stan and Pop dogmatically adhered to. But I'd done it only half aware. I had no idea why I had brought up smoking cigarettes. Snitching had not been my intention. I was just mad, and it was the first thing to come out of my mouth. I didn't figure it would be a big deal. Mom suspected all along

I'd been smoking, she could smell it on my breath. Not only that, she had been present a few times when Pop gave me sips out of his beer. So I think her being mad at him for letting me smoke was just an excuse. She was mad period, that's all.

Tillie climbed out of the chair and splashed in the pool and returned to the chair. A small animal was dead in the woods and from time to time its stench would waft along the breeze.

It was too bug-infested to keep sitting there, and I was tempted to go speak with Tillie. I suspected Stan might be inside the house, with Anya. These days he was always with Anya.

Around the front an engine started. That would be Anya's GTO. The thing always sounded like it was on its way to the drag strip. I heard it shift into reverse and back out of the driveway.

I got up, depressed.

Stan was in that car, and now he was gone. And I was surrounded by flies.

I returned home, hoping to get back into Pop's good graces. He was on the sofa, watching the day's first soaps. I sat beside him and asked a question or two and he answered in monosyllables. Whenever something funny happened on the TV I laughed out loud and looked to share it with him. But he wouldn't look back.

During a commercial I said, "Are you mad?"

He lifted his head, peered, and lowered it. "Leave me alone, I'm watching TV."

I went on down to my room and waited for Stan. Around

six Dickie Pudding rang the bell and asked if I wanted to pitch ball. But I was too keyed up. I didn't want to leave off monitoring the house for Stan's arrival.

I stayed awake 'til after midnight. Mom and Pop were in the front room, watching their shows and not speaking.

I had become hypersensitive to stimuli. Every time a car passed on the road I peeked out the window.

I kept falling asleep and waking up. I did that several times. Each time I could tell from the silence that Stan hadn't returned. I grabbed the clock from the dresser and held its face to the glow from the window. It was three a.m. No hallway light shone at the door. My parents had gone to bed. They didn't seem to care anymore how late my brother stayed out.

When dawn broke he still hadn't come home. Birds were singing, the room was growing light. And then I heard the rumble of Anya's GTO out front. Doors slammed, and the engine rumbled off into the distance.

Stan came in the house. . . .

I was anxious about whether I should speak or not. I prepared a greeting—"Jesus Christ, it's almost six, where have you been?" But he didn't come to the room and after a while the rehearsal grew stale. I waited and he kept not coming. Finally I couldn't stand it. I got up and looked in the hallway. There was a light on in the bathroom and I put my ear next to the door. Water was running in there, not only the shower water but water from the sink. The toilet kept flushing over and over. It sounded like he was tearing something up, fabric or clothes or something. I knocked on the door and whispered his name.

There was a pause. I figured he'd heard the knock and I waited anxiously for him to open up. Instead the toilet flushed . . . and then I heard another tearing sound. And then he grunted a little, as if he were lowering himself to the floor. Now it sounded like he was scrubbing the tub.

Christ, I thought, he's cleaning the bathroom.

I turned in the half-light of the hallway and saw a clown portrait on the wall staring back at me. Mom had brought it home from the Ben Franklin recently and hung it there. I don't know why she wanted that thing, clowns always gave me the creeps. And then I realized something. The thing looked like Stan, all sinister, weird and drug-addled.

I tiptoed back to bed.

My brother is on drugs, I thought. There's no reaching him . . . my own brother.

25

WHEN I WOKE UP I went to the creek, not the creek next to Anya's but a more communal creek in the woods north of our house. I took a pack of cigarettes and smoked a couple and waited for other kids to arrive and no one did. It's a curious thing, but whenever I was at the creek, kids who as a rule preferred to scorn me sometimes spent a pleasant hour hanging out. We were like enemy pickets fraternizing during truce. Class conflict requires so much vigilance, I guess, that even the hardest veterans need an occasional break.

The world was hot that day, too bright, too hot, too harsh, and I could tell already that turning thirteen would offer no advantages. In fact, something told me things were only going to get tougher. There is a hum, an undertone just behind the noise of the world. I have never liked silence. Besides, there is no such thing as silence. If there were silence I would cherish it and hold it to my ear like a seashell. . . . But maybe

I wasn't thinking along those lines when I was at the creek, probably I'm projecting backwards. But I did have intimations. I had been living in a cocoon and the cocoon was tearing and I was being thrust out against my will . . . and where would I go?

I went home and lay on the bed with my pillow propped behind me.

Stan woke in the afternoon. He didn't answer when I spoke. I wasn't his brother anymore.

He threw on jeans and a T-shirt and left the house. The fan in the dining room window sucked air through the passageways. The bedroom door was open. I was alone, and whenever the oscillating fan atop the dresser turned, it blew its breezy air upon me.

THE NEXT MORNING Reedy's patrol car cruised up. I heard the rumble of the engine. Stan was gone. Mom was at work. Pop was watching television.

The bell rang and I ran to the living room. I stood beside Pop as he answered the door.

Reedy regarded us gravely. He removed his hat, asked if he could come in. Pop stepped aside.

The cop was glancing all around, peeking in the corners.

He asked if Stan was home.

"I believe he went out," Pop said.

"Got a bit of a problem at the Joyners'," Reedy said. "Seems Gaylord has disappeared."

"Disappeared."

"Left the house two evenings ago, hasn't been seen since. Said he was going to Dogwood Downs, meeting Bruce Pendleton. They were supposed to go to a movie but Gaylord didn't show up. The movie started at eight, they were supposed to meet at seven-thirty. And then he didn't come home that night and now no one knows where he is. People say it's not like him to run off and they're worried something bad might have happened."

Pop's face darkened. Why would Reedy be coming to us? I was scrambling in my mind, trying to remember two evenings before.

"We were at Neuman's that night."

"You were at Neuman's Ice Cream Parlor?" Reedy quickly grasped at the information. He almost seemed relieved. "Your brother was with you?"

"Yes sir," I said.

"No, that was three nights ago," Pop said. "Tuesday night."

"Oh yeah, that was Tuesday."

"What about Wednesday evening? You were all here?"

"Why are you asking?"

"We're trying to find people who might have seen Gaylord. I'm going to all the houses around here, Mr. Witcher, I'm not singling you out."

"Well, no, we didn't see him. We don't have much to do with the Joyners."

"Mrs. Witcher was here in the house? And Stan?"

"Miss Witcher was here, but Stan was with his girlfriend."

"What time did he come home? You think there's a chance he might have run into Gaylord?"

"Maybe about ten. You can ask him when you see him. I doubt he ran into Gaylord, though. He stays at the Taylors' house most all the time these days."

"Wednesday night he came home at ten?"

"Yes sir."

Reedy held his eyes on Pop.

"Well, I'm going around the neighborhood and letting folks know. If you hear anything you get in touch with me, okay? Let me know."

"Yes sir, we'll do that."

Reedy hesitated, about to ask me something, but I stared at the floor and he let it go.

After he left Pop said, "I'll be damned."

He watched through the window 'til the cruiser pulled away. He cut the TV off.

"This ain't good," he said.

"Pop," I said.

"If anything's happened to that kid your brother will be first one they'll pin it on." He shook his head, thinking his thoughts.

I formed an image in my mind of the shack on Baskin Road. I got ready to say something and thought better of it.

Then I remembered Myra.

Up to that moment everything had been all abstract, and now I could see her fading away. She was getting fainter and fainter, like a radio station when you're driving out of town.

"Myra will hate me forever if Stan did anything to Gaylord."

"Your brother didn't have a damn thing to do with it. Kid's probably shacking up with some girl. He'll come home, you'll see."

"Pop," I said.

"Hell, when I was sixteen I took off and stayed three weeks. I remember Mama like to have a fit. I was in Asheville all that time, met a gal at a party in Hendersonville and she took me back to her place in Asheville. Older gal, you know." Pop gazed out the window, savoring the bawdiness of his bygone years.

"You told Reedy Stan came home at ten."

"So?"

"He didn't, he was out all night. He didn't come in 'til daylight."

"No, he came home at ten. I was right here watching TV, I remember."

"Then he must have gone back out."

"Nuh-uh, he was here. He sat with your mom and me and watched TV."

"Pop, you're getting your nights mixed up. I was awake when he got home. Anya's car pulled up around six in the morning and dropped him off and he went in the bathroom and stayed awhile. I was awake, I know."

"No, he was here Wednesday night. He was watching TV with me and your mom."

I knew this wasn't true and I was about to argue, but then Pop fixed me with an angry stare. "What's the matter with you,

you wanna get your brother in trouble? He was here Wednesday night, do you understand?"

"He wasn't here and you know it."

"You need to set your memory straight. If Stan gets in trouble 'cause of you I'll never forget it, you hear? And what about your mother, how you think she'll feel if your brother gets in trouble?"

"I don't wanna get Stan in trouble. If he didn't do anything there ain't no reason to—"

"This is not about what he did or didn't do. We ain't getting mixed up in it. Everybody knows your brother and Gaylord are enemies. Just the other day Deputy Dawg had to pull Stan off the kid with the whole neighborhood watching. You better believe if Gaylord's got himself in trouble first thing they'll do is point the finger at your brother. We don't want 'em even *suspecting* he had anything to do with it. Pay attention to me. I'm a lot older than you and I know the law. All they want is to find someone they can pin it on. They just want it off the books."

"Well I can't tell lies. If Reedy starts asking me questions he'll know right away I'm lying."

"Let him think what he wants. But Stan was here that night, you hear? That's what you tell him. He was home by ten."

Pop went in the kitchen. I heard him nervously opening drawers, looking into things.

"What's the number at the Taylors'?" he hollered.

"Call information," I hollered back.

I went to my room. I wanted to see Myra. I wanted to

show her I was on her side. Why did I have to belong to the enemy clan?

I carefully wrote her a letter, pausing to choose my words.

I heard Pop in the kitchen, on the phone.

After a while Anya's GTO pulled up. Stan came with her through the front door.

I read the letter back to myself:

> *Dear M,*
>
> *I am sorry to hear about Gaylord. If there is anything I can do let me know. I am sorry about my brother and how he treated your brother. I want you to know I am not like him. If you still want me to be your boyfriend I will be. I will be your friend if that is what you want. I hope everything turns out alright.*
>
> *Love,*
>
> *J*

I stuck it in an envelope and slid it in my back pocket.

When I came to the living room Pop and Stan and Anya were sitting there, grinning at me constrainedly.

"There he is!"

"Sit down, we're having a party."

Pop gave me a crooked smile.

They were passing a bowl of chips around.

"He's so cute!" Anya said.

Her eyes were dark and joyless.

I sat down and they faced me.

26

"HERE'S THE STORY," ANYA SAID. "We were together Wednesday night, Stan was with me the whole time. We were up in my room listening to the Doors and we didn't leave the house."

"Your parents were there, right?" Pop said.

"Yeah, downstairs. They'll verify we were at home."

They looked at me to see if I was getting the message. And then Pop changed the story. He told Anya she should lie. He said she should tell the cops Stan had left her house at ten.

"That's the time I told Deputy Dawg he came home," he explained.

Why were they training me what to say? I could smell the duplicity a mile away.

I took off like a bolt for Gladstein's, before they could shout at me to stop.

It was almost closing time and he was roaming about the

shop saying good night to his jewels. The prissy bell rang, the Yatzis yapped, and Gladstein turned to look. On the tip of his nose was a pair of narrow-framed glasses. I had never seen him in glasses; it didn't register at first what was different.

"Witcher! Where did you go the other day, you never came back."

I leaned against the counter to catch my breath.

"I need you to take me somewhere in your car."

"Did you run here?"

"Can you drive me to Baskin Road?"

"I suppose I can. . . ." Gladstein made a few puttering motions, took off his glasses, patted behind the counter.

"I'll only need a minute," I said, "and after that you can drop me off wherever you want."

He didn't ask any questions, which I thought was cool. He rounded up his dogs—they poured like water from the back room—and took me out to the parking lot. We got in the hot black Continental and he eased down the windows and turned on the air and after it started blowing cold he whirred the windows up again. He was able to operate everything from a panel on the driver's side.

"You have to tell me how to get to Baskin, I've never been west of the shopping center."

"Cross Karen and keep going on Matson. It'll change to two lanes when we're close to Baskin."

Behind me the dogs were panting against my neck. Gladstein set his glasses on the dashboard and put the car in gear.

The Continental cruised across Karen and headed towards where the suburbs ended and the country began.

These days the area off Matson is nearly teeming as China. Spanking-new houses made of high-tech clapboard shine through sparse trees and strip malls line the six-lane thoroughfare. Whenever you reach a rise in the road a steady line of headlights will be coming at you.

Back then narrow streets wound off the main road past stately manses that had once belonged to aristocrats and gentleman farmers. I remember an old FFV, a retired judge named Parham, who lived in a house on Baskin that had been standing since before the Civil War. Some years back Pop had been hired by the judge to renovate one of the bathrooms, and he took me out there to hang around while he worked. I must have been eight, nine years old. The judge was sitting in a book-lined parlor that might have come out of a Victorian novel. It was on the south side of the house, and there was a fireplace without a fire and a leather chair in which the judge sat perusing *Dombey and Son*. Pop was in the bathroom off the kitchen (the judge called it "the maid's bath") grunting and clanking his wrenches. I guess the judge took a shine to me, because he showed me a marvelous feature of the house. One of the shelves was phony. The books on it weren't real, they were spines glued to the surface. The entire shelf was really a door with a secret latch that released it, and when it opened you saw a tiny bedroom, a bed, a table, and a pair of antique reading glasses on the table. Judge Parham told me the secret room had been constructed during the Civil War so his ancestors could hide from the Yankees.

After that he took me behind the house and we wandered down to where some graves were. Off to the side, through the trees, stood the ruins of shacks where the slaves used to live. (The shack to which I'd intended to abduct Myra was one of them, about half a mile away.) All of the land around there, the woods and the fields and the houses, had once belonged to the Parham estate.

Now, as Gladstein got near Myra's shack, I asked him to pull to the side of the road. "I'm running up there to look at something, I'll be right back."

"You got a dead body there?"

I was holding the handle. Before I pushed open the door I said, "You shouldn't joke like that, Mr. Gladstein." Then I shouldered the door and ran around the rear of the car.

Gladstein tapped his horn and signaled he was going to cruise up the road and turn around. I nodded and kept running.

The shack was about two hundred feet off the road. Pop had shown it to me years before, after he'd invested in an easel and some paints so he could paint nature scenes. That hobby had lasted a year or so, long enough for him to paint the shack, once in winter and once in summer. There was a creek behind the shack, which he had included in his paintings, and one day when he was by himself he'd seen a UFO overhead, leaping and jerking across the sky. Several times he returned to the scene with Stan and me in tow, hoping we'd have a chance to see the thing too. I remember how excited and terrified I was. But we never did get to see it.

Now I was running through the thistles and briars, approaching the rotting shack. The sun was going down but there was still plenty of light and the air remained hot and humid. The sinister song of the cicadas kept rising and ebbing through the trees. Things were biting my arms and my legs. Everything seemed weak, depraved. The sun was dying in the sky, sending down heat that parched hands and feet and turned small animal carcasses into briquettes of corruption and stench. The shack was lopsided, off-kilter. It was as though the earth had jolted and its axis made to tilt.

The shack had no windows. There was only one way to see inside and that was through the door. When Pop and I explored it years before, we had found a pissy mildewed mattress on the floor. God knows who tossed it there. We could see it only because light was beaming through crevices in the walls. Next to it were torn-out pages from a girlie magazine.

I peeked in the doorway. The sun's angle was oblique and the interior of the shack was nearly pitch. I put a foot out and pressed on a board and something scurried away.

My heart liked to leap in my mouth.

I ran back to the road and arrived just as Gladstein's Continental was pulling up. I hopped in. His dogs were scratching and pawing at my neck.

"Did you find what you were looking for?"

I was trembling inside. It was like two hands had gripped a

vital stem and were shaking it up and down. My lips were shivering, my fingers were jittery.

Gladstein must have decided I was cold, because he reached over and tapped the vent in another direction to keep it from blowing on me. But I wasn't cold. It was so hot it might have been high noon.

And then I burst out crying.

"What's wrong?"

Gladstein had been kind enough not to ask questions and now here I was bawling like a child. It must have been years of crying coming out; I couldn't stop. In front of Pop and Stan you didn't cry.

"What happened? Did something just happen?" He twisted in his seat to stare at where I'd come from, expecting to see some culprit.

"Nothing happened," I said.

He drove away. He grabbed a few tissues from the glove compartment and handed them over. "You in trouble, kid?"

I wiped my nose. He turned onto Matson and headed towards town. We cruised for a few miles without saying anything. After we came to the third traffic light I pulled myself together. Gladstein had turned the radio to the country-western station and a Buck Owens song was playing.

"You like country music?" I said.

"Nah, I'm just trying to assimilate."

The light turned green. We were coming up on the shopping center at the top of the hill.

"Gaylord Joyner has disappeared," I said.

"Myra's brother?"

"He's been gone two days. He was supposed to meet Bruce Pendleton at the movie house at Dogwood Downs on Wednesday night but he never showed up. No one knows where he is now."

Gladstein whistled. He thought about that. "Were you looking for him just now, is that what you were doing?"

"If he got killed they're gonna blame my brother for it."

Gladstein took the Continental past the shopping center. "Don't be morbid, kids that age do all sorts of crazy things."

He turned into our neighborhood and dropped me in front of the house.

Stan and Pop were on the porch, watching when I got out of the car.

"No," I said, "he's dead."

27

POP'S AND STAN'S WORRIED EYES followed me through the house. Stan kept trying to make conversation. He trailed me to the kitchen, to the bedroom, to the bathroom.

Mom, of course, was oblivious to it all. Her work wore her out. She had to stand on her feet all day, and when she came home she had to cook, clean. After that she'd hit the couch and the lights would go out. I mean *her* lights. Sometimes she snored.

Pop was being friendly again. He came in the kitchen while I was fixing a sandwich, with Stan behind him.

"Why are y'all following me everywhere?"

"I was on my way in before you started. What were you doing with Mr. Gladstein just now?"

"Nothing, I went to see him at the jewelry store and he gave me a ride home."

Pop shot a glance at my brother.

"Man ain't funny or nothing, is he?" he asked.

Stan burst out laughing.

"What do you mean?"

"Well, put it together. What's a man his age want with a kid like you?"

"He's my friend."

"Why do you need a friend that old?"

I left the kitchen, taking my sandwich. Pop and Stan followed me to the bedroom.

"You know what Snead told me? He told me Mr. Gladstein has a house in Jefferson Ward."

"So?"

"Well, it's unusual, don't you think?"

"Maybe."

The peanut butter cleaved like paste to my palate. I wasn't sure I could swallow it.

"Gladstein's told you he lives in Jefferson Ward?"

"I was there when he told Snead."

"Huh," Pop said.

Stan swung the desk chair backwards. Pop was standing in the doorway. I kept working my jaws over the peanut butter. It wouldn't go down and I was afraid I might have to spit it out.

"So you feel sure about Gladstein, then."

"Sure about what?"

"That he don't have an ulterior motive."

"Like what?"

"You know, man that age with a kid like you."

"He believes segregation is wrong, that's why he lives in Jefferson Ward."

Pop puffed out his lips and nodded, pantomiming rational discourse. "Hell, I ain't got any problems with black people, Snead knows that."

My brother's face, unbeknownst to him, had grown all pop-eyed and obsessed, as though he was envisioning something ghastly or wicked. I wondered if it meant he was remembering what it was like when he killed Gaylord.

Pop saw what he was doing and said, "What's the matter, sport, you look like you seen a ghost."

Stan grinned nervously and snapped out of it.

I managed to swallow the peanut butter but it made me nearly retch, and Stan seemed to think the expression on my face had something to do with him. His eyes grew narrow, challenging me, and then he slapped his thighs and sprang out of the chair. He looked around at the floor as though he had misplaced something.

Pop moved along the hall.

Stan quickly left behind him.

I heard the screen door slam.

I got in bed.

My brother must have left for Anya's, because I was asleep by the time he got home.

IN THE MORNING I placed my letter in the mailbox (there'd been no Coghill pickup the day previous and I had retrieved it lest it fall in the wrong hands), then after a while I went and took it out. It was stupid to imagine Myra would be thinking about my letters when her brother was missing. Probably she had renounced me by now, anyway. I was a Witcher. How could she separate that from anything else?

I hung around the house, too timid to venture outside. On the radio and TV, reports were appearing about Gaylord's vanishing. I kept expecting them to say, "The prime suspects, according to the police, are the Witchers."

Finally, in the afternoon, I left. I wanted to find out what was happening. Officer Reedy hadn't returned. We'd heard nothing more about Gaylord, except that he was gone.

All was mournful silence. It was a Saturday and the adults weren't at work. They were in the yards, trimming the bushes, snipping at the borders of the walkways. They shot me glances and silently returned to their business.

I didn't go near the Joyner house. Instead I took the short-cut. Several kids on top of the drainage pipe turned their heads, although no one said a word. It was like walking through a suburb of the dead.

When I passed the Coghill house I saw Kathy cutting across the yard.

"Have you heard from Myra?" I called.

She shushed me with her lips.

"I'll be in the woods behind Dickie Pudding's place!" I kept my voice low but loud enough to hear. She turned her back and went in her house.

When I got to the woods I saw Mr. Pudding's car in the

drive, the doors flung open, the mats drying in the sun. A country station was playing on the radio. Dickie came around the side of the house and I waved and he went inside without waving back. I couldn't tell if he'd seen me or not.

I waited a half hour, sweating in the heat. Then Kathy came.

She didn't pass on the street. There was a pathway farther down and she turned in the woods.

This was probably the closest we'd ever been to each other. I knew her mainly from when I passed the Coghill porch. She was ten or eleven, and Myra's devoted slave. What distinguished her from her sisters was her smile, or actually, that she smiled at all.

I was surprised she had bothered to come. The Coghill blood must run mighty thin in her veins, that's what I was thinking. At any rate, she had put on a stern expression for the occasion. She didn't say a word, she just stood with her arms hanging down.

"Hi," I said.

She looked at me for a long time.

"Well, I guess you've heard about Gaylord."

"Yes," I said. "I've been worried about Myra."

"She won't stop crying. We've been with her all morning."

"I wrote her a note, but I don't know if I should send it."

"All she's thinking about right now is Gaylord."

"Has she said anything about me?"

Kathy cut her eyes away.

"They think my brother did something to Gaylord, right?"

"Why wouldn't they? Myra told me something in secret and

she said I could tell you if I saw you. She said she has feelings for you but she can't be your girlfriend."

"She said that?"

Kathy nodded.

"Tell her I understand," I said.

"All she does is cry. She won't stop crying."

I looked away. Down by the house Mr. Pudding and Dickie were watching. The moment I turned my head they began tending to the floor mats, putting them back in the car.

"Did your brother do anything to Gaylord?"

"I don't know, I hope not. What are the police saying?"

"They're searching everywhere. They've got men looking in the river. They're searching all the woods. The last time anyone saw him he was on Cherokee Road hitchhiking to Dogwood Downs."

"Why was he hitchhiking? How come he didn't take his Mustang?"

"Mr. Joyner says it has an expired inspection sticker."

"What does Myra think about all this?"

"She just cries and hopes he comes back. I was with her this morning. She has a picture of him on the table and she just sits there and looks at it and cries."

"I wish there was something I could do."

"No one can do anything, all we can do is hope he turns up. Unless you know something that might help the police."

"I don't know any more than anyone else."

"Is that true? You really don't know anything?" Kathy looked boldly into my eyes. "Not even for Myra?"

"Why would I know anything? I didn't do anything to Gaylord. It was my brother always fighting him, not me."

Kathy sighed. "If only you could see how upset Myra is."

"Will you tell her I'm sorry? Will you give her this note?"

Kathy took it. "I'll ask if she wants to read it, but she prob ably won't."

"Tell her I'm sorry. Tell her I hope Gaylord is okay."

"Why don't you just ask your brother?"

"Ask him what?"

"Ask him what he did. Then you can tell the police and maybe they can find Gaylord and bring him home." She kept eyeing me, hoping to provoke a moment of truth.

"That's jumping to conclusions. No one knows if anything bad has even happened." I made an effort to return her look. "Gaylord might have run off with some girl. Stan says he was at the Taylors' house that night, and so does Anya. And she was with him the whole night, so he couldn't have done anything."

"That's what he says."

"It doesn't mean it's not true."

"If he did something he wouldn't admit it anyway."

"Well, why would he say he did something if he didn't?"

"All right, I'm not talking to you."

She turned and walked away. I hadn't said what she wanted to hear. But why shouldn't I defend my brother? And what made her so sure I was hiding something incriminating?

"Tell Myra I like her!" I called.

What was the use? Kathy was speeding away with the same lightning efficiency she used in her mail delivery.

When I got home Reedy's cruiser was parked out front. Stan was leaning an arm against the top, speaking with the officer through the window. While I was crossing the yard I slowed down to watch.

Mom appeared at the door.

"Come in the house, that doesn't concern you."

She looked old, haggard and limp. Her hair was stringy, her face was gaunt.

I went inside thinking for some reason about how my mother didn't believe in God, how she had raised me to believe whatever I felt in my heart to be true. That was her catechism, the heart. She once told me she didn't understand how a loving God could have created a place so full of suffering as this world. She could never get past that, she said. Later I made the mistake of repeating these words to my teacher. This was in front of the entire class, during an impromptu discussion on freedom of religion. I was proud my mother had so much originality. Her not believing in God gave me a sense of the dignity of thought. But the class wasn't so admiring. Everyone grew quiet, and my teacher cleared her throat. She said something I couldn't make out.

Within days it got around that the Witchers were atheists.

28

ANYA WAS on the frayed carmine sofa, wearing one of her minidresses. Her legs were brown and bare and she didn't have any shoes on.

"Hey, handsome," she said.

I jerked my thumb towards the yard. "How come Reedy's here?"

"Oh, the pigs won't leave him alone 'cause he's got long hair."

"Is that what it is?"

"Of course. The minute something bad happens they're gonna go after the first hippie freak they can find."

To me Stan's long hair didn't make any difference. I remembered when he had a crew cut and he was the same then as he was now.

"He had to go and tell Gaylord he was gonna kill him," I said, "right in front of Reedy."

"Oh, that was just talk. That's Stan, it's the way he talks."

"It was stupid to say that in front of a cop."

"Your brother wouldn't hurt anyone, you know that."

"You haven't seen him when he fights," I said.

Mom backed away from looking out the door. "I've told him a thousand times he was gonna get in trouble someday. That boy runs around the neighborhood threatening everybody in sight and then when they suspect him of doing wrong he acts like some injustice has occurred. I told him a thousand times this would happen."

"But he didn't do anything," Anya said, "he was with me that night."

"Was he really?"

"Yes!"

Anya gazed at me, wide-eyed.

Mom was disgusted by the entire business. "So how come you're telling the police he left your house at ten?"

"That's what Mr. Witcher told me to say."

Mom tightened her lips and left the room.

"You told Reedy he came straight home?" I said.

"Yeah, I was talking with him a minute ago. He sent me inside, he said he wanted to talk to Stan alone."

I went over and parked myself next to her.

"Anya, I heard him come in around six that morning."

"I know, that's when I dropped him off."

We sat for a while, side by side.

I snuck a peek at her legs.

"How about little Mary, how's she doing?"

"Myra," I corrected. "Don't talk about her in front of Mom. Myra thinks Stan did something to Gaylord. She told Kathy Coghill she can't be my girlfriend anymore."

"Wow, Jack, I'm really sorry. How come everyone is so prejudiced against your brother?"

"He's caused a lot of trouble in this neighborhood. You don't know him the way other people do."

"Oh, come on, he wouldn't hurt a flea."

Reedy's engine started outside and Stan came in the house. He winked and put his finger to his lips.

No sooner was he in the door than Mom and Pop appeared.

Pop's eyebrows were lifted; he nodded towards the door. "So what'd he say?"

"Says he admires how 'streetwise' I am. Says he wants me to help him come up with ideas about how we might find Gaylord."

Pop burst out laughing, and after a dumbstruck silence Stan joined in. They both started guffawing at the top of their lungs.

"Deputy Dawg! How dumb does he think you are?"

Mom listened unhappily and walked out. Anya watched this male play uncertainly.

I headed for the door.

"Where you off to, sport?" Pop called.

I didn't answer. I left the house and went stalking through El Dorado Hills. People in their yards stopped what they were doing when I passed. No one taunted me. No one hollered. They even seemed to regard me with a sort of grisly respect.

Maybe they interpreted Gaylord's disappearance as payback for years of abuse. Maybe they were now realizing they had pushed the Witchers over the edge and we were behaving the way the downtrodden always behave. Maybe they had come to fear and respect us the way they feared Castro's Cuba.

I crossed the alleyway behind the shopping center and headed up the terraced slopes towards Gladstein's. But then I saw Snead's truck and realized it was a Saturday. I debated whether to go ahead or turn back, and finally I turned back. The truck had reminded me of Pop's plot to rob the store and I wasn't sure I could deal with Snead's being in the same room with Gladstein.

I passed the shops the way I had come, getting more and more depressed. My brother a murderer, my pop a jewel thief. What did that make me?

It was when I was crossing the alleyway that the trouble happened. Through the shrubs bordering Myra Street I saw sandals and tennis shoes and moving fabric, blue, white and green; and when I reached the steps Johnny Pendleton and two other boys appeared at the break in the fence. The boys were Chip Blevin and Barry Campbell, who lived across Cherokee Road where the houses were bigger. I didn't really know them, I just knew they were on the wrestling team with Pendleton.

All three of them blocked my way.

"Look who it is," Pendleton said.

I stopped. Chip and Barry stood like sentries on either side of him. They were keeping their eyes on him, not me. Barry was popping his knuckles.

"Where's your brother?" Pendleton said.

"At home."

"That's not very lucky for you, is it?"

They grinned. Chip rubbed a hand over his lips, as if to smooth a moustache. He darted a look behind to make sure no one was coming.

"Let me go by," I said.

"What are you gonna do if we don't?"

I looked over my shoulder and wondered if I could make it back to where the stragglers were still browsing before the shop windows. But the boys must have read my mind. Their feet raced down the steps and circled around behind me, and now Pendleton was blocking the pathway that led to the shops. "Sorry, are we in your way?"

Chip and Barry were flanking him. Chip had his eyes cut to the side, watching Pendleton. He seemed uneasy about what they were doing.

I turned and hurried up the steps and heard the drumming of their shoes as they rushed after me. "What did your brother do with Gaylord, asshole?"

I reached Myra Street, hoping I could get away without actually running.

Pendleton came up beside me.

"I asked you something."

"You tell me."

"I'm not playing games, Witcher, what did your brother do with Gaylord?"

"Same thing he'll do to you if you don't leave me alone."

Pendleton stopped in his tracks.

"What did you say?"

I kept moving.

"Did you hear? Are you guys witnesses? He just admitted it!"

I was nervous already about what I'd said. My motive had been to scare off Pendleton, but I realized if this got out it wouldn't do my brother's brief one bit of good. And what if it got back to Myra as well?

I turned around. The boys were babbling excitedly in the middle of the street, too preoccupied to notice I was heading back. When they saw me they broke off. They almost seemed scared.

"I take back what I said."

Pendleton scornfully drew up his pectorals.

"You can't take it back, we heard you."

"I don't know what happened to Gaylord that night. My brother was with his girlfriend, he didn't have a thing to do with it."

"You mean that hippie slut?"

"Don't call her that."

"If she's not a slut what would she be doing with a Witcher?"

Chip kept pushing at his nose, as though he wore glasses.

"My brother didn't do a thing that can be proved. Until you know what happened you shouldn't be making accusations."

"Oh yeah? Well, you can suck my dick. You and your brother and that hippie slut, you all can suck my dick."

I headed on down the street, uneasy about putting my back to them. I heard whispering, and then I heard Pendleton holler, "Where the fuck is Gaylord, you prick?"

A rock sailed past my ear.

I swung and looked. The boys were in the middle of the road. Pendleton's arms were at his side. His shoulders were sagging.

He brought his hands to his face and Chip threw a consoling arm across his shoulders.

I came to the corner, turned left and then right, which put me behind Dickie Pudding's house.

When I had walked a ways I snuck a quick look back.

The road behind me was empty. But what a cheerless acquittal it was.

29

POP HOOKED MY SHIRTTAIL as I was trying to slip past.

"Come on, let's take a ride."

"Where to?"

"We have to get your mother's headache prescription filled, she's having another migraine."

I peeked into the bedroom. One of her palms was next to her head, curled at the fingertips like a dead person's. A small fan next to the bed was making her hair tremble.

By now it was almost dark.

Pop assumed a curious position whenever he drove, twisted slightly to the left. He would fold his right arm over the wheel and bring his head so close to it you almost expected him to rest his chin. Garbage was piled up in the passenger-side foot-well, and paper bags and paper cups and balled-up napkins brushed against my flip-flops. Whenever Pop took a turn cans rattled in the back of the car.

"This guy Reedy figures he's got your brother cornered. He's this patrol cop playing detective and he thinks if he breaks this case he'll get a promotion. Man's gonna do everything in his power to pin this thing on Stan."

"He doesn't seem so bad."

Pop gave me a look. "You're getting awfully smart. What makes you think you been around long enough to know more than I do?"

I shrugged.

"Why don't you take the cotton out of your ears and put it in your mouth. I want you to listen to me for a change."

We rode along for a while without speaking, and then I said, "Okay, I'm listening."

"I don't want you talking to Reedy. Don't say a word to the man. He shouldn't be asking so many questions anyway. If he asks you anything you tell him you ain't saying a word without an attorney present. That'll shut him up, he knows the law."

"Pop, if Stan didn't do anything—"

"He didn't, but that's not enough for these cats. Stan is exactly the type of guy they like to pin stuff on. He ain't one of your refined Kellners or Joyners. Plus he run his mouth about killing Gaylord, which was his own damn fault."

"He's got a violent streak a mile wide."

"The kid ain't nothing but trouble, but we're sticking by him, hear?"

"Yes sir. But what if we found out he did do something?"

"We ain't gonna find that out."

"I'm asking, that's all. What if he did something and you found out. What would you do?"

Pop thought about it.

"All I know is I wouldn't turn him in. Wouldn't be my place to do so. Probably I would talk to him, convince him to turn his own self in."

"Witchers ain't snitchers."

"There you go."

"I don't guess we have to worry, Anya says he was with her the whole night."

"That's right, Stan couldn't have done anything. But we still have to say he left Anya at ten 'cause that's what we told Deputy Dawg."

To get the prescription refilled we had to go to the all-night People's on Main, because that's the only place that was open.

Pop ran in while I sat in the car and stared at the people passing in and out of the store. A black man in a porkpie hat strolled past and gave me a curt nod through the windshield.

When Pop came out he was beside a fat man, laughing hilariously over some ribald pleasantry. They parted with loud hollers and wholehearted waves. I'd yet to see Pop leave a store without making at least one new friend.

During the ride home he started up on Gladstein. "How come you visit that man so often?"

"I don't know, he was telling me how to make Myra my girlfriend. He sold me a ring real cheap, for fifty cents, and then he said I should try and kiss her."

"He said that, he told you to kiss her? That's a little weird."

"What's so weird, I did kiss her."

"You kissed that girl?"

Pop reached over and backhanded me. I gave him a grin and we rode along together, feeling warm. "A Witcher seducing a Joyner, I like that. You're gonna be a heartbreaker, kid."

I kept grinning.

"And now they think your brother offed her brother, that's too bad."

Which pretty effectively ended our warm moment.

"Listen, I want you to cool it with Gladstein, something ain't right about the cat."

I didn't say a word. I'd been expecting this ever since I heard him and Snead talking outside my window.

"He just came to this town to make trouble. Moving to Jefferson Ward, that's the craziest thing I ever heard. Black people don't want him, they don't want white people no more than white people want them."

He went on in this vein, and I let him talk. I stared out the window until the lights of the town began to dwindle and we were winding along the curves of Cherokee Road.

Pop was on a different tack by then. "You ever been in that back room of his?"

"Who, Gladstein's? No, I hang around out front, he never takes me in the back."

"Snead says he keeps his dogs in the back room."

"They're always whimpering behind the door. He's got three of 'em."

"Which is another weird thing, those fluffy dogs. You know who he reminds me of? Your mother had a cousin, Johnny Lee, I don't know if you met him, he only come to the house once or twice. Probably you were too small. He used to own a fluffy little Maltese and he'd put ribbons and bows on the thing and take it out for a walk. A man walking a dog that had ribbons and bows! I used to think, Man, this cat is cruising for a bruising. He was queer as a three-dollar bill, but he was all right, he wasn't too bad. He died of cancer two or three years ago. Your mother thought the world of him. Women always like queers."

Pop fell to musing and then he said, "I wonder what happened to the dog."

"I don't think Mr. Gladstein's a queer, he was married for twenty-five years."

"That don't say a thing. Man next door might be a queer for all we know."

"We don't have a man next door."

We were coming up on Lewis Street. As soon as we made the turn we'd be going past the Joyners', and my stomach got all fluttery, anticipating it.

"Does Gladstein have a burglar alarm?"

"He does, but it isn't hooked up. He told me he never got around to fixing it."

"He told you that?"

Pop searched my face, and I realized what I had said. I'd just sold Mr. Gladstein down the river.

"Well, I don't know, it could be I'm wrong."

"You said that's what he told you."

"Well—yeah."

I couldn't think of a convincing way to take it back, so I went on the offensive. "Why, you planning on robbing his store?"

"Of course not," Pop said, laughing.

He made the turn on Lewis and sailed down the road as fast as he could. I guess he didn't want anyone to notice us.

The cars were thick in front of the Joyners' house, probably people attending a vigil for Gaylord. All the lights were on and a few folks were standing in the yard smoking cigarettes. I could see the silhouettes of their heads as they turned to watch our battered car go past.

Pop's jaw tensed and he kept his eyes straight ahead. I craned my head to search for Myra, but I don't think she was in the yard.

When we got home I ran the headache pills to Mom.

I didn't switch on the light, because she couldn't bear it when one of her headaches was on. I brought her a glass of water and two pills and held her head while she drank. I knew from long experience that she wouldn't remember this the next day. When she woke up from her headaches she always had amnesia about the night before. My great-aunt Norma who lived in Lakeside used to tell me that Mom's not being able to remember was God's mercy at work. One time I challenged her and said, "Mom doesn't believe in God," and Aunt Norma said, "Do you really think that would stop God from being merciful?"

"If He's so merciful," I said, "why does He let her get headaches in the first place?"

She didn't have a good answer, and three days later she died. I always wondered if it was because of my question.

30

REEDY TRACKED ME DOWN the next day, just as I was step-ping into the woods next to Anya's house to do some solitary meditation. His cruiser turned onto Clark Lane and he tapped the horn.

He rolled down the window.

"This Joyner boy's disappearance is all over the news. You been watching the TV?"

"Yes sir."

"You aren't going in the woods to smoke cigarettes, are you?"

"No sir," I said.

He grinned to show he was only funning. "Those woods run up to the Taylors' property, don't they?"

"Yes sir."

He began to work his jaw. "This thing with the Joyner boy is a tragedy, ain't it? We still haven't heard a word from the kid."

I didn't say anything, I felt too much anxiety.

"I'm trying to remember," he went on, "where was it you said you were Wednesday night?"

"I don't think I should answer any questions. Pop told me I should have an attorney present if you start asking questions."

Reedy seemed surprised. "Hey, kid, I'm just making conversation. More information I have the better I'll be able to track the boy down."

"I was home Wednesday night, you can ask Mom and Pop."

"I don't need to ask them. Your brother was home too, right?"

"He was at the Taylors'."

"I thought your father said he was home."

"No, he was at the Taylors' earlier and then he came home at ten."

"You sure it was ten?"

What if the cop had gathered intelligence that Stan wasn't home at that time? I was afraid I might be walking into a trap, so I said, "Maybe it was later. It might have been ten but I don't remember exactly."

"That's funny, 'cause your father was dead certain your brother was home by ten. Said he was in the living room watching TV."

"I don't know, I went to bed early."

"So why did you just say it was later?"

"I said maybe. I was asleep, I don't really know what time it was."

I was getting hot from the exhaust of the cruiser. It was idling gently, rocking slightly while Reedy thought over what I said.

"You usually wake up when your brother comes in the room?"

"Most of the time."

"So you must have woke up that night."

"I don't remember, I was sound asleep. I mean, I don't know for sure. You probably should ask other people."

"So maybe he never came in that night. You'd have woke up if he came in, right?"

I looked down into the woods.

"I have to go, there's something I need to do."

"What, you have an important meeting in the woods?" Reedy winked. "Okay, pal, don't do anything I wouldn't do."

He put the cruiser in drive. Just before he coasted away he said, "Your zipper's down."

I dashed into the trees tugging the thing up.

The moment I was out of sight I whipped out a pack of Winstons. My hands were shaking so much I could barely scrape the match.

I moved down to the creek with the cigarette smoke puffing behind me like a locomotive. At the stream I jumped and kept going. I heard splashing in the Taylors' pool and the golden retriever barking. Probably someone was throwing the stick; but it wouldn't be Stan, because they had called him in to the Safeway store that morning to help with the inventory.

I sat at the edge of the woods and looked towards the pool.

After a while the gate creaked open: Anya was coming out with a towel around her shoulders. I called her name and she picked her way carefully to me in her bare feet.

"What are you doing?"

"Reedy was just asking me questions up on the road. I ain't that good at lying and I don't see why I have to say Stan was home at ten when I know he was here the whole time. Pop is crazy, he's messing everything up."

She glanced towards the house.

"Let me get my sandals, we'll take a walk."

It took her nearly half an hour. When she returned she was dressed in jeans and a peasant smock and sandals. Her hair stuck limply at her cheeks.

"Sorry, I jumped in the shower to wash off the pool."

We walked along the line of the woods and turned left.

The year before, Clark Lane ended at the turn, but then bulldozers and tarring machines came along and plowed an extension through the woods clean up to Cherokee. I'd always wondered who gave the order to do so, but none of the adults I asked knew. Now, as Anya and I walked up the extension road, we kept seeing ribbons and chalk marks on the trees indicating where the borders of the new yards would be. One lot had already been cleared so a house could be built.

"Wow," Anya said. "I guess ours was the first."

We walked along almost to Cherokee.

"So Deputy Dawg's been hounding you," she said, smiling at herself for putting it that way.

"That's because Pop is making me say Stan came home at ten. Reedy's getting suspicious and I don't see why it should be so important anyway."

"Your father's weird. I don't think he likes to be proved wrong."

That impressed me. Up to now Anya hadn't struck me as particularly bright. I wouldn't have thought to put it that way, but now that she said it I saw it was true.

"It makes me feel funny to say Stan came home at ten when I know it's a lie. And Reedy can see right through it. Why don't we go to Pop together, you and me, and get him to talk to Reedy and say he's been thinking it over and now he realizes he had his evenings wrong. I'd prefer saying Stan was at your house if that's where he was."

"Well, I don't know about that." Anya sighed.

"Don't know about what?"

Why was she sighing; why was she wistful?

She leapt up at an overhanging branch, tore away a leaf and held it to her nose. "What a drag, you can't even smell it, it doesn't have a scent."

"What were you getting ready to say?"

She smiled and shook her head, scolding my inquisitiveness. She dropped the leaf and resumed walking.

I fell in beside her, not taking my eyes away. Her changeability confused me, alarmed me. Who was this weird girl?

"This whole thing has been a comedy of errors from the beginning. I'll bet you didn't see *Blow-Up*, I guess you'd be too young to get in. That movie is so far-out! It's about this photographer that accidentally takes a picture of a murder, only he doesn't realize what he's got on film until he's in his darkroom that night developing his pictures. He'd been taking pictures of Vanessa Redgrave while the murder was happening, see, but it was happening in the background and they were in a park and he didn't realize what was going on until later when he's blow-ing up the pictures and he sees what he's got on film and it blows his mind in like a million pieces. It's like he filmed this murder and he didn't even know it, he was just out buying an-tiques or something. No, wait, that happens later, after he wres-tles with two chicks that don't have their clothes on. . . . I don't know, I might be telling it wrong. Anyway, the point is, he sees this murder that he has on film."

I had the feeling she was trying to tell me something perti-nent. It was a parable maybe, but I couldn't make heads or tails of it.

"And then later when he goes back to the murder scene to find the body it's been moved, which means maybe it was never really there, you don't know. And then this troupe of mimes comes along and they're playing tennis with invisible rackets and this invisible ball goes flying through the air and falls to the ground and the camera keeps following it even though it's invisible and you have to imagine that you're seeing it, which is the best part of the whole movie because it's like you can see the ball even though it's not there, I mean, you know it's not there but you can still see it and it's like if you're high it's so groovy because you're thinking, What's going on, man, this is so mind-blowing!"

"I don't understand why you're telling me this."

"Well, the point the movie is making is that you can't always trust what you think you see. Sometimes the things you see aren't really there, and then other times you don't see what's right before your eyes."

"Does that mean you saw something or didn't see something?"

She turned with a confused smile. "I didn't see anything, what are you getting at? I'm just telling you about a movie." Then she burst into a laugh that echoed up and down the doomed verdure of Clark Lane.

"Oh God, you must think—"

She dashed ahead and slapped at some overhanging leaves and tossed them to the road. When I caught up with her she shrieked and flung herself at me. Then she seized my shoulders; she stared at me severely and pushed me back at arm's length. "I'm gonna tell you something that you can't repeat to a soul. You promise? Not a word."

"What are you gonna tell me?"

I was too full of dread to hear more.

"I'm not telling unless you promise me first."

"Maybe I don't want to know."

"Okay, so maybe you'd be better off not knowing. That's groovy, I can dig that."

"No, tell me."

"You haven't promised."

"Okay, I promise."

"You can't say it like that. A promise is sacred, you have to mean it."

I gave it a few seconds and then I said, "Okay, I promise, I mean it."

Anya peered into the depths of my eyes. "You swear?"

And then she sighed, and we began to walk. "The truth is,

Stan wasn't with me the whole night, he went out in my car for a while."

"For how long?"

"Well like, there was this guy going to sell him a nickel bag and I let him use my car. He went downtown so he could meet the guy."

"He went downtown to buy grass?"

"Yes."

"Oh great, and here we've been telling Reedy—"

"Don't forget, you promised."

"What time was it when he left the house?"

"Around six-thirty, seven."

"But that's when—"

I sat in the road. I don't know how it happened. I was walking and then I was sitting and the asphalt was burning through my pants.

Anya covered her mouth and giggled. "Why did you sit down?"

I gazed up at her. "How long was he gone?"

"Oh man, the whole thing got all messed up. Once Stan got downtown the cat didn't have the dope because he had lost his wheels somehow, and they had to drive to some apartment complex in Southside and Stan says the cat they met there tried to rip him off, and you know Stan when someone tries to rip him off. I'm not sure what exactly went down, but when he came home he was all cut up and bloodied. It was around four in the morning and he still didn't have any grass, which was a bummer 'cause I'd been waiting all that time to get high. . . ."

I looked up . . . I saw a buzzard . . . the smell of a dead thing wafted through the trees . . . these crazy crickets in the woods were crying . . .

Anya stood over me.

"Here."

She offered her hand. I took it, got up.

"I've never seen anyone do that, you dropped just like a sack of potatoes."

"So now you're saying Stan wasn't with you when Gaylord disappeared."

"Oh, he was and he wasn't. Listen, if anything bad happened I would have known. I can sense Stan's presence even when he's not around. I can pick up his mood when I'm like miles and miles away from him. I feel his presence now, as we speak."

I brushed gravel and sand from my pants and started back the way we came.

"Where are you going?"

"Home. I feel like throwing up."

"Come on, Jack, he didn't do anything. He was just trying to cop some grass. Don't you love your brother? You should love him, everything is about love."

"Are you high?"

"Yeah daddy, on flowers and leaves. I'm high on that buzzard up there."

She caught up and walked me home.

31

I FOUND MOM in the kitchen, in misery. Her chin was on her palm and she was contemplating the dishwater fingers of the other hand splayed upon the table. She suffered terrible post-migraine depressions and every new attack brought her a fresh understanding of the brutality of existence.

I was in shock, meanwhile, from having learned, without the possibility of error, that my brother had done evil to Gaylord. I had suspected it all along, but now it seemed worse. Stan had returned to the Taylors' all cut up and bloodied. Bloodied! I looked at my mother and tried to tell her with my eyes. I was bound not to say it, so I tried to make her *perceive* my dread and apprehension.

Pop peeked in the kitchen and went away. Mom drummed her fingers once and stopped. I went over to massage her shoulders and she hummed "Mmmm."

"Where have you been?" she said.

"Out with Anya."

"Oh, that crazy girl . . ."

Her voice, perhaps her mind, had no reserves, no fight, and she surrendered languidly to the massage. I felt her shoulders grow slack under my kneading touch.

"Do you think Stan is going to marry that girl?"

I hadn't thought any such thing. My brother's marrying was the last thing I would have considered. But women's minds do run in that direction, and now I tried to imagine it: Stan and Anya in a neat house with a wooden fence. For some reason I pictured Grandma's house in Lakeside, my ideal of domestic success.

No, I couldn't see Stan in such a place.

"Anya is weird," I said.

"She's a hippie. I hope they aren't using drugs."

I didn't say anything, and she instantly picked up on what I was not saying.

"Are they on drugs?"

"I didn't say they were on drugs."

"You don't have to. They're using drugs, I know they are."

"Don't go accusing Stan of using drugs, he'll think I told you."

"Why would he think that?"

"It's the way he thinks. Mom, they are not using drugs."

"You promise they aren't?"

"Why is everyone making me promise them something?"

"Who else have you been promising?"

"Well, Anya."

Mom was quiet. Then she said, "What did she make you promise?"

"I can't tell you what she made me promise. Just drop it."

Yet I did want to tell her. Why was I doomed to know, by myself, that Stan was unaccounted for when Gaylord disappeared, and that he came back to Anya's hours later, "bloodied"?

Bloodied!

"Since when did you and Anya become so close?"

"We're not close, I only know her through Stan."

"Did she tell you something about that night?"

"What night?"

"The night Gaylord disappeared."

Why would she ask unless she was wondering? I arranged a telling expression on my face in case she turned around. My eyes would inform her, but my lips would reveal nothing. . . . I massaged her shoulders until my hands got tired. Pop came in with an empty glass and filled it with water and gulped it at the sink, staring over the rim.

"Feeling better?" he asked.

He left the room without an answer.

I tried to make my voice casually curious. "Do you believe Stan did something to Gaylord?"

In Mom's memory lurked a whole catalogue of Stanley Witcher violence. It began in kindergarten, during his first school days, when he would return home on the bus each and every day ripped, bruised and bloodied. Eventually it got to the point that she was asked to attend weekly conferences with the teachers, all on account of Stan's bullying. He didn't get any gentler with age either; maturity brought no tendency to count to ten. In fact, the assaults only grew more violent. He would beat kids over the head with cylindrical objects, kick their nuts, bite their ears, twist their arms. Two years ago Pop had been forced to pay for one kid's stitches. And yet with Mom, Stan would be so affectionate, tickling her, hugging her, kissing her, telling her she was sexy. Even with me, even with his brother, he had his generous moments. They were fewer and further between, it's true. A smile from Stan was like a summer's day in Siberia. But they did happen.

Mom said, "I don't want to say that about your brother. I don't even want to think it."

Still, it must have crossed her mind or she wouldn't have been so curious about Anya. She was looking at me, trying to gauge what I might know. "He was with her, right? They were at her house listening to Beatles records that night."

"The Doors."

That was her consolation, as it had been mine up to a half hour before.

What could I do? I didn't want to lie. Nor did I want to break any promises. So I said nothing. I let my eyes speak.

Mom kept looking. And then I saw her shudder. She hid her face in the length of her piano-playing hands. She sat with her elbows on the table, face buried.

Pop peeked in. His eyebrows arched, he mouthed an inquiry. Is she okay?

What a family.

Mom wiped her index finger under her nose. For a moment I thought she had been crying, but then I realized she was hot, that's all. The big fan in the dining room window kept sucking warm air through the rear screen door. All it did was make us hotter.

"How's Mr. Gladstein?" she said—a topic I found as painful as the possibility of my brother's foul play. I'd been so wrapped up in the Gaylord business I hadn't had time to brood about anything else. Now I remembered telling Pop that the store's burglar alarm didn't work. Why on earth did I tell him that?

Mom was watching, suspecting me of things.

"You know what Pop says, Witchers ain't snitchers."

"What is that supposed to mean?"

"I was just thinking about it, that's all. They used to say that in Hendersonville."

"I know all about Hendersonville," she said curtly.

One of Pop's best friends came from a bootlegging family in North Carolina. This man got so good at outrunning cops on the mountain roads he later became famous as a race-car driver. Years before, Pop had taken Stan and me to see him race in Charlotte. Unfortunately, the celebrated friend had outgrown Pop, what with his riches and his trophies. All he did was shake our hands. He was too busy heading towards where a passel of women was waiting on the side of the track.

Mom cringed whenever the subject of Hendersonville came up. There was plenty in Pop's past I didn't know about, and I wondered if I'd ever get to hear the good stuff, like after I turned twenty-one. What irked me was that Stan knew about things I never heard tell of. Maybe there was something in Pop's younger years everyone knew but me that would explain why Mom couldn't put her doubts to rest.

"You're as much a Kirby as a Witcher," she said. "You don't have to do everything like the Witchers."

"Yeah, but I still don't wanna be a snitch."

"That's not what I meant. And why are you thinking so much about that? What are you hiding?"

"Nothing," I said.

She glowered in the Kirby style. When Kirbys get mad they drop their faces and stare from underneath their brows. That's what Mom was doing, and I shifted about uncomfortably.

"Myra told me she can't be my girlfriend anymore," I blurted.

I said it to distract her, and it worked.

"When did you see Myra?"

"I didn't. She sent a message through Kathy Coghill."

"Oh Lord, why did my kids have to get mixed up with the Joyner kids?"

"You don't believe in the Lord."

"That doesn't mean I can't pray. Everyone wants divine help. I read this book once, a religious book I found at a yard sale over on Stanley Street. It was written during the Middle Ages and it said that when you pray you shouldn't use a lot of words, you should just say 'God' or 'Sin' or 'Love' or 'Help.' It said if you find yourself in a crisis you should use as few words as possible. Like when your house is burning and you shout 'Help' and that's all your neighbors need to hear. God is the same way, according to this book. All you need to say is 'Help.' Because if you use too many words He might not get the message, what with all the prayers He must be hearing. Everything just becomes a big jumble to Him, I reckon. So that's what I do. I pray 'Help.'"

"I thought you were an atheist."

"Maybe. But I don't see how praying can hurt anything. Might as well stay on the safe side."

"Mr. Gladstein gave me a chant to say," I said.

"A chant?"

"Yeah, a syllable. It's got the power to help you, but you have to believe. It's all in the mind," I said, tapping my temple.

"God, my children are crazy. The whole world is going crazy. All these riots and protests and wars, and now we have these mind-blowing drugs and that crazy psychedelic music to go with it. I thought Mr. Gladstein was a nice man."

"He is a nice man."

"Did you know he lives in Jefferson Ward?"

"How do you know that?"

"He told me last time I saw him, at the shopping center. That man talks so much I always wonder if he'll let me go, once he gets started. And to think he lives over there with the colored people. What on earth is he thinking of?"

She buried her face in her palms and I went out to the porch so I could sit and think by myself. That's all I'd been wanting, ever since Reedy derailed me in the morning: some solitude, a little time for reflection.

And then I noticed the red flag was standing on the mailbox.

32

I GRABBED THE NOTE and dashed with it to my room.

> *DJ,*
>   *Can you meet me tomorrow (Monday) behind*
>   *Dickie Pudding's house at one in the afternoon? I need*
>   *to see you.*
>
>   *M*

I penciled a declaration of intent to be in the Pudding woods, took it to the box and raised the flag. Kathy Coghill was only moments behind, as if she'd been positioned nearby with binoculars. This time I didn't let her get away. I caught up with her at the corner and called out, "Hey, tell her I'll be there."

Kathy turned, incensed.

"You're not supposed to be following me." It was broad day-light and anyone could see. "This is just great. If Myra gets in trouble it'll be your fault."

"I thought she was grounded."

"Not after what happened. Don't be stupid. And stop fol-lowing me. We shouldn't be talking out in the open like this. Be there tomorrow. For Myra."

I returned home, properly rebuked.

A little later, the boy who killed my girlfriend's brother came home.

We sat at the table and ate egg noodles mixed with ground beef and tomato sauce, a fabrication my mother had christened "goulash." Stan ate silently, pushing the hair from his face. Oc-casionally he would look up sharply, as though mindful of our conjectures.

I couldn't look at him. He kept giving me evil glances. I didn't want to be in the same room with him. I headed for the bedroom and he followed me in. "Punk," he said. He put his loud funky music on. I split for the kitchen and hung out until he left for Anya's.

Snead came over and Pop pulled out his harmonica and I went to the yard and studied them for signs of plots and con-spiracies; but all they did was sing the blues. Snead was ill-tempered and short with Pop. He wanted the drink and the music, not the conversation. Around eleven I went to bed, thankful the house had so many fans blowing at full speed. That rendered it impossible to hear their voices underneath my window.

The next afternoon I was in the woods behind Dickie Pudding's house.

The sun was blazing, and shouting drifted up from the Pudding house. Conglomerations of gnats kept molesting my air. The hum of the world was louder than ordinary: high-speed traffic on Matson, appliances sucking and blowing and churning, the gears of Gehenna slogging through the bedrock; wasps and flies and gnats and mosquitoes; air conditioners jutting from windows, dripping on the grass below; airplanes in the clouds, helicopters, UFOs, whirly beasts you couldn't see; two-way radios, shortwave sets operated by men in basements; TV antennas, electrical towers zapping the sky.

That morning Pop had shown me where a county cop was quoted in the paper as saying that the department wasn't treating Gaylord's vanishing as a criminal case. "Nine times out of ten kids that disappear come back home in a week. They need to get away from the pressure, blow off some steam. Usually they're with a member of the opposite sex," he sensitively observed. My brother wasn't mentioned, to our relief. Accompanying the article was a school photograph of Gaylord in a coat and tie and a 1966 flattop, humbly aware of his husky gentility.

The heat coagulated in my throat.

I spotted Gaylord in a cloud.

I saw sixteen-year-old Pop with his Asheville moll.

I pictured Myra, a child Niobe, weeping over the morning paper.

She appeared at the curve in the road, stopped and peered and stepped cautiously into the brush. Her eyes were all swollen.

Rusty had come along, and he barreled himself right into me.

"Hi, Myra, I'm really sorry about everything that's happened." Rusty was propelling me backwards and it caused the words to fluctuate in my chest, so that they came out like this: "I'm re-e-a-l-l-y so-o o r ry about everythi-i-i-ing that's ha-a-a-pppened." I snagged his paws. His hot breath blasted me and I pushed him away.

"I know you didn't have anything to do with it," she told me.

"I've really been worried about you, I want you to know that."

"I know, everyone's being so nice. Jack, I shouldn't have snuck out of my house that night. If I had known how much pain my parents would be in I wouldn't have done it."

"Well, how would you know? I feel bad too, now."

"We're just kids," she observed.

I suspected someone had been counseling her. It sounded like she was repeating revelations gleaned from some wise adult. But as far as us being kids, so what? I couldn't see what distinguished kids from adults, apart from size.

I'd already run out of things to say. I stood there waiting for her to speak and she looked back at me, repentant and heartbroken. And brainwashed.

"The reason I wanted to see you is so I could give you back your ring and bracelet."

"I want you to keep them," I said.

I understood she could no longer be my girlfriend, but still I found the declaration painful. Myra was breaking up with me! We would no longer be going steady! This was it, the fated moment, the thing that must occur when a Joyner gal and a Witcher boy collide.

"I can't have these in the same house where Gaylord lives. You understand that, don't you?"

Why was this girl so pretty? Her eyes were too big, her nose was lopsided, her beatific smile would easily be deemed a symptom of idiocy by anyone less infatuated. I remember how in the old days I had considered her pogo-stick strut ungainly. And then came that fateful morning when she had congratulated me on my grades. At that moment Myra Joyner became my ideal of feminine grace and mercy.

Now her face was soiled and shadowed by tears. And yet she was more beautiful to me than ever. Tragedy had brought out some preternatural womanness in her.

While she dug in her pocket for the jewels I said, "You know, he's my brother, I was born with him, I didn't have any choice in the matter."

"I know. It's just the way people think."

"Who cares?"

"I do."

She fished out the ring and the bracelet and offered them.

Recklessly I flung them over my shoulder.

"What did you do that for?" she cried.

"If you don't want 'em I don't either."

She peeked around to see where the jewelry had landed.

"You're not going to leave them on the ground, are you?"

Tossing away material goods was a major impropriety in El

Dorado Hills, and Myra wasn't all that appreciative of my contempt for such trifling vanities.

"They're just things," I proclaimed.

"No they aren't, they mean something."

"It doesn't seem like they mean that much to you."

"Do you think this is easy for me? I wanted to keep that ring!"

She began to cry. Her chest heaved with aching sobs and I took her into my arms.

"Mom found out about us. I told her, it seemed like the right thing to do."

I patted her back and held her. From his haunches Rusty gave me a wink.

"You're the only boy in school as smart as I am. I tried to tell her but she said—"

"I'm a Witcher."

I felt her tears seeping into my shoulder.

"Myra, I don't want the ring. If you won't keep it, why would I want it?"

"Oh, Jack, that's so—"

She stopped. "What if someone comes along and finds them? Then they'll be wearing my ring and my bracelet."

"So what, let them."

"But it could be anyone, some low-class person . . ."

The truth is, I was already feeling a little guilty. In my mind I saw Gladstein's accusing eyes. Hadn't he told me the ring possessed magic qualities? I had never really swallowed that line, but the story surrounding it, the heroic exertion, the triumph of the will, the stolen kisses, all that did give the ring a certain value.

I searched for a while through the dirt and the leaves, kicking things around. The bracelet I found immediately, but the ring seemed lost, gone forever.

"Oh well, I'll look for it more after you've left."

Myra nodded distractedly. Her mind was formulating a question, trying to find the horrible thing she needed to say.

"Do you think your brother could have . . . do you think he did something to Gaylord?"

I shook my head. I couldn't tell her what I knew and what I knew I didn't want to know and not wanting to know was, if you stretched it, as good as not knowing. Gaylord was gone, that's all.

"If you knew where we could find him you'd tell us, right?"

I gave her a puny nod.

"Do you?"

"Do I what?"

"Do you know anything that might help us?"

The words came from Myra's lips, but they belonged to her mother. Her mother had designed all this, the meeting in the woods, the surrender of the jewels, maybe even her tears. Everything, all of it, the entire scene, it had been scripted by her mom! The notion made me rebellious and I studied Myra with suspicion.

She saw it in my eyes. Her lip trembled, and silently she begged me for mercy.

How could I do anything but sympathize? Her grief, her loss, her brother's photograph in the papers.

"What if it turns out Stan did do something," I said, "will you hate me forever?"

She considered the question myopically, straining to see her thoughts.

"It would be hard not to, but I wouldn't hate you."

"You know I really like you, Myra."

"I know, and if it weren't for all this . . . even though you're a Witcher and all . . . I mean . . ."

I was staring at the tiny rise where her breasts were developing.

"Can I kiss you?"

"No, I couldn't, not with Gaylord being gone."

We looked at each other.

Her eyes kept digging into mine. Probably she thought I was holding out on her. And no doubt her mother was at home on tenterhooks.

"I have to go," she said, "people are waiting for me. Come on, Rusty, let's go."

But Rusty stayed.

She took the path that led to where the road curved. Before she stepped out she turned to look back.

I kicked at the dirt, brushing aside leaves and debris. But I couldn't find the ring. It must have taken some erratic hop when it hit the ground.

After I left, Rusty stayed behind, sniffing and pawing and trying to find it for me.

33

EVERY TIME I THOUGHT about Gladstein I felt pangs for my faithlessness; frankly, throwing away the ring bothered me more for his sake than Myra's. I returned to the Pudding woods twice to search for the thing. I knocked on the Puddings' back door to see if Dickie had come across it. (No one answered, which I found depressing, since I had heard voices inside just before I knocked.)

Gaylord Joyner's disappearance was big news. Mrs. Joyner kept showing up on the TV, with Myra sniffling beside her. Search parties were formed. People spread out in groups to comb the woods beside Moccasin Road or they piled into flat-bed pickup trucks and headed to the next county to look for Gaylord there. Rivers and lakes were plumbed. Tips came into the police department: suspicious noises in a basement, a white kid buying drugs in Jefferson Ward, a drifter in a motel room who looked like Gaylord. Mimeographed signs were tacked to telephone poles and taped to shop windows. A $1,000 reward was offered in the newspaper.

Eggs were thrown at our house. The rear tires on our Ford were slashed. Shouts and jeers from passing cars were a nightly event. Mom got accosted at the Ben Franklin by two ladies who denounced her for harboring a fugitive.

"I'm not harboring anyone. He's my son, he lives with me."

"He's a murderer!"

The commotion nearly got out of control, until Mr. Harris unctuously ushered the ladies from the store.

Mom took to her bed with a headache.

Dickie Pudding had ditched me and I didn't have a soul to call friend, unless it be Anya. I went to the Taylors' pool twice that week, padding along the hot street to get there. Reedy would cruise past in his Plymouth, giving me a two-fingered salute off the brim of his cap. And then, on top of everything, I would remember Pop and Snead and what they planned to do, and in my mind I would see Pop behind bars, and Stan in the next cell, and Mom and me in the poorhouse.

Anya told us the detectives were coming to her door with questions. They had heard about the incident on the day of the pool party. They were canvassing the entire neighborhood and yet they never visited our house, which we found alarming. Such was our paranoia: it was bad news when the cops came and it was bad news when they didn't.

One day I ran into Snead. I was flip-flopping along in my bathing trunks, on my way to the pool, when his truck turned the corner. This was down by the woods that ran to the Taylor house. He pulled up, inclining his face towards me. The cigarette was hanging from his mouth. "You going swimming with the rich folks?"

"Hi, Snead. Yeah, my brother goes with the girl that lives here."

"So I hear."

"What are you doing around here?"

"Got a job on Stanley." His cigarette gestured in that direction. "How come you ain't been to Gladstein's lately?"

"I don't know, I just haven't been there."

"He asked about you yesterday."

"Gladstein did?"

"He says you ain't coming there no more."

"I'll go see him then."

"I'm going to his house Saturday night. Man lives in Jefferson Ward."

I felt the blood running to my face. "I have to go," I said.

"I ain't keeping you."

Snead put the truck in gear.

I sat by the creek and smoked a cigarette and thought about what he'd just told me.

Saturday was the night, then.

I flicked away the cigarette and went to the pool. Anya and Tillie were there. (Basil was away lawyering.)

"How's that good-looking dad of yours?" Tillie said. She was in her white bathing suit.

"He's fine. So is Mom."

Anya pulled me into the pool, giggling and splashing water. Tillie watched us, nervously tugging her fingers. "Where on earth could that Joyner boy be?" she shouted.

"Oh, Mom, I'm getting so sick of hearing about that," Anya said.

"We told the police Stan was here. You don't have to worry, he has an alibi!" Probably now the whole neighborhood knew, the way Tillie was shouting.

Did she really believe Stan was inside her house when Gaylord vanished? But in that castle how would she have known if he'd left?

A rivulet flowed from Anya's nose; she cupped water and tossed it at me. Then the phone rang. Tillie went inside and came out and hollered for Anya.

That left me alone in the pool.

I lifted my arms and let water cascade from them.

Up above, from a second-floor window, Tillie peeked out and waved. . . .

Snead had never been sold on the scheme, that was plain. The whole thing was Pop's doing, and it might not be terribly difficult to talk Snead into calling it off. Anyway, there was a wall between Pop and me. I couldn't talk to him. Every time I tried to bring it up, the words wouldn't come. Around Pop I was afraid of not being Witcher enough. But I was afraid of something else, too. I remembered how he'd been staring at me at Neuman's that night, I remembered the coldness in his eyes. . . .

I figured it wouldn't be hard to locate Snead. But I had to leave right away. He had said his job was on Stanley, and all I had to do was stroll along 'til I found his truck.

I left without fanfare. I could hear Anya's voice in the kitchen, talking on the phone. Tillie had never returned. Too wet to hoof it through the woods, I took to the streets. By the time I came upon Snead's truck the sun had dried me off. This was two or three blocks past the Coghill house, beyond the turn into the Pudding woods. Snead was hauling old lumber from around the back of a house and loading it on the flatbed. He came stumbling along with both arms full and his cigarette poking out of his mouth. When he got to the truck he tossed the two-by-fours on the flatbed and slapped his palms.

He turned his cigarette to me. "What you doing here, Witcher?"

I was all fluttery from the butterflies in my stomach.

"We have to talk about something. All right? It won't take long. . . ."

What was I saying?

The smoke from Snead's cigarette burned at his eye, but he never so much as blinked.

"All right?"

"Well, go on, I ain't got all day."

"I heard you and Pop talking the other night."

"What night, what are you talking about?"

"I don't know, some night. The fans weren't on, I could hear you outside my window."

"So?"

"Y'all were talking about robbing Gladstein's store."

Snead's eyes liked to bug out. I could see them through the cord of smoke climbing from his cigarette.

"I don't know what you're talking about."

"Come on, Snead, I heard you. You're supposed to go to Gladstein's and let Pop know the coast is clear. You know the combination to the safe in the back. I heard you."

"Boy, you must be crazy. You must be on drugs."

"I'm not gonna snitch. Gladstein doesn't have to know anything. I just want you to call it off, that's all."

He turned to rearrange the boards in the truck, fanning them out so they'd rest against the tailgate evenly. "You better not be spreading tales, Witcher."

"I won't say a word to anyone. Come on, Snead, you know it's true."

He spun around and set his mean brown eyes upon me.

"If you ain't out of here in five seconds I'm gonna smack you upside your head. What right have you to come around here telling lies? You're out of your mind, boy."

I was backing off, holding his gaze. "You can't do it, Snead. If you do I'll call the cops. I don't want to, but I will."

"Boy, your pop is gonna kick your little ass. You keep your mouth shut. Now get out of here."

"Just don't do it, that's all. I don't want any trouble. I like you, Snead."

I was moving away, wondering if he might hop in his truck and come gunning for me. I wouldn't have been surprised if another rock had sailed past my ear.

I was walking fast, hoping to find some people in their yards. I figured Snead wouldn't come get me if he knew people were around. When I got farther along I came upon Karla and Kitten on the Coghill porch, attended by a Pendleton or two.

I walked straight past with their eyes following me. I was chanting Gladstein's syllable to keep my mind occupied. I was praying the way my atheist mother had taught me. All these damn eyes. Maybe getting beat up by Snead wouldn't be so bad after all.

34

IT DIDN'T TAKE POP long to find out. The next day he flung open the bedroom door and stared at me and closed the door. He didn't say a word.

At the supper table we were grim-faced, silent. Stan was just home from the Safeway, Mom from the Ben Franklin. I went to the living room and turned on the news and saw Lyndon Johnson's face and left the room. Pop came in the bedroom behind me and shut the door.

"What's this I hear from Snead?" He was yanking his neck, getting rid of the creaks.

"About what?"

"He says you came up to him the other day and started talking nonsense about him and me robbing Gladstein. What the hell is that about?"

"That's what I heard."

"Heard where?"

"I heard you and him talking outside my window one night. Your voices were so loud I could hear you."

"So?"

"Y'all were talking about robbing Gladstein's store."

"You're hearing things, kid."

"I heard it loud and clear."

"You really think I'd break into a man's store? That's how low an opinion you have of me?"

"I heard what you said, that's all."

"You heard something, you got that right. You must have little green men in your head."

"I heard what I heard."

I wanted to be defiant. But I began to doubt myself. What if my imagination had been playing tricks?

"I don't appreciate your going to Snead like that. You have something to say you say it to my face."

"Yes sir."

"Snead must think we're a bunch of lunatics in this house."

"We are," I said.

He snorted grimly and left the room. While he was going out Stan was coming in. They edged past each other in the doorway.

Stan sat next to the desk and looked at me, on the bottom bunk. His shoulders drooped. He clasped his hands between his thighs. His hair hung near to his shoulders. His bosses at the Safeway had been getting on him lately about cutting it. He took off his sunglasses, played with them, walked them across the top of the desk. Then he stopped.

"What's Pop's problem?"

"I don't know."

"He seems mad about something."

He kept looking at me with his murderous eyes. "Wanna come to the drive-in with me and Anya tonight?"

They were going to a Hells Angels movie.

I told him no, I didn't want to go. I didn't trust these overtures he was making. Probably he figured his generosity would keep me quiet.

"You're a punk, you know that?"

"Why are you getting mad?"

"How come you don't wanna go to the movie, what's your problem?"

"I don't like Hells Angels movies."

"Punk. Fuck you, punk."

"I have a right to not go."

"Fuck you," he said, "I oughta put your lights out."

I got up and left.

In the hallway I bumped into Pop, who was heading towards the room.

"I want a word with you," he said.

"Let's go somewhere else, I don't wanna talk around Stan."

We went to the backyard. I sat on one of the swings and Pop picked up a branch and tossed it so that it twirled through the air like a boomerang. There was still plenty of light, and several dogs came along to greet us.

"I'd like you to tell me what you think you heard that night."

A spaniel I'd never seen before came up and greedily licked the back of my hand. I wiped it on my shorts.

"Just what you and Snead were saying. You wanted him to call from Gladstein's house so you'd know the coast was clear. I heard him say he had the combination to the safe. Pop, just the other day you were asking me questions about Gladstein's burglar alarm."

He grinned. "You're a little fool, you know that? We were joking, that's a standing joke we have, about robbing Gladstein. We joke about that all the time."

"Okay, I didn't know it was a joke."

I was happy to play along if it would keep me out of trouble.

"You're getting more like your mother every day. She doesn't have a sense of humor either."

"I guess I don't," I said.

"You really think I was planning on robbing Gladstein?"

"Not if you say you weren't. Whose dog is that?" I wanted to get off the subject. I didn't want to hear him lie anymore.

"I don't know whose dog that is, I ain't never seen him before. Come here, pooch."

Pop massaged the spaniel's head and neck lavishly.

"Wanna go get some ice cream?"

"I'm not hungry."

"Come on, you're getting too skinny, we gotta put some meat on those bones."

"I'm not in the mood."

"You're still mad, aren't you? You really believed I was gonna hurt that Jewish friend of yours. You've been mad at me ever since I lost my job."

"Well, it's not as if you've been out looking for a new one."

"There you go, that's what this is about, me losing my job."

"I didn't say a word about you not having a job."

I stood. I had seen Stan walking along the road, on his way to Anya's, and now I could go inside if I wanted.

Pop watched me go. A few minutes later Mom came into my room, just as I had anticipated.

"Were you arguing with your father?"

"All I want is people to leave me alone."

I folded my arms sternly across my chest, so she could see me wanting to be left alone.

"Me too? You want me to leave you alone?"

She was only being kind, but that was worse.

I threw a pencil across the room. I shoved past her and darted out the door. I ran outside. I was just waiting for the first taunt to come at me. I was liable to punch somebody. I didn't care if my brother did do Gaylord in. I wasn't going to take it anymore.

I pounded the streets, walking really hard, and then I heard Reedy's cruiser pull up beside me. I couldn't believe it, it was seven at night. Didn't this guy take any time off?

"Hey, Jack," he said, stopping the car.

I kept walking and he inched along beside me. "What's the matter?"

"Leave me alone, I don't have to talk to you."

"Why, what are you hiding?"

"This is against the law," I said, "you can't question me unless I have a lawyer present."

"I can ask anything I want. You don't have to answer, but I can ask."

We came to a standstill.

"Don't waste your breath," I told him.

"Come on, kid, tell me what I need to know."

I thrust my face into his.

"I killed Gaylord Joyner. I'm the one that did it."

Reedy jerked his head backwards. And then he burst out laughing. "You're a comedian, I get it!"

His car accelerated. I went back to the house and saw the mismatching tires on the rear of the Ford (Pop had replaced the ones that got slashed)—the commode that Pop had left in the side yard—a rusty lawn mower in front. That was Witcher House. . . . I sat on the porch. It wasn't two minutes later that Snead's truck pulled up. I moaned and scrambled for my room. As I swung the door closed it jammed against something, and Mom moved her foot away.

She pulled me to the bed and took me in her arms.

"I can't hold you forever," she told me.

"What if Stan killed Gaylord?"

"Don't say that. Your brother might be mean but he would never kill anyone." She tightened her hold to prevent me from saying anything else.

"I think he would kill someone. I think he'd kill me if he got mad enough."

"How can you say that?"

"Mom, look at the guy."

She didn't say anything.

"I told Reedy I killed Gaylord Joyner."

"What!"

"He's trying to get me to tell him something so he can arrest Stan."

"Why on earth did you tell him you killed Gaylord?"

"He laughed when I said it."

"Are you crazy? That's gonna make him think the Witchers had something to do with it even more."

"I do think Stan killed Gaylord, I really do."

"Stop that, I don't wanna hear that kind of talk."

She left the room.

I got in bed. I heard indistinct voices at my window and chords coming from Snead's guitar.

I snuck out the back door and ran across the lot to the north end, where Pop and Snead wouldn't see. Then I went in the other direction, not wanting to pass Myra's.

Two or three kids were messing around at the drainage pipe and I changed my mind about going there. I went past the Coghills' and up the road behind Dickie Pudding's house and then I got on Myra Street and hoofed it 'til I came to the rear of the shopping center.

Gladstein's Continental wasn't in the lot. He had closed his shop for the night.

Across Matson from the shopping center was a tiny apartment complex. I was familiar with the grounds and I knew where there was a small laundry separate from the other buildings.

I found a few hard chairs in there and threw myself down. No one was using the room; the washers and dryers were perfectly still. A fluorescent light winked and hummed above me. Occasionally it made a waspish noise and flickered like a strobe lamp. Somehow that lulled me into sleep.

When I got home it was six in the morning. Mom was lying on the carmine sofa, using her hands for a pillow; she raised her head when I came in. She didn't say anything, she just told me to go to bed.

I admired her for that. It would have been so easy to yell, and she didn't.

35

I BARRELED to Gladstein's Saturday afternoon, hoping to get there before Snead came with his buffer. As I was entering the store I noticed a "Missing" poster in the window, with Gaylord's name on it.

"Witcher!" Gladstein hollered. "What has kept you away so long? What other tragedies are plaguing our El Dorado Hills?" He was wearing the doleful countenance of a veteran actor whom people get sentimental about too late in his career.

"Hi, Mr. Gladstein." I took a quick look around the store. "Last time I came you had customers."

"Did you take a picture? I might need it as proof." I heard his dogs sniffing at the back room door. "I meant proof I had customers," he said. He thought I hadn't got the joke. "So tell me," he went on, "have you been out with the search-and-rescue parties?"

"I don't think they'd want a Witcher coming along. Everybody thinks my brother killed Gaylord."

"What do you think?"

I just shrugged. "Myra gave me the ring back," I said.

"Boy, you two are like Romeo and Juliet."

"I feel you should know: when Myra gave me the ring I threw it over my shoulder, and now it's lost in the woods."

Gladstein took this harder than I expected. He bit his lip and wrinkled his brow.

"Is it still lost?"

"Yes sir. I've gone back a couple times looking for it. I do have the bracelet, I found that."

"You threw the bracelet away as well?"

"Yes sir, I'm sorry."

I offered the bracelet and he snatched it. He unlocked a drawer with the key around his neck and placed it carefully inside.

"You have to find that ring, Witcher, this is no joke."

"I'll go back and look."

"You can't throw magic away like that. Magic will turn against you. I'm serious, I could be affected by this too. What did you throw it away for?"

"I don't know. If she didn't want it I didn't either."

Gladstein shook his finger at me. "Now I might lose my protection."

"From getting robbed? Oh no, you won't get robbed."

"Who said anything about getting robbed?"

"Well, when you told me about the burglar alarm you said you never got it fixed."

"Yes. Well, guess what? I've had it fixed! I took your asking as an omen. I called the burglary people and they came and repaired it."

I had saved Pop! If only he knew!

Gladstein and I grinned back and forth.

And then he frowned.

"Witcher, listen. I have never worried about getting robbed. Do you seriously believe we take anything with us when we leave this world? People are fools, vain fools." Gladstein shrugged, philosophically surveying the world from atop his stool.

We mulled this over for a moment. Then, seizing the opportunity for further reflection, I said, "Do you believe in God?"

"Well, I don't know. Magic I do believe in. That's in the Bible too, you know. Moses, Aaron, they were world-class magicians. You don't mess around with the Big Guy, He'll send plagues and frogs. It's all very supernatural."

"My mom doesn't believe in God."

"She doesn't? And what about you?"

"I believe in God, it's people I don't believe in."

"Smart kid. You might have a future."

"I'm sorry about the ring," I said.

"Where is it, exactly?"

"In the woods behind Dickie Pudding's house."

"Yes, I'm acquainted with Dickie Pudding's father. Something tells me he isn't exactly pleased with people of my per-suasion."

The extent of Gladstein's intelligence on neighborhood matters always surprised me.

"That was the friend's father I was telling you about, the one that's in the KKK."

"Well, it's settled. If I go in the Pudding woods I'm likely to be lynched. Which means it's up to you to find the ring." Glad-stein rested the side of his head against his fingertips. He stayed that way a moment, prayerful, and then he said, "So your mother is an atheist."

Through the window I saw Snead's truck trundling into the lot.

"Here comes Snead," I said. "He told me he's coming to your house tonight."

Gladstein glanced absentmindedly towards the window and turned back, awaiting my reply. We were still staring back and forth when the prissy bell announced Snead's entry.

I bolted immediately, avoiding Snead's eyes, and ran to the Pudding woods. I searched high and low. I kicked aside leaves and turned over rocks. I traversed the entire system of paths. I stared cynically at the scampering squirrels: what if one had absconded with Gladstein's ring and buried it for the winter? I sat on a flattened tree trunk and observed the people sauntering along the road, on their daily trek to the shopping center—mainly kids. Then I heard the sound of high heels.

I straightened up.

Mom!

This was the end of one of her working Saturdays (she worked every other weekend), and now she was on her way home. I watched her figure pass, obscured by the trees. Her head was bent. Her lips were moving silently, preparing briefs and justifications for her life. Seeing her made me want to pray. I squeezed my eyes and saw an image of Gaylord's corpse instead.

I dashed out of the woods and fell in behind her. By the time I made it around the curve she had already turned on Stanley. She was ahead of me by the length of a football field.

Only a few people had ventured outside that day. Many were on vacation, and those with air-conditioning had found shelter in their dens and TV rooms. There would be no gauntlet to pass through, and for Mom's sake I was thankful. Poor Mom. She was the quiet Witcher. No one knew how to place her; hers was guilt by association. And yet she had committed the one unpardonable sin. She had spawned new Witchers. For all that, the better sort of people pitied her. They knew about her vocabulary, her mastery of show tunes. Many in the neighborhood attributed my good grades to her genes, to her influence.

I was coming up on her heels and preparing to call her name, but the sudden memory of the image of Gaylord's corpse slowed me down and made me not want to go home. The very idea of seeing Pop and Stan filled me with dread. What if Pop went ahead with it, what if he robbed Gladstein anyway?

After I passed the drainage ditch I veered off course and thrashed through the weeds all the way to Matson and walked along the side of the road. I could feel the traffic at my back. Occasionally a car would honk and some kid would shout at me as it flew by. I passed the front of the Pudding house, where Mr. Pudding was cutting a swath across his sloping lawn with his riding mower. He didn't return my wave.

I wound up at the laundry near Gladstein's store, the one I'd slept in the other night. This time dirty clothes were tumbling in the washers and people were coming in to fold and sort; but no one paid attention to me.

When it was dark I crossed over to the shopping center. Gladstein's Continental and Snead's truck had vanished from the lot. I peeked in the window of the jewelry store—still as a movie set. I trotted around and passed the sewing store. In the alley I took a position behind Gladstein's shop, on the grassy hill behind it. I rested my back against the chain-link fence. Soon a white lady came along, picking up bottles and throwing them in a bag. Then a black man passed through the alley singing "Cool Jerk" by the Capitols.

I sat until I grew hungry and then I ran to the vending machine in front of the gas station at Karen and Matson and bought a bag of peanuts and a Coke and brought 'em on back. I must have hung around until eleven—I stayed a long time, I know that. Eventually I could barely hold my eyes open and I was bored out of my mind. So I went on home. Mom and Pop were on the couch in the living room, watching TV.

Seeing Pop with his legs stretched across Mom's lap made my vigil seem quixotic, unwise. He was a poor sap uselessly quagmired in the sludge of domesticity, that's all. I almost felt a pang of sorrow for him. And then he gave me a slow-burning slant of the eyes.

"Where on earth have you been?" Mom said.

"Out."

"Well, no lie! Where did you go?"

"I needed to go somewhere and think."

"You were with Myra Joyner, weren't you?"

"Forget Myra Joyner."

Pop swung his legs away from Mom's lap and followed me down to the bedroom. I was worried he was coming to hit me, but I stayed cool. I switched on the overhead light and he closed the door behind us.

"You see I'm here."

"Okay," I said.

"I'm here, I ain't breaking into jewelry stores."

"Fine," I said.

"So your little fantasy didn't mean a thing. Your friend is safe, you see that."

"Yes sir."

"All right then. Just keep your mouth shut about what you think you know about me." He gave me one last evil glare and stepped out of the room.

I was on the bed, gazing at the shut door—even the door seemed disgusted with me.

My brother was gone and the dread night had passed. I was dead tired, and I wanted to be light-years away in sleep by the time Stan got home.

36

IN THE MORNING I found him at the table slurping cereal from his bowl. A news report came on the radio about the search for Gaylord, and Stan reached across the table and turned the radio off. He belched sonorously and Mom said, "Stop it, you pig."

Pop delivered a jab to my shoulder. "What's the word, sport."

"Nothing."

Stan slid back his chair.

"Where are you off to?" Mom said.

"The pool. You coming?" he asked me. I'd have happily taken a dip on this hot and humid day, but not with him. I told him no.

He headed out the back screen door, slamming it.

"Let's take a ride," Pop said.

"Where to?"

"To the park. I'll grab my sketchbook, I wanna do some drawings by the lake."

I shook my head. I didn't want to be seen with him in public. I thought he had quit drawing, anyway.

"Come on, don't be a stick-in-the-mud."

"I'm not feeling that well."

Pop kicked back his chair and left the room, irritated. Mom flicked her eyes towards the door, indicating some thought she was having.

A little solitude, that's all I needed. And yet the less I wanted to be around Pop and Stan the more they wanted to be around me.

In the afternoon Stan returned with Anya and asked if I wanted to go to the quarry. He meant the old granite quarry on an island in the river that could be reached via a footbridge. The quarry had flooded years ago and now locals hung out there on hot days, somersaulting in.

Anya was laughing against Stan's shoulder, making faces. Every time she looked at me she burst out laughing all over. Mom was keeping an eagle eye on her.

I nudged my toe against the rug.

Stan left the room.

"What's so funny?" Mom said.

"Nothing." Anya bit her lip.

Stan reappeared holding an orange juice carton.

"I hope you aren't drinking out of that," Mom said.

He swigged from the carton deliberately. "You coming to the quarry or not?"

"Mom told you not to do that."

He yanked Anya away with him. We heard the GTO fire up and rumble off and then Mom padded down the hall in her slippers. I sat on the sofa, staring through the window panel with the missing screen. Pop stepped in; he had been in the yard. He snapped his fingers as he passed through the room. He went to the kitchen, came back.

"Come on, let's take a ride."

"Where to?"

"It's Sunday, let's take a ride."

"Why, so you can give me a lecture?"

"What's wrong with you?"

I followed him outside. The Ford was glaring and broiling in the yard. We always kept a towel across the front seat to keep it from scorching us when we got in.

"I don't wanna go riding, it's too hot."

"Come on, we never do anything anymore."

I was scared of him and my brother and I wanted them to leave me alone. I was going to be a lone wolf from now on.

"I don't wanna go, Pop. Just let me not go."

"How'd you get to be such a pain in the ass, will you tell me that?"

I went inside and grabbed a Mark Twain book from my room and took it to the brackish creek and sat against a tree, reading. A yellow smell, sulfur or something, was emanating from the creek. The song of the insects swelled and receded. Chiggers were biting. I kept scratching red marks on my legs. An hour passed, and then I heard someone thrashing through the brush.

I looked up, and here came Stan with Anya.

"I thought you were going to the quarry," I said.

"Changed our minds."

Stan rolled a joint with quick, kneading fingers.

Anya fell next to me, out of breath. "What are you reading?"

I showed her the cover, *Pudd'nhead Wilson*.

"What's that about?"

"Fingerprinting."

"That's all?"

"It's about an amateur detective who takes people's fingerprints for fun and later he solves a murder because he has the prints of the guy that did it."

"What are you looking at me for?" Stan said.

"I'm not."

The insects sounded like they were laughing. Flies and mosquitoes buzzed around our ears.

Stan lit the joint and passed it to Anya. It smelled foul, sweet, sinister. I didn't like being around while they were smoking grass. I stood up and dusted the seat of my pants.

"Where you going? Come on, take a hit."

"No, I'm leaving."

Anya ballooned her cheeks, spat smoke, snatched my ankle. "Come on, Jack, don't go."

"I don't like being around that stuff."

"He's such a good boy," Stan sneered.

"So? It's sweet."

"Witchers ain't sweet."

Anya tugged at my ankle. "Come on, sit down."

I fell to a sitting position.

"Tell us more about your book."

"It's by Mark Twain. It's a detective story."

"Why are you interested in detective stories?" Stan said.

"I've always liked Mark Twain."

"Kid should be a librarian, at night he reads books under the covers with a flashlight."

"Wow, that's what they call being good in bed." Anya giggled.

"Who gets murdered in the book?" Stan said.

"The judge, but they blame it on these Italian twins who are passing through town. It was really a white guy who did the murder, except he's not white, he's black. He got switched in the cradle by his mom who's a slave and she put the judge's son in place of her own child and then he grows up thinking he's black. I've read it before," I explained to Anya, who was listening bewilderedly. "Back then even if you were one thirty-second part black they could sell you into slavery. Sometimes you couldn't tell the whites and slaves apart. There were people as white as you and me that got sold into slavery, that happened all the time."

I figured this would astonish them, but they just burst out laughing.

"Jack doesn't need drugs," Stan said.

"Come on, Jack, get high with us, this grass is so good."

"Tell the truth," Stan said. "Are you reading that book because of Gaylord?"

"What would Gaylord have to do with it?"

"Well, that's kind of a murder mystery, ain't it—I mean, what happened to him?"

"I don't know. You tell me." This came out far more sardonic than I intended. Stan and Anya picked up on it and a weird, stoned silence fell.

The singing of the insects faded away.

"Jack thinks I killed Gaylord."

I shook my head. I didn't want him thinking things like that.

"Tell Anya," he said, "tell her what you think."

"I don't like talking to you when you're high on grass," I said.

"You're such a pussy, you don't even know what being high is like."

"Hey, be good, you two. The vibrations are getting weird."

"Why don't you tell her how I killed Gaylord," Stan said. "Play the detective, go on, pretend you're whatever his name is. Pudd'nhead."

I got up to leave and he grabbed my arm. "Where do you think you're going?"

"Let me go," I told him.

"I'll let you go, but you have to stay, you can't leave." His face was so close I could smell his breath. He had head-butted me a couple times, and I thought he was about to do it now. Once he let go I had to struggle against an impulse to dash through the brambles.

I sat on the ground.

"Don't fight, you two," Anya said. "Peace, remember? It's about peace."

"Shut up, Anya, butt out of it."

She seemed shocked. She drew herself up and her mouth fell open and stayed there. This is the typical facial arrangement of those who are wasted (I was beginning to know these things), but something like understanding was struggling into her vacancy. She gazed at a fixed spot before her eyes. I don't know, maybe no one had told her to shut up before. She looked scared and hurt, and for a second I thought she was going to cry.

Stan, meanwhile, kept nodding behind his sunglasses. There was no getting to his eyes.

All three of us were very quiet. And then Anya rose. She placed her palms flat out in front of her as though calling a halt to some proceeding.

"I'm going home," she said.

"Why?"

"I need to go meditate."

"Like Yogi Bear?"

"Don't laugh at me, Stan, I'm really upset."

"What for?"

"I don't like the vibration here. You guys are acting weird."

"What are you talking about? Come back here."

But she leapt across the creek and climbed the wooded rise that led to the civilization of the Taylor household.

37

THAT LEFT ME ALONE with my brother and the laughing insects.

"Bummer," he said, "I better go calm her down." But he didn't leave, he just leaned against a tree.

"What's she so upset about?" I said.

I knew exactly why she was upset, because my brother was a psycho, but I had decided to mimic the kind of thinking Stan used in situations calling for sensitivity and insight. I was hoping it might keep me from getting my ass kicked.

"Well, I tell you," Stan said.

He didn't say anything else.

His sunglasses were like doorways into dark rooms. He turned them towards me and I had no way of knowing what was in there. I kept hearing all these insects, flies, crickets, gnats, bees, wasps. Add to that the roar of jet fighters leaving vapor trails in the sky, the traffic on Matson, the appliances and the air conditioners and the window fans and the power lines.

An old spider rattled across my flip-flop and I shook it off.

"You never told me," Stan said.

"Told you what?"

"How you think I killed Gaylord."

"I never said you killed Gaylord."

"Yeah, but you think too loud."

The sunglasses tilted away. I couldn't tell where he was looking.

"What do you think, did I use a gun or a knife?"

"I never said you did anything of the sort."

He grinned; moved closer. "Let me tell you something you oughta know. I saw Gaylord right before he disappeared. That very afternoon. Me and Anya were driving past his house and he saw us coming and he waved us to a stop."

"Really? Wow, I didn't know that," I said, gushing to allay the danger.

"I know, I'm telling you. He leaned in the window and said he wanted to make peace. He said he was tired of all the anger. He gave me his hand to shake. And I told him I might think about it. If he was good. That's what I said, I said he had to be good."

"Really?"

"Go ask Deputy Dawg, he knows. He's already asked me about it. Whole neighborhood was watching through their windows, seems like."

"So y'all made friends."

"Hell no. I only told him that so I could take him by surprise the next time. I wanted to make him think he had a chance."

"Did you see him again?"

"If I did, I'm the last one, right?"

"Then you didn't," I said.

"I never said I didn't."

He still had that evil grin going. The darkness of his glasses turned in my direction and he nudged his chin for me to come on over.

"Come here," he said.

"I don't wanna come there."

"Okay, I'll come to you."

He came and sat beside me. He made a big production about it, sighing and groaning while he lowered himself. He picked up a stick and twiddled it between his knees. I shot a look at the path that led out of there, but running was pretty much out of the question.

Stan leaned close to my ear. "I hear you know my secret."

"I don't know any secrets."

"Anya told me she told you. Like, you know I wasn't at her house when Gaylord disappeared."

"That's none of my business. I never asked her anything. I can't help what Anya says, what she says is none of my business."

"But you're my brother, right? You go steady with what's-his-name's sister. Plus Deputy Dawg has been coming around and asking his questions. I would think that might make it your business."

"I'm not gonna say anything, don't worry about it."

Stan tossed the stick. It twirled in the air and made a splat when it hit the sulfurous creek. And then we heard a gurgling sound as if some monster had emerged from the turgid deep to devour it. Stan laughed silently in appreciation of nature's dark comedy. His shoulders moved up and down.

He turned his dark glasses towards me. "You know damn well I'd kill you if you said anything. If it's the last thing on earth I did. I swear to God, I would fucking rub you out."

"I would never say anything to anyone, you know that. Why are you acting this way?"

I saw two of me in his sunglasses. Which might have been Gaylord's last vision: two Gaylords, choking and dying, one for each lens. On the other hand, who knows, maybe my brother hadn't hurt a single soul. It's just he was crazy enough to enjoy it that other people suspected he did.

"Hey, little brother. We're friends, right?"

"Of course we're friends."

He pinched the collar of my T-shirt and yanked me close. "We damn well better be friends."

He let go and we sat and listened to the laughing of nature.

"You know, if I put your head into that creek water you'd be dead in five seconds, damn thing's so full of pollution. It's those damn factories and plants you see out there on the interstate when you drive past. They pump their fucking chemicals in the river and then that shit gets in our creek and we can't enjoy it anymore. Look at that goddamn water, it's like acid."

I shook my head. "It's bad, it looks bad."

"Corrode your fucking face off, that's what it would do."

That wasn't a prospect I wanted to entertain.

"I wonder if Anya's okay," I said.

"Fucking businessmen, goddamn companies, they don't give a shit about Mother Nature. And you know damn well Mother Nature's gonna get her revenge someday."

He laughed at the thought of it.

I nodded at his sagacity and spied the path that led out of the clearing. I wanted to go home so bad I could taste it. I wanted Mom to hold me. I didn't care if I was thirteen.

Stan didn't say much else. I suppose he was too wrapped up in Mother Nature and her implacable ways.

I was waiting for him to let me go. I opened my book and stared at a page, and he, next to me, tilted his head to read along.

After a while he hoisted himself, stretching and groaning.

"Wanna smoke a joint with me?"

"Nah, I'm too young."

He burst out laughing. "Shit no, you're exactly the right age. I wish I had started turning on when I was your age. People should turn on early, man. We wouldn't have so much trouble in the world if everybody got high. Look at that shit in the creek, just because those creeps can't stop making their money. That's all they think about, their booze and their cars and their country clubs. People don't have no fucking conscience."

"I know. I agree. But I don't want to smoke grass just yet. Maybe next year."

Stan let out a yawn and said, "Well, I reckon I oughta find Anya. What was she so upset about?"

"I think it's because you told her to shut up."

"I didn't tell her to shut up. When did I tell her to shut up?"

"I thought that's what I heard, probably I was wrong."

Stan nodded, looked around.

"Well, kid, you take it easy. And remember, if you say anything to Mom and Pop I'll carve your eyes out. Think about that whenever you get the urge."

"Okay, Stan. Don't worry about me."

"I ain't worried, believe me."

He leapt across the yellow creek and strutted up the rise, leaving me to marvel over the graciousness of his personality, his remarkable joie de vivre.

I got out of those woods as fast as my legs would carry me. I ran back to the house and arrived covered in sweat. Mom was coming out of her bedroom, fresh from a nap.

I sat on the carmine sofa. My arms were crossed. I stared straight ahead.

She sat beside me.

All along I'd been thinking Gaylord would never, ever get in a car Stan was driving, even if he was hitchhiking. That had been my last hope. But now I knew Stan had led him to believe that they'd made peace. Which meant Gaylord just might have climbed in.

"Did Stan go to the quarry?" Mom asked.

I didn't say anything. I had already decided never to say another word. Not ever. To anyone.

"Where's your father?"

In fact, the Ford was not in the driveway, but I wasn't going to be the one to tell her. She could go check for herself.

She peeped out the door. She came back.

"Do you want a sandwich?"

I followed her into the kitchen and sat at the table with my arms crossed.

"Cat got your tongue?"

She fixed me a cheese and peanut butter sandwich, my favorite, and sat catty-corner from me.

"Would you massage my neck like you did the other day?"

I stood.

"Finish your sandwich first."

After I finished eating I dug my fingers in her neck, flexing and unflexing them. Mom rolled her head and told me I was a good boy. I didn't say a word. I stuck to my mute policy.

Later, when Pop came home, he tried to make conversation. I just stared at him with my arms crossed.

"He's not speaking anymore," Mom explained.

"Not speaking!"

Pop's whole world was falling apart. Mom wasn't speaking to him either, and she didn't even have a mute policy.

"Why is he not speaking?"

"Ask him."

"How can I if he won't tell me?"

I got in bed and clenched my eyes tight. I was hoping I might fall asleep before Stan got home. Every sound I heard reminded me of his imminent approach. I was listening for noises I didn't want to hear. Whenever a car turned on the road my heart stopped. My ears would follow it as it drove past. If Mom or Pop rattled something in the kitchen I attended to it with the greatest alarm. It was no use: the only thing that might possibly put an end to my dread would be the appearance of what I dreaded.

Finally he came home. I listened to him rustling about in the dark, climbing up to the bed.

Now, maybe, I could fall asleep.

As I was drifting off he called out, "Good night, kid."

"Good night," I called back.

That meant infringing against my mute policy, but I was afraid he'd kill me if I didn't answer.

38

WE WERE INTO AUGUST, and still no Gaylord. Weeks had
passed since he'd disappeared. Cicada season was over. But I
could hear them anyway. Their song belonged to the hum behind the humming of the world. It was enough to make a
person crazy.

I'd go see Mom at the Ben Franklin, say hello to Mr. Harris,
visit with Mr. Gladstein, knock on the Pudding door, search
with chastised heart for the abandoned ring; perch on the back
porch with my arm around Rusty, pounding his ribs. Or I'd go
to the woods, the different ones, the woods where Stan and
Anya didn't go, and smoke cigarettes and watch the other kids
messing at the creek. They didn't like my being there, yet they
dared not taunt me. I was the bogeyman of my age group: Stan
Witcher's brother. Nobody would speak to me, which wasn't
unusual; but lately they had taken to nodding with a sort of
dour respect whenever I showed up.

I would sit under a tree, doing my best not to think my thoughts. And yet the thoughts kept coming: memories of my brother, like how when I was nine or ten and the boys at school had started to pick on me he took me to the yard and taught me how to defend myself, showed me how to hit, duck and wrestle, how to kick boys in the balls. One time he made me punch him in the lip until he bled. That's how he coached me past my squeamishness, he bled for me. And he'd bled for me in other ways. God help anyone who taunted or threatened Jack Witcher. It got to the point that I would never tell him if someone crossed me. You better believe, a lot of kids owed their lives to me without knowing it, simply because I had kept my mouth shut.

We Witchers each had a reason to hold Stan in our hearts. Take the way he was with my mother. It was just harmless joshing when he told her how sexy she was, but who else ever told Mom she was sexy? With Pop, Stan shared adeptness in the manly arts, like fixing engines, punching guys and seducing gals. On such recondite matters they might hold forth for hours, going well into the dark of night. Occasionally on an evening they would up and take off, leaving me at home, so they could indulge in what Mom called "boys' night out." What did that mean? She assured me when I was old enough I'd be invited to go along, and I used to sit at home invoking images of dirty movies and tumbling dice and girls wearing pasties. I couldn't wait to come of age, which according to Pop's notion of legality meant I had to be sixteen.

Families live on loyalty more than love, and it wasn't fear

alone that made me keep my mouth shut. I could never forget that Stan had bled for me. And yet I was terrified of him. He and Pop had made some kind of pact, or that's how it seemed, and I had a suspicion Pop knew what Anya had told me. I had become the enemy, in Pop's and Stan's eyes. They shared a repertoire of gestures, winks and nudges. Whenever they were in a room together their words, even when addressed to Mom or me, seemed to hold implications they alone could decipher.

One day, when the Witcher men were at home and Mom was at work and Anya was "on the rag" (as Stan put it), Pop and my brother, with remarkable composure considering that the search for Gaylord was still on and Stan was still the only suspect in his disappearance, asked me to go to Fairglade with them. Fairglade was a park in the center of town with a tiny petting zoo and a bamboo forest.

Pop had his sketchbook tucked under his arm. His hair was dampened and slicked back and he looked almost sweet, like a child.

Every time Pop and Stan invited me to go someplace with them I imagined being tied to the pissy mattress in the shack off Baskin Road. I remembered the mad humming around the shack and the living thing inside when Gladstein drove me over that time.

The minute they weren't looking I shot out the door. I headed for the woods, the good woods where Stan and Anya didn't go, where the creek didn't smell like sulfur, where I had a private nook in the trunk of a tree. I sat and watched the minnows curve through the water like highway arrows. The day before, some kids had tried to dam the creek with bricks and blocks of wood and since then the water had broken through. It was still dammed near the remnants, and I went down there with a stick and toppled the dam to release the backup and watched as the blocks twirled downstream and came to rest against the left bank. I wiped my fingers, pulled out a Winston. The humming was barely audible when you weren't listening, but otherwise it was louder than a freight train.

Car doors slammed on the road above. Pop's shrill whistle (he used two fingers) sounded through the trees. Stan came down the path and stopped fifty feet up.

"Come on, we're going to Fairglade!"

"How did you know I was here?"

"I didn't, I just came down to check."

"I don't wanna go to Fairglade."

"Pop says you have to."

"Why?"

It was out of family character to be ordered to do something if it wasn't necessary. I reluctantly climbed to my feet and followed Stan up the path. Through the trees I could see the road and the battered Ford and someone moving beside it. When I got closer I spotted Pop. He was pacing beside the car. His hands were clasped behind him. When he saw me he nodded. "I want to pose you in front of the bamboo forest so I can draw you."

"Why don't you get Stan to pose?"

"He's too ugly." They laughed, wanting me to laugh with them.

The Ford was idling. I was at the edge of the woods. I didn't want to die in the bamboo forest among the stalks.

"Hop in," Pop said.

He had his sleeves rolled up. Pop never wore short sleeves, not even in summer.

"I don't want to go."

"We'll only be an hour or so. I'll drop you off here when we're through."

I started thinking about the hot shack and the pissy mattress and the cicadas. I saw myself lying in all that stink with a knife in my chest. Meanwhile the gnats and the mosquitoes and the bees and the flies and the wasps kept buzzing. Add to that the airplanes and the jet fighters leaving vapor trails and the helicopters and the lawn mowers on Lewis Street and the vacuum cleaners and the other appliances and the fans and the air conditioners and the traffic north on Cherokee and the traffic south on Matson and the trains on the tracks beside the river and the chemical and pharmaceutical plants next to the interstate pumping pollution into the air and the barking of neighborhood dogs and the frogs croaking along the banks of the creek and the snapping and buzzing from the satellites circling the earth and the cicadas in my mind that never stopped singing.

I broke into a run. I dashed past Stan and swerved around Pop (he was reaching out to snatch me) and hightailed it between the houses until I came to Lewis Street. Pop and Stan were hollering behind me; the doors to the battered Ford slammed shut and the car got in gear. At the corner I swung right and took the shortcut and came out on Livingstone. I was already winded and cramping up, but I kept running as hard as I could. I headed along Stanley and took the road behind Dickie Pudding's house and reached Myra Street and slowed to a walk, holding my side and looking back. When I got to the break in the fence I turned into the shopping center and mounted the terraced walkway just as the Ford pulled into the lot.

I started running again. Some old lady who was window-shopping gave me a stern look and told me to slow down, and when I got to the Ben Franklin I busted in and leaned against the counter, panting.

Mom said, "What on earth!" She was all embarrassed because a customer was with her.

I couldn't talk. I shook my head.

The Ford pulled up and I pointed through the window. "They're making me go to Fairglade with 'em and I don't want to. Tell 'em I don't have to."

The customer picked up her bag and left with a smile and a shake of the head for the vagaries of children. Pop dashed in, exasperated and glaring at me. "Will somebody tell me what is going on?"

I glanced at Mom.

"He says he doesn't want to go to Fairglade."

"All right, fine, he doesn't have to. But why is he running from me?"

"He's upset, let him be."

"What's he so upset about?"

"I don't know, just let him be."

"Well, damn it, he doesn't have to act like I'm a leper."

Pop looked self-conscious, as though he'd unduly exposed himself by coming in the store. And maybe he had.

"Can I see you a minute?" he said to Mom. She left the store and they stood on the sidewalk.

Mr. Harris came walking up and said, "Hello, Jack."

"Fuck you," I said.

"Excuse me?"

His brow wrinkled. He went to the register and stared blankly into the drawer. A lady with palsy approached and placed a few items on the counter. In his bafflement, Harris had neglected to inquire how she was doing. Outside, Pop and Mom were moving their lips. Occasionally they would toss a glance towards the store.

Mr. Harris rang up the items for the lady with palsy, and Pop went back to the car. Mom held the door for the palsied lady, who stopped to say a few palsied words.

Behind them the Ford was backing out and Stan's sunglasses were moving in reverse with the car. Mom was patting the palsied lady's hand, nodding.

She came in.

"Your son just swore at me," Mr. Harris said.

"Don't pay attention to him, he's upset at something."

"Well, so am I," he said. He strutted off, showing his indignation. He kicked an empty box in the aisle.

Mom watched him leave. She turned to me and said, "I have two hours before I get off."

"I'll go see Mr. Gladstein and when it's time for you to leave I'll walk you home."

After that I went up the steps to the jewelry store, feeling sheepish and defiant at the same time. What a mess I had become! Who was I?

It must have shown on my face. Gladstein pulled a stool from the back room and let me sit behind the counter. When customers came in I was allowed to unlock the display cases; he showed me how to work the register.

After a couple of hours the prissy bell tinkled. Mom had come to pick me up.

"Hi, Margaret."

"Hello, Moses."

My ears pricked up.

I swung my head to check out Gladstein. He was leering at my mom with that hot-sausage-demon grin of his.

"Just coming to get my boy," she said.

"Came to the right place, huh?"

He gave me a wink, and Mom allowed him a smile. I was looking back and forth at them.

39

JUST WHEN, I wanted to know, had Mom and Mr. Gladstein started calling each other by their first names?

"His name is Moses," she told me. "Isn't that funny? God must have given him the Ten Commandments." She laughed out loud at her little joke.

We were on Myra Street, walking home.

"That doesn't answer my question," I said.

"What's your problem? We've been having lunch at the drugstore."

"Does Pop know?"

"Of course he does. Moses is a friend from work."

"You don't work in the same place, how can he be a friend from work? And how come you never told me?"

"I didn't realize it would be so important."

"Not important! Mr. Gladstein is my friend."

She laughed. "Well, I'm not trying to steal him from you. I

like Moses," she said. "He's different from the people around here, he's not so judgmental."

We walked quietly for a while. I kept looking back over my shoulder.

"What's wrong with you, you're acting like the Fugitive."

She meant the TV series.

"I think I might be getting an ulcer. Can't you get ulcers from worrying too much?"

"Are you worrying too much?"

"Do you ever hear cicadas in your head?"

"What?"

"I think Pop and Stan want to kill me."

She didn't say anything. She walked beside me thinking about what I'd said.

"If anything happens, if I disappear, that's what happened, they killed me."

She hugged me close. "All this has been too hard on you. You're too young for all this stress."

We walked along without saying anything, and then she said, "We're good people, we are not trash. My parents didn't raise me to be trash and I didn't raise you to be trash."

"I'm not crazy."

"I never said you were crazy. This has been too stressful for you. I wish I could protect you from the ugly side of life."

"I wish you could too. But you can't. And Stan is crazy, and I have to sleep in the same room with him. The night Gaylord disappeared he came home at six in the morning. I heard him in the bathroom and he had the sink and the tub running and he was tearing something up in there and he kept flushing the toilet over and over. And Anya told me he wasn't even with her that night, she doesn't know where he was or what he was doing when Gaylord disappeared. He went out in her car about the same time Gaylord was hitchhiking and Gaylord might have got in the car with Stan because he thought they made friends."

She just blinked at me. "What are you talking about?" she said.

I don't know why I was telling her. Maybe it was because she had acknowledged how hard it was on me. I couldn't carry this anymore. My brother might kill me and she needed to know.

"Stan told me he saw Gaylord earlier that day and they shook hands and made friends."

"Are you saying Anya told you that Stan wasn't with her that night?"

"Yeah. And when he came back to her house he was all cut up and bloodied."

My mother gaped at the horizon and back at me. Her darkest fears, everything she secretly believed, it was all passing before her eyes.

"God damn them!" she said.

I don't think I'd ever heard her swear before.

"What are they lying for? What are they hiding?"

"I think he did something to Gaylord."

"Don't say that."

"Well, how do you explain it?"

"I don't know how to explain it."

We were passing the Pudding woods and I took her hand and pulled her in.

"Where are you taking me?"

"You have to help me look for my ring. It's here somewhere."

"What ring?"

"The one Mr. Gladstein gave me."

"Can't we look some other time?"

I kicked at the earth. I dug at the dirt with a stick. Mom wasn't helping. She was standing in the woods, wearing a dress. Down at the Pudding house Dickie and his brother were staring. Dickie came on up.

"What are you doing?"

"Looking for a ring. If you find a ring in here it's mine, okay? It looks like a diamond but it's not."

Dickie watched me uncertainly. He stood next to Mom. They both had their mouths open.

"Jack, let's go home, you can look later."

"Give me five more minutes."

Dickie watched for a while and then he said he had to go.

The cicada song, that humming in the world, kept playing, and I could hear the traffic on Matson. Trucks flew past and shook the rafters of the Pudding house.

. I came upon an exposed root that belonged to an oak and tugged until I got the spine slightly out of the ground.

I peeked underneath.

"When did Anya tell you Stan wasn't with her?"

"One day when we took a walk. And now Stan knows she

told me and he said he'd kill me if I told anyone. So you can't tell him. Because if he finds out I'll be dead for sure."

"Stan is not going to hurt you."

"Mom, he killed Gaylord."

This time she didn't deny it.

I kept scraping with my feet and brushing leaves to the side. Jet fighters were leaving vapor trails; sometimes they're up so high you can hear them even when you can't see them. There'll be a sonic boom and the whole world will shiver.

Insects were buzzing, little balls of mites were tussling next to my head.

Mom took me by the arm.

"I am not standing here a moment longer. I want to go home and get out of this dress."

"You can't tell Stan what I told you," I said.

She didn't answer.

We followed the curve in the road that led to Stanley Street.

"We can't keep telling the police lies," she said, "they're trying to solve a crime."

"You didn't tell them a lie, you told them what you believed."

"No, I sat right there and listened while your pop lied, and I knew he was lying. It's just I didn't see what difference it made at the time. I thought Stan was at Anya's that night."

"Well, he wasn't, he was out murdering Gaylord."

"Will you stop saying that?"

"It's the truth. And he'll kill me too if you say anything. Remember that. If he kills me it's your fault."

"My God, my two sons, the boys I gave birth to."

"You don't believe in God."

"I can't believe what I'm hearing. All this talk about killing. You're my baby boys!" She burst into tears.

"If we had the ring it might've protected us, that's what Mr. Gladstein said."

"Oh, he's as crazy as the rest of you."

I patted her back.

"What are we going to do," she said. "We can't keep living a lie like this."

"Sure we can. Mom, don't tell anyone, please, I'll get killed."

We came to the house and saw the Ford in the driveway. Pop and Stan hadn't gone to Fairglade after all. But what would be the point in going to Fairglade if I didn't come along to be strangled and left in a ravine?

And then I noticed something. The flag on the mailbox was up!

"You go on in," I told Mom.

As soon as she was out of sight I grabbed the note and stuck it in my pants.

I went inside. I heard Mom and Pop in their bedroom. I peeped into our room, the room I shared with my brother.

He wasn't there.

I snuck to the kitchen. I took the butcher knife from the drawer. When I got to the bedroom I slid it underneath my pillow. How could I bear my brother's hard eyes and grin? How could I plunge a blade into his heart? Doubt made my legs grow wobbly. I gazed about the room, searching for a way out. The night at the window grew black. I raised the screen and jutted my head out.

I read Myra's letter. It was terse and unromantic, full of business. She said she needed to see me. Would I be in the Pudding woods the next afternoon at one?

I stuck the note between the pillow and the pillowcase. I lay on the bed and listened.

Snead didn't come to visit that night. I wondered if it was over between him and Pop. I wondered if I had destroyed their friendship. Maybe Pop could no longer look him in the eyes. That would be another reason for Pop and Stan to murder me.

Atop the dresser the oscillating fan swiveled on its pivot. The thing had developed a rattle.

I practiced pulling the butcher knife from under my pillow so if I needed it in a hurry I'd know to grab the handle and not the blade.

Around eleven Stan came home. He stayed in the living room with Mom and Pop for a long time. I prayed Mom's "Help" prayer. After a while I tried chanting Gladstein's syllable.

I didn't want to know my brother. I wanted a new Pop.

I engaged in a fantasy of coming home to Mom and Mr. Gladstein instead of Mom and Pop and of Gladstein regaling us with jokes while Mom tolerantly listened. I could hear his booming voice in my mind. And then I remembered. If Gladstein were my pop I'd have to live in Jefferson Ward.

I heard footsteps.

Stan was just outside the door. The handle turned, stopped.

"What?" he called.

Mom's voice was speaking from down the hall. I reached under the pillow and touched the handle of the butcher knife. Stan said something back and the doorknob turned and he came in the room.

He took off his shirt. He climbed to the bed above me.

I had my hand on the knife, under the pillow.

Stan was quiet.

Then his voice penetrated the dark.

"You little prick, you told."

I felt the blood in my legs go cold. I breathed in; held it in. Fear spread like a dark wash over my body.

We lay in perfect silence. The oscillating fan rattled and blew and revolved away. That's all I could hear, the rattle, the electric blowing. An hour, two hours passed. It felt like forever.

I heard Stan stir. I gripped the knife. I held it under the sheet, next to my leg.

He slid down to the far edge of the bed and hopped to the floor. I saw him through the dark. He was putting on his shirt.

The bedroom door opened and he left.

I strained to hear. The front door to the house creaked open.

I crawled to the window. Stan was passing across the yard, heading in the direction of Anya's house.

I tiptoed out to the hall, opened Mom and Pop's bedroom door. Their window fan was blowing and it was hard to hear anything but the roar.

I hoarsely whispered, "Mom!"

Her head lifted.

I backed out and pulled the door closed.

She came to the hallway, clutching her robe.

"What are you doing with that knife?"

"Protecting myself. You told. I asked you not to and you did it anyway."

"Jack, he's not going to hurt you."

"I trusted you."

"We can't just let him lie like that."

"So what, are you gonna call the cops now?"

"I want Stan to tell the police. I'm giving him the chance."

"He just left the house," I said.

"He's not here?"

"I'm afraid of what he might do to me. Can I sleep in your room?"

"Go to bed, I'll sit with you."

"You have to stay all night. That's what you get for telling. Plus I'll never trust you again."

"Fine," she said. "Give me the knife."

She came into my room and sat in the chair next to the desk.

"When I fall asleep you can't leave, you have to stay."

"My God," she said, "my crazy sons."

After some time passed she said, "Your brother didn't do anything. He was afraid, that's all. He didn't want to be arrested for something he didn't do." She was quiet awhile longer. Then she said, "I should think I know my own son. If I thought for one minute he hurt that boy I wouldn't be able to live with myself."

I didn't say anything.

She stayed all night. I know because I was awake. At one point she started to leave and I raised my head to challenge her.

"I'm just going to the bathroom," she said.

The fan rattled and oscillated air across my face.

"For God's sake," she added.

"You don't believe in God," I said.

When the morning came Stan was still gone.

40

ONCE MORE, for the last time, I went to the Pudding woods to await the coming of Myra. Dickie Pudding kept peeking out of his back door. After a while he strolled up to where I was.

"How come you're always hanging around my woods?"

"Don't worry about it."

"It's my property, I have a right to ask."

"Suck my dick," I said.

He left and I killed time by trying to find the ring. But I was too demoralized. Obviously I'd never find it, and now it seemed stupid to have tossed it over my shoulder. I'd done it only for effect, to impress Myra.

I was jumpy from the night before. In my pocket was a pocketknife I'd filched out of the desk drawer, not nearly as effective as a butcher knife but still good to jab someone's eyes with. While I was walking to the woods I'd hugged the shoulder of the road in case I had to make a dash through the yards. Now I was listening for the rumble of Anya's GTO.

Myra already seemed to belong to a remote time in my childhood. The last I saw her she was on TV, weeping next to her mother. Now, as she came around the curve and stepped into the woods, her cheeks were dry, her face was clean and dignified. Rusty charged forth to greet me and Myra smiled a smile that said, "I have experienced great tragedy and my feelings for you are compromised by bitterness and agony, but I am willing to bestow this wary sign of regard."

Then she flailed her arms and leapt back, believing some invisible thing was attacking her. I'd never known anyone as goofy in the woods as she was.

Finally she came on over.

"Hi, Jack. I'll bet you were surprised to get my note."

"I thought you had told me good-bye forever."

"This time it might have to be. But I wanted to give you something."

She held out the ring.

"Myra!"

"I came back and found it. I was walking home that day and it kept driving me crazy that you'd thrown it away. I couldn't believe you would do such a thing."

"I've been here almost every day looking for it."

"I know, Kathy told me. She passed by one day and saw you. She said you were practically tearing the woods to pieces."

"Keep it, I don't want it."

Myra regarded the jewel fondly in her palm. I was reminded of those ads where they pose a blonde in front of a velvety backdrop and she's looking at her ring in raptures while thinking about some jerk whose beaming face hovers in a circle in the corner.

"No," she said, "I can't, I just can't."

"To remember me with."

"I'm not sure I want to remember you, to be perfectly honest."

"Come on, don't forget me, I didn't have anything to do with . . ."

I didn't finish, but she knew what I meant.

"You're his brother. Every time I think about you I'm going to remember."

"I guess," I said.

She handed me the ring and I dropped it in my pocket without looking at it.

"Anyway," she said.

She stared down at the Pudding house. "How's Dickie doing?"

"He doesn't talk to me anymore. No one around here does."

"I'm sorry," she said.

"It doesn't matter, I never had a lot of friends."

And then out of the blue she got all teary and her face flushed. "I know, and that makes me so mad! It doesn't make any sense! I always argue with people, I tell them, 'It doesn't matter that he's a Witcher, he's smart and he's nice and we should be nice to him.'"

"You tell people that?"

She nodded, all choked up. "I still think that. You can't help who your family is."

"But my family . . . I mean—" I looked around. "My mom is nice," I said.

Myra nodded. "She seems nice, it's just the way she looks."

We were wringing our hands, awkward in farewell.

"Anyway," she said.

We both swung our heads towards the Pudding house at the same time, as though for an impromptu snapshot . . . and then her tiny chest heaved, remembering that the occasion was sad.

"My mother is right pretty when she puts on her makeup," I said.

"Oh, she *is* pretty, she's just different, that's all."

I patted her arm for being nice. I suppose that's why I made my decision. I was dead anyway, and now I knew Myra had defended me against my enemies. In spite of everything she had believed in me. I had to keep one thing in mind—this was Myra, not just anyone. And I knew from books what a man owes a woman. There is a crazy nobility in attacking one's doom, if it's done for the right reason. Just as it's crazy and noble to believe what's written in books.

"There's something you need to know, Myra, and I'm not gonna ask you to keep it a secret."

I paused, waiting for her to look at me.

"I found out something about that night. My brother's been telling the cops he was at Anya's house and that's what Anya's been saying too. But we were out walking one day and she told me Stan wasn't with her the night Gaylord disappeared. He drove off in her car around six-thirty, which is about the time Gaylord started hitchhiking on Cherokee. Anya said Stan didn't come back 'til four in the morning. She wasn't with him during that time and she doesn't know where he was or what he was doing." I didn't mention that he was all cut up and bloodied.

Myra's face was a blank. I don't think what I had said registered. She was preoccupied with other thoughts.

"You should tell your parents," I instructed her.

"Tell them what?"

"You don't understand, do you? Stan lied about where he was the night Gaylord disappeared. He might have done something. No one knows where he was or what he was doing."

"You mean he wasn't at that girl's house?"

"That's what I'm trying to tell you."

"How long have you known this?"

"I don't know. Awhile. I didn't know at first, but one day Anya told me."

Myra's face when she was about to cry screwed up gradually, so that you could chart the progress of her emotion. It was like watching a bowl fill with water. Her face grew sadder and sadder until finally it was the very image of derangement and grief.

The next thing I knew she had landed a punch on my chest.

"Damn you, Jack Witcher! You knew all the time and you didn't say anything?"

She hit me again. Then she began to thrash blindly through the bushes, bawling and weeping. She didn't know which way to turn. Nettles and branches were scratching her limbs. Uselessly she thrashed her arms.

"Myra!"

I caught up with her and pulled her around.

"I'm sorry! Stan said he'd kill me if I told."

Rusty remained in the clearing, watching.

"He killed my brother, that fucking asshole!" Myra pounded my shoulders.

"I'm sorry, I should have said something, it was wrong of me. But I was afraid."

"You're a Witcher, that's what you are."

Sobs wracked her frail body and she stopped and sucked in air. I thought she was about to choke and I touched her arm to steady her. And then she cried out and hit me again.

She slapped me, three times on the face.

And then I began to cry too.

We faced each other, weeping. Her face was all screwed up and so was mine. We kept looking at each other, blinking and wiping our noses and bawling our eyes out.

Finally she came into my arms and let me hold her. I patted her back until she calmed down, and I said, "You should tell your parents what I told you."

She nodded.

There were sounds on the road. Someone was passing, but I didn't care, and neither did Myra. Or maybe she didn't notice. Her sobs were so loud I imagine the whole neighborhood could hear them. I'm sure the Puddings had got their fill.

"If they arrest my brother it'll be fine with me," I said.

"I hate your brother."

Her tears were making me wet.

She drew away and said, "I'm going to tell my parents what you just said."

"I want you to."

"What will happen to you?"

"To me? Why would anything happen? School will start and I'll go and people will make fun of me. I'm used to that. But you know what, Myra? I have a feeling things are gonna get better when I'm older."

"Not me, I'll never be happy again," she said.

Even then, even with my limited thirteen-year-old perspective, that struck me as a dismal thought for a girl to have. But it was true. I believed her. And I, Jack Witcher, I conceived at that moment a rage against my brother that has never quite left me, not even now. I wanted to hit him, punch him, kick his balls, claw his eyes, bite his ears, maybe cut him with the butcher knife.

I said, "You do what you have to do, Myra."

"I'm sorry, Jack. I wish we could be friends."

She pulled up the tail of her shirt and wiped her eyes, and I wiped mine on my arm. Our tears were more or less finished.

We gazed at each other for a long time, the way people can when they have cried together. Then she came close and kissed my cheek.

"Mom knows I'm here. I have to tell her everywhere I go now. She made Kathy follow me."

Through the trees, where the curve began, someone, Kathy I suppose, was hanging around beside the road.

"I can't stay any longer. I'm sorry, I have to go now."

"Okay. I understand."

"Come on, Rusty," she said.

But Rusty stayed.

I went home to fight my brother. Maybe to kill him.

41

THAT WAS THE DAY I found out Stan was on the lam, after I got home and came to the conclusion that we'd been robbed. Then I saw that everything I owned was accounted for. Only Stan's stuff was missing: his clothes, his stereo player, his James Brown records. The essential things.

I called Mom at the Ben Franklin and she told me to go to the Taylors' to check if he was there. I cut through the woods, jumped the creek and surveyed the Taylor yard. There weren't any cars in the driveway and the house looked shut.

When I got back I phoned Mom and she said she would try to leave work early. Then I sat on the carmine sofa and waited. And then I got spooked. What if Stan hadn't gone on the lam? What if he came home? I pulled the butcher knife out of the kitchen drawer and returned to the sofa.

I peeked through the window. Rusty, lying in the yard, inquisitively raised his head.

Mom came home at the usual time. By then Pop was home, and I took both of them to our bedroom.

"I don't know, maybe we did get robbed," Pop said. "Why would a kid take his stereo with him if he was leaving?"

"It's portable," I said, "you can pack it up and carry it."

"But why would he just leave without saying anything?"

"Look, Pop, all my stuff is here. What robber would come straight to this room and take only his stuff? And then not go to your room?"

"True." Pop shook his head, thinking. "But would he be running through the streets with his clothes and his stereo player? He can't be carrying all that stuff, can he?"

"I'll bet Anya helped. Probably they loaded his stuff in the GTO."

"We should go to the Taylors', maybe they're home by now."

We got in the Ford and drove over.

Basil's Dodge was not in the driveway, but there was Tillie's Cadillac, still warm and ticking under the hood. We parked on the street and Tillie came to the door, newly coiffed and wearing a fine pearl necklace. She eyed our Ford with distaste and quickly appraised Mom's dress, but her demeanor was pleasant enough. She had just this second got home, she told us, she'd been to her hair and nail appointments downtown and stopped by Basil's office on the fifteenth floor of the NVB building and together they had gone to the tearoom at the Tabbot & Reeves department store for a slice of banana cream pie.

Pop was hanging back, awed by the majesty of the Taylor spread.

Mom got right to business. "We think Stan might have run away. His clothes and his stereo player are gone. I'd like to speak with Anya, maybe she knows where he is."

"Well, her car's not here, can't you see? She must have gone out."

"But Stan couldn't have carried that stuff by himself and we're thinking someone with a car must have helped. And Anya does have a car. . . ."

Tillie, nervously enlightened, kneaded her fingers and blinked her eyes.

"Why don't y'all come in?"

We walked through the cavernous front room and tacked up the steps to the second floor. The floors were hardwood, an oddity in that era of wall-to-wall carpeting, and we sounded like a small marching army.

Tillie brought us to Anya's room and, turning her back, swung the door open like the lady who reveals the prizes on a game show. We sheepishly hung in the hall while she stepped in before us.

She crossed directly to the walk-in closet. "My God, half her clothes are gone! Look, her green and yellow paisley minidress! And that blue blouse we bought at Tabbot & Reeves. And her jeans, her smocks!"

She turned to the bed. "Oh!"

She put her fingers to her mouth.

"What's the matter?" Mom said.

"Her Teddy is missing!"

We figured that must be bad. We shook our heads.

"She doesn't go anywhere without her Teddy."

"They must have split together," Pop observed.

"You mean run away from home?"

"Well, that's what it looks like to me."

"But why would she run away from home?"

We waited. We knew what was coming.

"It's that damn boy of yours, I told her to stay away from him."

"He's not a damn boy," Mom said.

"What's Officer Reedy's number? I'm calling the police right this minute!"

"Won't do much good," Pop said, "she's old enough to go where she wants."

"After what happened to the Joyner boy? I'm calling the police."

"Don't go jumping to conclusions, that's all."

"Her Teddy is gone, what other conclusion can there be?"

She left us alone. We were quiet a few moments and then Pop said, "I wonder how much a head start they got. They could be all the way to North Carolina if they been on the road two hours."

"You sound like that's what you want," Mom said.

Pop shrugged. "Well . . . when you gotta go you gotta go." He gave me a wink.

"You know what makes me mad?" Mom said. "He promised me he would go to the police. He said he was going to tell them where he was when Gaylord vanished. He swore to me he would do that."

"Must have changed his mind."

Mom made a sound under her breath, and we heard Tillie on the phone, downstairs, spelling out Anya's name. "A-N-Y-A . . . No, it's not a Russian name, what difference could that possibly make?"

"I wonder why she didn't use this one," Pop said, indicating the untouched Princess on the nightstand.

"That's Anya's private line," I explained, "it's different from the one downstairs."

"Well, heck, you can call the cops on this just as good as any other."

The mysteries of rich people were beyond our comprehension. Just take Anya's bed: that thing was big as a swimming pool. Its backboard looked like it was made out of the same material they used to produce the banquettes at Neuman's Ice Cream Parlor. And in the corner of the room stood a console stereo player made out of maple wood, with its lid open. Pop and I strolled over to examine it.

"No wonder they took Stan's stereo," I said, "they could never have got this in a car."

The downstairs phone jangled as it hung up, and Tillie called: "Excuse me! People! Would you like to come down?"

We descended to the enormous front room with the ski lodge ceiling.

Mom wandered over to look at the piano. Tillie asked if we wanted a Tab and we said no. This was business, not pleasure.

Mom asked Tillie if she knew how to play the piano.

"No, that daughter of mine is supposed to be the pianist in

the family. First we bought her the thing, and then we spent a small fortune paying for lessons. But all she wants to do is to listen to the Beatles and the Doors. And now there's this colored boy Jimi Hendrix, that's all she talks about anymore."

Mom was nodding, relating to what she was hearing. "Does he play this psychedelic music they're listening to?"

"Yes, those screaming guitars. And those lyrics about drugs."

Mom and Tillie pursed their lips.

After a while we heard the rumble of a police cruiser as it pulled up in front of the house.

"I wonder if that's Deputy Dawg," Pop said.

"Who's Deputy Dawg?" Tillie said. "Why are you making these tasteless jokes?"

We elected to greet Reedy in the yard. It always took him forever to get out of his car and Tillie was impatient to speak.

"My daughter appears to have run off with their son," she hollered, dashing over the lawn.

Reedy called through the window, "Ma'am?"

We trailed Tillie to the cruiser.

"My daughter has run away, and so has their son. They went in her car. It's a candy-apple-red GTO. I can give you the license number, I have it written down in the house."

"Yes ma'am. How old is your daughter?"

"Eighteen."

Reedy looked at Pop and Mom.

"Your son went with her?"

"He's eighteen," Pop said, "it's legal."

Reedy cocked his head. "There isn't a whole lot I can do if she's of age."

"Of course you can," Tillie said, "you can find her and convince her to return."

"Do you know where she went?"

"Isn't it your job to find out?"

The cop met Mom's eyes. She was staring a hole through him. He raised his eyebrows and said, "Why would your son skip? What do you think must be going through his mind?"

"I wouldn't call it skipping," Pop said. "When I was his age I run off all the time."

"Spare us the sordid details," Mom said.

Pop missed the sarcasm. He turned to Reedy with a furrowed brow, showing his concern. "Have they found the Joyner boy yet?"

"No sir, we're still looking."

Reedy was watching my mother.

She said, "Why don't you take Jack home, I'd like to speak with Officer Reedy alone."

Pop slowed down his gum-chewing. "What for?"

"I think it's time he learns what we found out from Stan."

Pop's eyes grew large as buttons. His mouth halted, mid-chew. He nodded at Reedy, his way of offering an "Excuse me," and then he said to Mom, "Could we have a word?"

He pulled her way up in the yard and began to whisper histrionically. We couldn't hear a word they were saying, all we could do was watch. It was like they were arguing in pantomime. Pop was uneasy, and Mom had lowered her Kirby brow.

There wasn't going to be any talking her out of what she was set on doing, I could tell that a mile away.

Tillie shrugged and returned to Reedy. "They might be heading to Pennsylvania. My sister lives there, she married Paul Thatcher of Harrisburg."

"Then you know what you should do, ma'am? You should phone your sister and tell her to be on the lookout for your daughter."

"That's not very helpful. A crime is being committed and you don't even seem to care. That boy could have kidnapped her."

"Excuse me, but doesn't your daughter have relations with the Witcher boy?"

"What do you mean, 'relations'? What are you insinuating?"

"Well, isn't she his girlfriend?"

"I don't think I like your tone."

Reedy was only halfway paying attention, anyway; he kept craning his head to see how Mom and Pop's dispute was progressing.

I wandered off. The evenings were growing shorter and there was a blue tinge to the air. When I got to the corner I looked behind. Mom and Pop were still at it. Tillie was still berating Reedy for ignoring her.

I turned off Clark and headed home. Rusty, lying in front of Witcher House, labored to his feet and came loping along to greet me. . . .

A half hour later Pop stomped through the door.

"Your mother's telling Deputy Dawg no one knows Stan's whereabouts at the time Gaylord disappeared."

I got up from the sofa and went to the window. Reedy's patrol car was idling in front of the house. The Ford was in the driveway and Mom was in the front seat of the cruiser next to Reedy. Rusty was at the edge of the yard looking in.

I turned around. Pop's hands were trembling. He lit a cigarette and stared at me wildly.

42

THEY FOUND THE BODY a week or so later: Pop and I saw it on the news.

That was when they swore out the warrant.

Stan, it turned out, gave the cops quite a run. By the time they busted into the crash pad in San Francisco where he'd been holing up (we learned about that later) he was long gone.

Months passed, and the murder of Gaylord was no longer news. No one was interested outside of the families and a few neighbors. During this period Pop and Mom separated. I don't know the details. He split in the night while I was sleeping. Mom said he was staying in a cheap hotel in Southside. She didn't know if he was coming back.

The upshot was, we were now living in the house by ourselves. It didn't seem any bigger with just the two of us, but at least I didn't have to worry about being killed for snitching. Pop and Snead were no longer playing the blues in the front yard, which must have made Mr. Pudding happy; and the junk at the side of the house had ceased accumulating, which no doubt pleased Mr. Kellner. So I guess everyone was happy.

Snead was being real friendly whenever he saw me. One day he came over with his second-oldest son and they scraped and painted the house. Snead said he couldn't stand seeing that word TRASH peeking through the cheap paint Stan and I had coated on. Which was right nice of him. All he charged us for was the paint.

The other major change was my school. After my first week back, the principal and other functionaries had a meeting with my mother and suggested it might be less traumatic for everyone involved if I were discreetly placed in a school in the next district. I had already passed Myra twice in the halls and both times her lower lip had started blubbering, so to my way of thinking this wasn't such a bad idea. We lived on the border between the two districts, and the new one wasn't any farther away than the old one. As a matter of fact, I liked the new school. The name Witcher didn't mean anything to the students there, although it eventually got around that my brother was wanted for murdering a boy. Which was a plague on me in many ways. There were moments, fleeting moments, when I would feel a young boy's unreasoning happiness, the kind you might feel on an autumn afternoon when you remember that the world is huge and full of girls and you have your whole life ahead of you. And just like that the sharp blade of a shadow would cut through my light and I would see Gaylord's grimacing image and accept his violent demise as a curse on the race of Witchers forevermore.... Not that I was tempted very often by joy. I would kill it whenever it threatened me.

Just before the school year began Mom came in my room and gathered up my dirty clothes for the wash. While she was going through the pockets she found Myra's ring.

"What's this?"

Of course, I'd already informed her about the ring I got from Gladstein. Now she examined it curiously.

After a while she gave me a little peek. "Can I wear it?"

For some reason that pleased me. It seemed like the perfect ending for the ring.

"Sure, Mom, you'll be my steady girl now."

ONE DAY LATE IN OCTOBER, as she came home from work, she was met by two men clambering out of a small car with a big 6 stenciled on its side. One of the men, with a dimple in his chin, was holding a microphone. The other, less telegenic, was bungling about in the background with a huge camera. They wanted to record for posterity Mom's bemused reaction to the news of the arrest, in Portland, Oregon, of Stanley Witcher for the murder of Gaylord Joyner.

She had heard nothing about it until that very moment. She said, "What was he doing in Portland, Oregon?"

That didn't satisfy the man with the microphone.

"How do you feel to learn your son has been arrested for murder?"

"Not too good, this is the first I've heard of it."

"Do you think he did it?"

"Did what?"

"Committed the murder."

She began to murmur something low and the man thrust his microphone forward to catch what she was saying. That only flustered her, and she quit.

"Would you mind repeating what you just said?"

The man with the camera was angling around, trying to get a better shot.

"I was praying."

"For your son?"

"No, it's just a thing I do. You go into the cloud of unknowing and ask for help. That's all you ask for, is help. I got that out of a book I read."

The man lowered his microphone.

I guess her reaction didn't have enough human interest to satisfy the station, because she didn't make the news that night; but if you ask me, the reporter missed a splendid chance to run a provocative story on The Praying Atheist of El Dorado Hills.

That very evening Stan phoned from Oregon; I was listening from the next room. "Stan," I heard Mom say, "I want you to tell me the God's honest truth. Did you kill Gaylord Joyner?"

She was silent awhile and then she said, "I see."

When she hung up she told me Stan claimed he didn't do it; he said the cops were after him because he had long hair and had attended antiwar demonstrations when he was in San Francisco.

We never said another word on the subject.

Certain esoteric procedures were undertaken so that my brother could be extradited to our town to stand trial. A week later he was transported to the county jail in handcuffs. I saw it on the news. The man with the dimpled chin was covering his arrival.

From time to time a phone call would come in from the jail and Mom would take a taxi so she could visit her incarcerated son. I never went with her. I was out of touch with the Witcher men, although sometimes she would tell me, "Your father says hello."

To contact Pop you had to dial a service station across the street from this motel where he was staying and speak with some guy named Jeff Davis and then you'd have to wait for Pop to call back, which might take hours. I spoke with him a couple of times and he said he wanted to get together, but he never acted on it.

I wasn't interested anyway. I had taken up stamp-collecting.

SHORTLY AFTER MOM'S APPROPRIATION of Gladstein's ring, she came in my room and gave me a look. It was a school night and probably I was studying for a test. Or maybe perusing a philatelic volume.

"What?"

"I need to ask you something."

She gazed all around the room. It was mine now. I had found an old 45 record player in the attic and placed it on top of the desk where Stan's stereo used to be. My taste in music ran to the 5th Dimension and Dionne Warwick.

"How much did you pay for this ring, you never told me."

"I didn't, I traded another one in for it."

"But you got the first ring from Mr. Gladstein too."

"Yes ma'am."

"So how much did you pay for the first ring?"

"Fifty cents."

Mom was sitting in the desk chair. Her hands were in her lap. She wasn't wearing the ring, she was rolling it between her fingers.

"You know, ever since I found this I've been having doubts about it. I've been looking and looking at it and thinking, 'Something here isn't right.' Well, today after I got off work I took it to the jewelry store at Dogwood Downs so I could have it appraised. And do you know what the jeweler there told me? He told me this is a genuine diamond."

"You're kidding. Let me see that, Gladstein told me it was fake."

"Well, he wasn't being truthful, although God knows why."

I held it to my eyes. "Maybe he didn't know."

"He had to, he's a professional jeweler."

The thing was sparkling luminously between my fingers as it never had when it was mere crystal. I lowered it and gazed at my mother in amazement.

"How much did the guy say it was worth?"

She shook her head. She wouldn't tell me. She reached out and I handed the ring over.

"We have to take this ring back to Mr. Gladstein," she said.

"No way! It's mine. I gave it to Myra and she had it on her finger. I can't give it back." Parting with the ring seemed a heartbreaking prospect, even though I had once tossed it over my shoulder.

But I could see Mom was going to be adamantine about it. She'd put on her Kirby brow, and now she was glowering at me from across the room. "This ring is too valuable," she said. "You're telling me you paid fifty cents for this, and that is not right. I don't know what Mr. Gladstein was thinking when he gave you this ring, but we can't accept it."

"What do you mean, 'we'?"

"I should think I'm involved in this."

"It's my ring, not yours. I'm the one that paid for it."

"Fifty cents is not a reasonable price to pay for this ring."

"How much did the guy say it's worth?"

Mom lowered her head. "He offered a thousand dollars on the spot."

"A thousand dollars! Give me that ring!"

"Hold on, you just wait."

"That's my ring!" I shouted.

"It is not your ring, it's Mr. Gladstein's."

"He sold it to me! I bought it and it's mine!"

I was ready to cry. A thousand dollars!

"It wasn't right of him to let you have this ring for fifty cents."

"He can do anything he wants with his rings, they're his!"

To me it was pretty cut-and-dried. Mom's scrupulousness was going to cut me out of a fortune rightfully mine, and all because she wasn't a Christian and therefore had to prove to everybody how good she was. I was furious she'd allow her atheistic niceties to come between me and my ring. We argued all night. I accused her of meddling where she didn't belong. And to think I'd been nice enough to let her wear it! She slipped the ring back on her finger, which meant the only way I could get it off was to use force.

My fury was justified, and righteous. I shouted in a way I'd never shouted at her. I cursed her, I called her dirty names. I wanted to hurt her. I wanted her to know the strength of my feelings.

She grew stern and insisted I apologize, and I wouldn't. There was a lot of storm and stress—hollering, slamming of doors, etc. In the end we agreed to take the matter to Gladstein.

It so happened I had been visiting Gladstein's shop after school. He would allow me to sit behind the counter and say "May I help you?" to the customers if they came in. Our friendship had deepened during that period. Actually, he was the only friend I had.

By now he knew all about Myra's returning the ring during our final rendezvous. He had listened to the story with great interest, laughing out loud and energetically lifting his eyebrows. What a rip-roaring tale it had turned out to be, what with my brother bludgeoning and burying Gaylord while Myra and I carried on a forbidden romance. He insisted I should keep the ring forever. He told me to stay open to its power: "Always remain ready, that's the romantic attitude."

Needless to say, I was counting on him to back me up in my argument.

The next day we went to his store. Gladstein's initial response when Mom challenged him on the value of the ring was to play dumb. She told him about the jeweler at Dogwood Downs, a guy named Bledsoe, whom Gladstein, apparently, knew very well.

"Bledsoe said the rock is real? I'll be darned, let me see that thing."

He put the knob in his eye.

"Yes . . . amazing."

He took the knob out.

"Well, looks like Bledsoe might be right. This does appear to be a diamond."

"Moses," Mom said. "Stop acting so innocent, you knew that ring was real."

"No no, I just didn't look closely enough. These things happen. I must have reached in the drawer and . . ." He snuck me a quick peek. I remembered perfectly well he had fetched the ring from the safe, but I certainly wasn't going to say so.

Meanwhile Mom was tapping her toe and assessing the diplomatic approaches to deceit altruistically motivated.

"Moses, you must have known."

"Nah, I just handed him the first thing I came across. He wanted to impress his girl, you know."

"You mean Myra Joyner, whom I specifically asked him not to associate with."

"You did? Well, I didn't know that. I'm acquainted with Mrs. Joyner. Knew the boy too, the one that, you know . . ."

Mom said, testily, "I would like you not to interfere in the way I raise my sons."

"Interfere! I love this kid. I was trying to help, that's all. In fact," Gladstein bellowed, laughing, "the kid came out a lot better than I did. Right, Witcher?"

I grinned, futilely.

"He didn't come out any way," Mom said, "because we're returning the ring."

"Well, do what you want. But the kid paid for it. I mean, sure, I charged the wrong price, but that's my tough luck, that's business."

"Moses, he did not pay for it. He traded you a fifty-cent ring and I don't want my son growing up thinking life is that cheap. I want him to learn the value of things."

Gladstein clawed at his goateed jowls while the dogs sniffed at the door.

"I don't think life is cheap," I said.

"You shut up," Mom told me.

"How am I going to learn the value of things if I'm not allowed to own anything valuable?" I looked pleadingly at Gladstein.

"What can I do," he said, "the kid paid fifty cents, it was a legitimate sale. The ring is his."

"It's not so hard to figure out, Moses. Return the fifty cents."

And that's what happened. Gladstein deposited two quarters into my palm and Mom steered me out of the store. When I turned to glance back at him, she shoved me along.

"I hate you," I said, walking home. "I could have sold that ring and had money for college."

I figured college would fill her with regret.

"That's nice, telling your mother you hate her."

When we passed the Pudding woods I flung the two quarters out of my hand and heard the faint thud of their falling amongst the trees.

"That was real grown-up, Jack. How old are you? Let me tell you something, you're going to be a lot harder than your father or brother ever were. You'll never do anything wrong, not you. But my God are you going to be hard."

I didn't know what she meant by that. Her saying it filled me with anxiety.

I tried to reconcile myself to being hard. I even liked the image—me, hard. But then it began to bother me, mainly because she stopped speaking right after she said it. It was as though my future character defects already were filling her with loathing.

For the rest of the evening I followed her around. I didn't say anything, because I didn't want her to believe I was apologizing. Still, I followed her. If she went in the kitchen I followed her. When she went to watch TV I sat nearby. I was waiting for her to take back what she said.

It was like I had been cursed.

43

EVENTUALLY SHE DECIDED to divorce Pop.

To break the news she utilized her most earnest tones of heartbreak, sorrow and concern. But she needn't have bothered. Pop's absence didn't make that much difference. As long as she had to work full-time I didn't see why we needed him. All he did was lie around all day watching soap operas.

I told Gladstein my parents were getting divorced, and he beetled his brow and smoothed his goatee. "Is she still mad about the ring?"

"It doesn't make sense she's so worried about being good. She doesn't even believe in God."

Gladstein winced. He didn't like that.

"I've asked her to lunch a few times," he said, "and she keeps telling me she's busy. What does that mean? Busy at lunch? Lunch is when you take a break."

But it was true that Mom had her hands full. Her son was

in jail, and we'd been saddled with a rookie court-appointed attorney who lacked the proper gravitas and needed too much bolstering. He would phone Mom every day to ask if he was doing all right, which hardly gave her confidence. On top of this, she had to arrange her own divorce.

"What caused your mother not to believe in God? Atheism often stems from religious trauma. Were her parents preachers?"

"No, she just thinks the world is a bad place."

"Well, there is tragedy in the world, one can't deny it. But there's magic, Witcher. There's magic in the world."

"If you say so."

"Sure there is." Gladstein gestured about, inviting me to examine his shop as proof. And you know what? He had no customers. The air was stale. His dogs were whining and scratching at the back door and I could smell their shit. Gladstein on magic just wasn't convincing anymore. He had promised so much, and yet I never even got to see Myra's breasts. All that happened was my brother murdered her brother and wound up in jail.

Days passed. Gladstein fretted, pined and worried. He asked about my mother constantly. Finally he decided he would accept her coldness no longer.

He arrived at Witcher House one day in his Continental, hoisting his bulk out one leg at a time. I was in the front room, watching. It was Sunday and Mom was off work.

"Mom, Mr. Gladstein is here," I called.

"Moses? What does he want?"

"He's brought flowers."

His hair was slicked back and he was wearing a jacket with a carnation in the lapel. He had shaved his goatee, making him look denuded and perverse.

He grimly approached the door, bearing his bouquet. Mom appeared just as he was entering.

He thrust the flowers at her.

"A token of apology."

"Apology for what?"

"For the ring. For interfering."

"Well, thank you, Moses, this is so nice of you. We'll let bygones be bygones. Come in the kitchen, let's have a seat."

She was touched, I could tell. Not even Mr. Harris at the Ben Franklin had brought her flowers.

We went in the kitchen and sat. Mom stuck the flowers in a glass, placed it on the table. They were gardenias, I believe— I don't know flowers very well.

"Think of them as a token," Gladstein said.

He seemed uneasy. Perhaps not being on his stool made him uncomfortable. The kitchen chair was inadequate for his bulk, which kept spilling over the side. Poor Mr. Gladstein was alien to kitchen chairs.

"Sweet domesticity," he said, gazing around.

Yeah, you haven't tried her goulash, I thought.

"It's been so long since—"

"What?"

"You know, I was with Sophie for years, I never knew anybody else."

"She sounds like such a nice person."

"She had a lot of compassion for the poor, a highly developed sense of social justice."

"She sounds like she was a real nice person. I've always said that."

"Which is why I thought . . . this ring, it's . . ."

Mom seemed nervous. She cut her eyes towards the glass and said, "Those are such pretty flowers."

"Yes, and I want to tell you something, Bledsoe was way off the mark when he said that ring was worth a thousand dollars. He was trying to take advantage of you—that ring's worth a lot more than a thousand."

"Really? I don't know a thing about diamonds. Somehow it looked genuine to me, that's all. I only took it to Mr. Bledsoe out of curiosity. I never would have sold it."

"You should be wearing that ring, Margaret. It belongs on your finger."

Mom's hand flitted to the gardenias and began to rearrange them.

"That sounds like a proposal." She laughed.

"Of course, we have to wait for the divorce to be final. How long will that take?"

"Wait, stop. I was only joking."

Mr. Gladstein stared at me in terror.

Mom's eyes plunged downwards.

"Jack, why don't you leave us alone a few minutes," she said.

I was glad to get out of there. I sat on the porch, blushing for all three of us. I couldn't believe Gladstein would be so art-less. What did he know about women? *I* knew more. And this was the man who had promised me magic, who had counseled me on Myra.

At that time of year the evening should have been forbid-ding and cold, but it was balmy instead. The hum of the world was not driving me so crazy anymore. Perhaps the gods had been appeased. Maybe they were enjoying the nice weather too.

I sat waiting for Gladstein to finish his foolishness.

It took longer than I expected, maybe an hour. By then it was dark and finally growing cold. I was just standing to fetch a sweater when I heard the scrape of chairs in the kitchen. (The door was still open, I could hear them through the screen.)

Gladstein stepped out.

"Walk me to the car."

I went to the Continental with him. He turned the ignition and whirred down the window. The dogs were not in the back-seat. I imagined them yapping behind some door in Jeffer-son Ward.

"She turned me down. She said no."

"She's not even divorced yet," I told him.

Gladstein bit his lip. He stared ahead, nodding at his thoughts. "Back in the old days matchmakers used to take care of things like this."

"Maybe you should try again in a year."

"That's what your mother told me."

"She did?"

I was stunned. I had offered that only as a false hope.

"I'm not out of the game yet, no sirree."

"She said she might marry you in a year? Does that mean we'll have to move to Jefferson Ward?"

He wasn't paying attention. He was already arranging the rabbi, the huppah, the date.

I liked Gladstein, but I couldn't picture him as a father. I was Pop's son, even if I never saw the man again. I was a Witcher. This is where I lived. In Witcher House.

"Boy, let me tell you, I'm glad that's over with."

"How come you like her so much, Mr. Gladstein?"

"Class, Witcher. She has good qualities. I've always thought she was too good for your father . . . but maybe I shouldn't say that."

"You should go home," I said, "take care of your dogs."

"A woman like her craves affection, someone who will appreciate her, give her attention. Women like attention, Witcher. She needs magic, she has no magic in her life. People need magic, and I could give her that, I really believe I could."

He shot me an anxious look. "How would you feel if your mom and I got married?"

"I'm not sure I'd want to live in Jefferson Ward."

"What's wrong with Jefferson Ward?"

"We're white, have you noticed? We've got white skin."

Gladstein swiveled his baggy eyes away from me.

"What a world," he said, "what a sad world. No compassion, no feelings for others."

He wiggled his fat fingers in farewell. And drove off.

44

IT TOOK THE JURY sixty minutes to return with a verdict. I imagine they went to the jury room and passed around potato chips and chatted about TV programs they had seen.

The evidence that convicted my brother was largely circumstantial, but there was plenty of physical proof, like hair and fibers from Anya's car and traces of blood swabbed from the seats of the GTO and from the cloth shower curtain in our bathroom. Anya, incidentally, no longer was in love with my brother. By the time the trial began she had taken up with a pharmaceuticals salesman ten years her senior. It so happened she had reappeared on Clark Lane the very day the news broke that Gaylord's body had been found. She'd last seen Stan in San Francisco, which is where she ditched him after she caught him practicing free love in a Haight-Ashbury crash pad with a hippie chick who, apparently, gave him a dose of clap. He and

Anya had argued about it, and he had punched her, and she had come to the conclusion that he was a loon.

People I never dreamed of were called to the witness stand. A gas station attendant. A late-night hamburger clerk. A farmer whose shovel got stolen from his porch the night of the murder. Bruce Pendleton, whom Gaylord was supposed to meet at the movies and never did.

A local guy, some dope who'd been ambling purposelessly along the side of the road that fateful evening, reported seeing Gaylord in the passenger seat of the GTO right before he disappeared. That was a pretty big deal, and our defense attorney was too inept to trip the guy up. Reedy testified about the threats Stan had made in his presence. Anya and my mother bore witness about Stan's real whereabouts, and I was called to tell the court about the early-morning hours when my brother returned home and ran the water in the bathroom. While I was being questioned Stan, at the defense table, doodled on a pad.

His alibi was easily destroyed. Not even his haircut helped him. He had trash written all over him.

They sent him to the state pen. I went to visit him once with Mom. I was around fifteen. The guards shook me down. I was led through a courtyard surrounded by barred windows, and from the windows the bellowing of hundreds of inmates echoed off the walls.

We sat across a table from each other. Stan was in a prison shirt and pants. His hair had been buzzed and his complexion was bad. He had pimples. His skin was pale.

He didn't have much to say. He had always blamed me for his imprisonment. He blamed Mom too, but he needed her care packages so he didn't come down on her so hard.

"I hear the Joyners left the neighborhood," he told me.

I nodded slowly, hating him.

He saw that I hated him and he changed the subject.

That was the only time I saw him after he got put in prison.

I HAD a pretty hard time forgetting Myra, not least because my last name was repeatedly linked with hers in the papers. Gaylord Joyner and Stanley Witcher would remain in perpetual association. And I was having nightmares about Gaylord, dreams I don't wish to tell.

One day, even though everything that could be said had already been said, I wrote her a letter.

> *Dear Myra,*
>
> *I am sorry I didn't come to your brother's funeral, but I felt it would be too hard on you and your family. I am sorry for what you are going through. If there is ever anything I can do for you let me know.*
>
> *Your friend,*
> *Jack*

I used the postal system, and five days later a letter came back.

Dear Jack,

Thank you for your letter. It was good you didn't come to the funeral. I don't blame you for what happened, but I will always hate your brother. I hope your life is better than his.

Yours truly,

Myra

I would daydream about her, invent scenes where we laughed, talked, hugged. I'd course her name during class across my notepaper. I inscribed *MJ* on the edges of all of my books. I fantasized that there would be a day when she'd come bobbing along and say, "It's no use, I tried to get over you but all the other boys are dummies. You're the only guy as smart as I am."

Roaming the halls of the school where I'd been banished, sitting on the stool behind Gladstein's counter, lying in my brotherless room—at so many moments my thoughts would wander to Myra. Where is she? Who does she talk to? What does she think about? Everything was about her: the Pudding woods, the shopping center, the sewing store near Gladstein's. Rusty, of course, was a faithful reminder, since Myra and I had been his best human friends. I would bend to pet him and say, "Hey, Rusty, how are things next door to the Joyner house?"

I saw her during our senior year of high school. This was at a party thrown by a kid whose parents were out of town. As soon as her eyes lighted on me she spread out her hands and beamed in surprise, as if we went way back and had wonderful memories. She crossed the room, hesitated, and gave me a warm hug.

"Look at you," she said. "I hear you're going to Harvard."

She'd grown up over the past five years. I had recognized her only by her pogo-stick walk, a residue of adolescent gawkiness. Otherwise she looked like a girl you could see anywhere, pretty and self-assured. But a pretty, self-assured Myra would never be any girl. Not to me. Not even now.

"Can you believe it?" I said.

"That doesn't surprise me, I always said you were smart."

"What about you?" I nearly asked if she was going to Duke, but I didn't want to bring Gaylord to mind.

"I'm sticking around," she said.

She was going to a local college, she didn't want to leave her father alone because her mother had just died and he was having a hard time adjusting to that.

I told her I was sorry to hear it.

"I'm sorry about everything," I said, "especially about everything that happened back then."

"It wasn't you, Jack, everyone knows that."

She gazed at me kindly, but in her eyes lurked something awful: fear, anxiety.

"I can't help it," I told her, "I've always felt so bad about what happened."

She looked away and I wondered if I should stop.

My girlfriend hadn't been able to come to the party that night, and all I wanted now was to go off with Myra and talk about the ring I once gave her and the kidney-shaped pool at Anya's house and the kisses we once exchanged.

She smiled and said, "Okay, bye, I just wanted to come over and congratulate you on getting into Harvard."

"Do you ever see anyone from the old neighborhood?" I asked.

She patted my arm and went away.

After a while I saw her leaving the party with an older guy who played guitar in a band called Black Death. Later I found out she was dating him.

I left the party after that. The only reason I'd stayed was for her. I had been hoping she would leave with me.

WHEN MOM AND GLADSTEIN got married he sold the house in Jefferson Ward and bought a split-level off Baskin Road. That's where I spent the remainder of my adolescence, up to the time I won my scholarship.

A line of trees behind the house functioned as my woods. I would go there whenever I wanted to be alone.

When I was sixteen I actually made a few friends. My girl-friend was named Deborah and she lived one road over: a nice Jewish girl with a wide smile and an exotic nose. For years after we broke up she wrote me sad, introspective letters. Later she married a dentist. Before her wedding she told me I was the only one she had ever truly loved.

On the day I left for college Mom and Gladstein were busy packing the car to drive me to Boston.

I left to say good-bye to Deborah. She was crying, and I was sad. We knew it was over, even though we kept protesting that it wasn't.

She had been accepted into the same school Stan would have gone to had he not been enrolled in the state pen. In fact, it was the school Myra wound up attending.

After we said good-bye I strolled thoughtfully back to the house, wondering why I never felt things the way I should.

Pop was waiting for me. He had come to say farewell. I think it was the first I'd seen of him since Christmas, when he had come by to drop off my gift—a gilt-edged copy of *The Last of the Mohicans*, the only book, I believe, he had ever finished.

"Harvard boy, good golly. Must be your mother's genes 'cause it sure ain't mine."

"Must be," I said.

"You gonna write?"

"Would you write back?"

I hadn't seen much of him over the years. It wasn't until Mom phoned to tell him I'd been accepted to Harvard that he got excited about me again. He had remarried and redivorced. He was working as a mechanic in a garage in Southside.

"Come on, let's walk to the woods," he said.

Our house was on a cul-de-sac, and there was a patch of trees at the end that separated our subdivision from the next. That's what he meant by "the woods."

Pop was wearing glasses and he was fat. He steered me away from Mom and Gladstein, who were loading up the new Lincoln with my belongings. Mom hollered at me not to take too long.

"This is quite an accomplishment for a Witcher," Pop said. "I don't think any Witcher has ever gone so far. If your brother had gone to college he would have been the first Witcher to do so."

"But being a Witcher, he didn't."

"Don't be bitter," he said. "You got your whole life ahead of you. It's gonna be a heck of a lot easier than mine was."

"What's so bad about your life? You've always had plenty to eat, a roof over your head."

"Man does not live by bread alone."

We came to the cul-de-sac.

Pop was fidgeting with his fingers. He had something he wanted to say, but now that the time had come he didn't know how. He gave me a pleading look, as if he thought I might help him.

"I think they're ready to go," I said.

We returned to the car, and the whole time he kept darting looks at me.

I thought, Who is this fat man with glasses?

We drove off and he stood watching. I gave him a glance as we drove by and then I looked away. I was hoping we'd get out of there fast, but Mr. Gladstein, or Moses as I called him now, saw a ball bouncing across the road and carefully braked the car. It was irritating, because the ball was plainly off the road and the kid it belonged to was waiting for us to pass.

"Go," I said.

Mom spun around to give me a reproachful look and then her eyes were diverted by something behind me.

"Your father is waving. Turn and wave good-bye to him."

But I didn't.

I wasn't going to look back ever again.

a note from the author

When my friends and I were twelve or thirteen, the arbiter in matters of taste, fashion and style was a kid who lived at the end of my street, named Barry. Barry had a subscription to Arnold Gingrich's *Esquire*. He wore the first alligator shirts I ever saw and he made known to us the importance of the alligator for pectoral adornment, as opposed to the horse, or the dolphin. This was in 1967, when kids all over the country were sporting love beads and Nehru jackets. I myself was well on my way to becoming a hippie until Barry set me on a (perhaps) less evolved track. Still, I thought he knew everything worth knowing. Looking back, I believe it might have been Barry, more than my parents or the Catholic school I attended, who truly educated me.

One thing I learned from him was how crucial it was to have nothing to do with the Smiths. (Let's call them the Smiths.) My neighborhood was a tidy place, a working neighborhood, Southern in tone without being redneck. The people were decent. They kept nice houses and nice lawns. In those days there was no guarantee the neighborhood kids would go to college. I remember how shocked I was when a guy who sold pot to the neighborhood kids got accepted into Princeton. I never even knew him to read a book. He must have done it on the side, when no one was watching.

The Smiths lived on a marginal road that had been cut through the trees to allow access to other, nicer streets. Theirs was the only house on the road. There was no pop in the house, just a mom and several hyperactive kids. The mom was a sight to behold, bone-thin, scraggly, narrow-lipped. At another, more populist time she could have been a heroine in a Steinbeck novel. When she called her kids to supper she shrieked. She was abusive and drunken, an irrationally angry woman. No one in our neighborhood had much compassion for her, or, for that matter, for any whose tough luck placed them low on the social scale. I guess we were only a step above that horror ourselves. It's why the folks on my mother's side, who were kind of country, didn't like country music. It was too close to home.

Maybe that was the problem people had with the Smiths. People never want to be reminded of what they might have been, or might be. One of the Smiths, named David, was my age. He used to come around on his bicycle to harass us, but only because we never let him play with us. He'd shout names and we'd tell him to get lost. He never fought, he just came around and hollered obscenities. I remember his face, livid, purple, contorted by pain, rage and rejection. There was something ritualistic about his interaction with the neighborhood. We let him know he shouldn't be there. It wasn't his neighborhood.

Barry had laid down the law concerning him. Smith was *scum*, *white trash*. His name was never mentioned except in the most contemptuous of tones. "Get out of here, no one wants you." "Who invited you?" Occasionally, in a weak moment, David would catch your eye and try to appeal to you, looking for reason, civility and gentleness. That was tough. Then you'd have to put him in his place.

I remember one day, against all convention, he parked his bike and sat on the steps in front of Barry's house. Barry made a point of hosing the steps down afterwards.

For all I know, David might have been a nice boy. He might have had talent, decency and goodness. Since I was no kinder to him than anyone else was, I never found out. I didn't insult him to his face, but I took care to speak of him behind his back with the appropriate measure of scorn.

Now I wonder why. Being Catholic, I was out of place in that WASP neighborhood. My friends went to public schools, I to parochial. I rode a different school bus and stood on a different corner every morning waiting for it. I was overly sensitive to such differences. The dormer windows on my house faced the backyard, whereas every other house on the block had dormer windows facing the front. Our telephone exchange began with 288. Why did everyone else have 282? Did the others take note? Did they see that I was marked? And then there was my father, who was an auditor with the IRS. My friends' fathers were bricklayers and truck drivers. Their fathers taught them the basics of baseball, how to fish, how to hunt. My dad painted depressing street scenes from his impoverished New Orleans childhood and took me on long drives into the country, looking for UFOs.

I wasn't ostracized but socially I felt myself on thin ice. I liked books, and I hid what I was reading when my friends came to visit. One time my buddy Stanley told me his parents wouldn't let him hang around with me because I was a Catholic. I talked him out of that. Another friend's dad expressed his jubilation when JFK, that Vatican front man, got shot in Dallas. (Remembering himself, he later offered me an apology.) I had the deep longing of the outsider, the genuine outsider, to be an insider. The worst thing anyone could call me was "weird." "Wetta, you're so weird." I was told that constantly, often at moments when I was priding myself on seeming normal. What was so weird about me? It didn't matter that the words were spoken with affection. I wanted to be like everybody else.

Considering the level of brutality kids suffer when they're thought of as outsiders, I never had it all that bad. My friends accepted that I couldn't fish, couldn't fire a gun, didn't know how to fix cars. They adjusted to my limitations, seemed to like it that I was wistful and poetic. I dated girls; I got invited to parties.

A kind of tolerance exists even among those who might be considered narrow. Tolerance from working people is the real thing because there's nothing patronizing about it. The people I grew up with were polite and agreeable, which must have made it all the worse for David Smith. What does it mean when everyone is friendly and pleasant and gets vicious only when you come around? Like I say, I never had it as bad as he did. But maybe I felt things might turn if I wasn't careful. It's a good idea to be normal.

The Smiths of the world serve a cautionary purpose. There's something sacrificial about them. They perform a social function. They set a bottom, a defining limit, to what we dread and fear about ourselves, and reassure us that we haven't reached it yet.

What happened to David Smith? Did he become a criminal, a sociopath? Maybe he adjusted. Maybe he's a saint. When I run into people from the old neighborhood they usually can tell me something about the whereabouts of our contemporaries. But no one ever says a thing about David. I've thought about him many times over the years and even suffered for his memory. To tell the truth, this book was written, if anything, as a kind of homage to him. Still, I've never bothered to ask anyone what happened to him because I'm sure no one would know.

if jack's in love

discussion questions

1. How do the social and cultural pressures in Jack's town compare with what we experience in our towns today?

2. When you were growing up, were there people in your neighborhood who had a reputation like the Witchers'? How were they treated?

3. Do you think Stan committed the murder? Does the author attempt to create a mystery about it?

4. Why is Jack so conflicted in his feelings about his father and his own friendship with Gladstein?

5. Jack believes that the ring Gladstein gives him is magical. Why does Gladstein lead him to this belief?

6. Why do you think Gladstein chooses to live where he does?

7. Have you ever felt that your family has a reputation like the Witchers'? How can people deal with the stigma of being ostracized?

8. Usually in wartime, communities are brought together. *If Jack's in Love* takes place during the Vietnam War. Does the war have any impact on Jack's community?

9. Jack feels that his father openly socializing with a black man is looked upon by the neighbors as taboo. In what ways are his concerns justified? Are those concerns relevant today? Why or why not?

10. At the end of the novel, Jack seems bitter toward his father. Is his bitterness justified? Should he have made more of an effort to reconcile with his father?

acknowledgments

I would like to thank Amy Einhorn, Alice Tasman
and Anna Jardine for their advice, encouragement
and support.

about the author

Stephen Wetta grew up in the '60s and '70s, was influenced by the music and the literature of the time, drank, used drugs, got into financial trouble, and spent far too much time reading and writing. He knocked around for years at different jobs, didn't like any of them, and got sober without wanting to. Somehow he wound up with a Ph.D. and worked for ten years as an adjunct. His academic career was singularly undistinguished, and he was eventually hired full-time by a school that couldn't get rid of him, shortly before he was jailed for tax evasion. *If Jack's in Love,* his first novel, won the 2011 Willie Morris Award for Southern Fiction.